Maggie Ling was previously published as an illustrator and cartoonist before choosing to work with words alone. Her stories have been placed in numerous international short story competitions, including a shortlisting for the Bridport Prize, Cold Snap, her only ghost story, winning an Asham Award. Her work has been published in *Unthology 1* (Unthank Books, 2010), *Something Was There*, the Asham Award-winning ghost story collection (Virago, 2011), *Unthology 5* (Unthank Books, 2014), and online by Seren Books (2017) and Fairlight Books (2019). She lives in Norwich, a UNESCO City of Literature.

APPETITES

stories of love, sex and death

MAGGIE LING

Death and the Maiden was first published in the short story anthology *Unthology 1*
(Unthank Books, 2010). *Bird Brains* (2014 and 2015), *Reflections* (2010), *A Life* (2016),
Body Language (2017), *Black and White* (2013), *Red Fox Morning* (2011), *One Slip* (2014),
Porkies (2012), *Running Away* (2012, 2013 and 2016), *That Day* (2010) and
Another Time (2014) were all listed in international short story competitions. *Dick's Life*
first appeared in *Unthology 1* (Unthank Books, 2010). Online, *Let Her Go* was Seren Books'
Short Story of the Month (October 2017, serenbooks.com), and *Bird Brains* and *Running Away*
were published by Fairlight Books (May 2019, fairlightbooks.co.uk).

Matador
9 Priory Business Park,
Wistow Road, Kibworth Beauchamp,
Leicestershire. LE8 0RX
Tel: 0116 279 2299
Email: books@troubador.co.uk
Web: www.troubador.co.uk/matador
Twitter: @matadorbooks

ISBN 978 1838591 144

British Library Cataloguing in Publication Data.
A catalogue record for this book is available from the British Library.

Printed and bound in the UK by T J International, Padstow, Cornwall
Typeset in 11pt Minion Pro by Troubador Publishing Ltd, Leicester, UK

Matador is an imprint of Troubador Publishing Ltd

Contents

A well-governed appetite is the greater part of liberty.

Lucius Annaeus Seneca

Death and the Maiden

W atching him had become a comforting pastime, a part of her life. Something she did when washing the dishes. She seldom used the dishwasher now. He was someone to look down on as she hand-washed her 'delicates' – delicates previously tossed into the washing machine without a thought. These so-called delicates now extending to barely worn sweaters and shirts, all clearly labelled 'machine washable', yet all lovingly immersed in soapy bubbles in the kitchen sink.

She had not gone out of her way to observe him. No. She was just going about her daily routine. It was *he* who had placed himself in her line of vision. He, two floors below, who had given her – looking down from her top-floor casement on the other side of the square – an 'open-curtained' view of his life. And the most comforting thing of all was, he was always alone. Had been alone for weeks. Or was it months? Yes. He had been alone since early November – though he had gone away for Christmas. Home, she supposed. Wherever that might be. This had saddened her at first. But then, late Boxing Day afternoon, she had seen slits of light filtering through the Venetian blind, and, come the morning, there he was, back at his desk again. She even found herself able to enjoy a film that afternoon, curling up on the sofa, quite relaxed, halfway through going to the kitchen for refreshments, looking down, and seeing him still sitting there. Had he, she wondered, moved his desk to that position purely out of consideration for her? She had not seen him move it. It had been there when she returned from work, two weeks after he'd moved in.

She had gone to the sink to fill the kettle, expecting to see only the glow of a hall light leeching through a half-open door, to be met by the sight of him, sitting at his computer, the desk lamp's glow highlighting his face. And instead of putting a teabag in a mug, as she might have done, as she had always done, found herself searching for an unopened packet of loose Darjeeling she thought she still had, setting the tea to brew in her large, largely unused, teapot, pulling out a stool to drink it there in the kitchen.

It was at breakfast time the next morning that she noticed a large filing cabinet had replaced the exercise bike previously visible in the corner of the room. So he would no longer expose his half-naked torso to her gaze, no longer lie there stretching, lifting weights, doing energetic push-ups, before, half-disappearing behind the half-drawn curtains, she would see his feet pedalling to nowhere on the bike.

Now he barely disappeared from view, the blind was always up and he, more often than not, was always there. Though not there in the mornings: not before she went to work. And seldom there on Saturday mornings. But almost always on Sundays. Another considerate move on his part. Sundays had always been difficult. Although, shuffling into the kitchen like that, seeing him there, she had felt quite slovenly. Had made a New Year's resolution: vowing never again to spend most of Sunday in her dressing gown, going out the following day to buy three pairs of pull-on lounging trousers with matching tops, bargain price, in the sale.

I've seen her up there, up at that window, looking down. Saw her soon after I moved in here: those first few days when I used this room as my exercise space. I know the park's only ten minutes up the road, but, at the beginning of something, I barely go out. Like to keep my head down, keep concentrated – even when there's nothing much to concentrate on. 'For fuck's sake!' my wife used to say. 'How the hell can you write about life if you never live it?'

I remember once countering this much-used insult of hers by quoting a much-quoted bit of Socratic wisdom: 'Well,' I said, with all the irony I could muster, 'the unexamined life and all that…'

'Words! Words! Words!' she said, slamming the door.

I had put my desk under the window in the living room. But this block being right on the T-junction, I found looking out on the wide, busy street leading straight north to the park quite distracting. Especially since, even in early November, the Christmas lights were already twink-twinkling from dawn to bloody dusk. No way was I ready for such jollity. Not this year. Sorry. Not *last* year. Is it really already mid-January? How is it that time can drag, yet, at the same time, speed by in a flash?

Anyway, as soon as I'd pulled down those dreary curtains, put up a cheap blind (which, since the room's too dark when it's down, I needn't have bothered buying) and dragged the desk here under the window, I felt the slightest tug-tugging of something: an upturned thought, bordering on a vague idea, beginning to surface in the dishevelled bunch of nervous ganglia that constitutes my brain. Felt this the right space to be in – work-wise, that is.

There's something sombre, something punitive about sitting here, looking out from this tall sash window (Georgian; in itself quite elegant) into the dingy funnel of buildings out there, all looking in on themselves. Such a contrast to the living room. The other side of the block all glittering lights, all spend-spend-spend neon, while this side smacks of Grub Street. Or worse. Don't know if anyone really uses that dark square down there. Occasionally an echoing cough splutters up to me. Every once in a while I hear what sounds like a rubbish bin, the old-fashioned galvanised sort, being scraped across the ground; hear the shuffle of feet. Picture a chained-together ring of prisoners circling the square; an animated Doré etching, straight out of Newgate.

Becky used to tell me I was *chained* to my desk. Ironic, really. Though I didn't think I was then, I most certainly am now. Thanks a bunch, Becky.

I thought she might stop looking down at me – the woman on the top floor, not Becky; don't think Becky'll ever stop looking down on me. Thought the woman up there might be a bit of a middle-aged perv; one who, for some unfathomable reason, got off on my OK torso. Figured when she saw me tap-tapping away down here – or, most likely, *not* tap-tapping away – she might stop looking. I mean, that woman spends half her life in that damn kitchen. Surely there's more to her flat than one room. I can just about make her out – the woman up there, not my wife. Thought I'd made Becky out a long time ago. My mistake.

Some might think it a good thing, feeling you have some understanding of another human being, believing they have some understanding of you, and finding a degree of contentment in that. I imagined Becky and me to be in that mythical place. But, truth is, my wife, for all she says now, was never really into contentment. No. Becky has some mistaken notion about women and mystery. Has a need to hold on to it, hold a part of herself back in some misbegotten, misguided, *mysterious* way.

I think I've seen her, the woman up there: seen her in the street a couple of times. I'm pretty certain it was her. Anyway, if it was/*is* her, she's a brown sort of woman: brown hair, brown coat, brown boots – brownish skin, even. Not brown-skinned. Not Afro-Caribbean or anything. Just a tad muddy. Swarthy, you could say – except you can't say that now without it sounding like an insult. Her skin has the 'lived-in' quality of someone not overly concerned with her appearance. Not *not* concerned, you understand, not one stage off a cardboard box and a street corner, just someone unbothered by such things. And, perhaps, since we're here in the heart of the city, where a complete makeover is the bat of a false eyelash away, a woman not too flush with money. Maybe, right now, she and I have that much in common.

This woman – the woman I *think* is this woman – looked a couple of decades older than me. Although I suspect she might look a bit older than she is. She's not tall, but not tiny, and has a kind, if slightly tense, face. The kind of woman who looks a little out of place in this part of town. Looks of another age. One in which Being had more clout than Looking – in the sense of looking good, of caring how one is perceived. Looks the sort who would be more at home in the country, where she might dissolve into the monochrome, clod-brown winter fields.

I was born in a field in October 1959 – or so my mother told me, six years later. I can still remember her telling me the story of my birth. Except, after she told me, I somehow managed to reconfigure her words, and for some time – beyond a time when I should have known better – I remembered it this way: *You were born of a field*, imagining my childhood self emerging from Mother Earth, pushing through her fertile surface like a plump, ripe seed, bursting into life.

I had chalked up almost a decade on Mother Earth before my schoolteacher sought to correct me on this basic principle of life. 'Heavens, child! Did your mother not tell you how you arrived in the world?' I pretended my mother had not told me; this retelling of my life story coming as a sudden disappointment to me. Now I was like everyone else. I had come into the world, not free, not self-determined, not, as I had thought, in control of my arrival, but, quite literally, tied: chained by flesh and blood to another flesh-and-blood human being, to my own flesh and blood, to my mother.

My father was not present at my birth. Though only two fields away at the time, turning the last of that season's stubble, the thrum-thrum-thrumming of the tractor and the caw-caw-cawing of seagulls circling overhead quite enough to drown out my mother's hopeless cries for help.

More than an hour had gone by before, in need of his long-overdue refreshment, making his way back to the house, my father came upon his wife and newly born child – his only child – tied together as one in the damp meadow grass, his flask of tea and trencherman's supply of sandwiches fallen to the ground beside them.

Sometimes I think I too can remember that day, can call up from deep within my unknowing, floating self, the slimy pond creature who slithered out onto the grass, squirming on the end of the umbilical cord, unable to break free. For, even now, when I think of it, I see white clouds scudding above my head, feel my heart racing, as a baby's heart races, with joy or with fear, think of this first sight of the world and wish I could see it again, could begin again.

Thing is, the Brown Woman up there is beginning to bugger up my plot line.

'Yeah,' my editor says, skimming over the synopsis, 'it'll do fine, Grant. But you'd better crack on. *Fast!* You know we're planning to catch the Christmas market next year. We'll just have to rush this one through. Still, you're such a pro. You've managed a book in six months before now… So?' Duncan gives me one of his raised-eyebrow looks.

So? I nearly say. *Write the damn thing yourself, why don't you? Because, y'know what, Duncan, I've had enough of pleasing you, pleasing my agent, pleasing my publicist – even pleasing my readers. Had enough of being a book factory: churning them out just because I can, just because they sell –*

just about. Just because my name's embossed on the moody, monochrome covers; just because I'm Kindled, am beloved of supermarkets – as well as a few kindly independent bookshop owners; because I sell at three-for-two, as well as, every once in a while, precisely the price I should sell at. Because of this, everyone's happy. Everyone except me. But hey! Who cares? I'm just the writer. And, irony of ironies, this time, even Becky's happy.

My estranged wife dared to call me the other evening. 'How's it going?' she dares to ask in her soft, caring voice.

'Fine,' I say. 'Don't worry. The mortgage will be paid. I won't renege on promises made. Just as long as you don't call me. Email, if you must. Otherwise the cheque'll be in the post, as and when – or, rather, in your brand-new bank account.'

Having finally got myself a plot line, as crap as that plot line may be, I, quite literally, cannot afford to waste time on this one. We're nine months behind schedule, you see. Interesting, that time frame.

My mother never sought to inform me of the physical processes involved in my growing from child to adult. Which may partially explain why I have never quite made it in the world of adults; why, after all these years in the city, I still feel apart from them, feel more connected to the earth than to its people. But at least here you can get lost, can melt away, can lose the past – or try to lose it.

As a child, I remember observing traces of blood in the toilet bowl. Thinking my mother had contracted some internal, terminal affliction, I waited, fearing for her life, saying nothing. Nothing happened. In fact, my mother blossomed. Again I said nothing, never expressing my fears, or even my relief – if that emotion was felt. Our relationship, you see, was not one enamoured of intimacies. We dealt with the very basics of life, she and I. The everyday acts of eating and sleeping, the only subjects worthy of our daily discourse, her daily cross-examination; the same dialogue tossed back and forth, without thought. *What* I thought mattered little to her. What went on beneath her daughter's cranium could remain a mystery as far as my mother was concerned.

Menstruation, the curse we had in common, was something else she chose not to share with me. I was fourteen years and eight months old when I had my first period, and fifteen years and nine months old when I had my first child. Both events were washed away in a similar fashion.

Does that woman have no friends? Hey! Who's talking? Is it the work, or is it me? Or has Becky been ratcheting up the ante? Whatever it is, most of the time it *is* just me, this room, this computer, and a stream of emails – plus the odd harassing call from Duncan. And, as nice as it is to have *someone* call me, Duncan is not someone I need right now.

I should call, text around, send a few emails, say, *Listen, folks! It's not how it looks. I have* not *walked out on my butter-wouldn't-melt-in-her-mouth pregnant wife. Why would I want to do that? It's* she *who has walked out on me. It's just, she's walked out by staying put.* Well, what else could I do? Though I might've got more empathy if

I'd reassembled a couple of those cardboard boxes I'd been dutifully flattening, handed them to Becky, and booted her straight out the door.

'Grant...?' she says, in her sweet, girly, questioning tone. 'Are you busy right now?'

'Hmm?' Looking down at a flattened box, thinking, *What Einstein of the cardboard universe works out how to cut this stuff in such a way that it assembles and disassembles like this? Makes writing a damn detective story look like child's play.* Then, tuning in to what Becky is saying, I hear the word 'baby', hear myself saying, 'When? *When* did you say this baby's due?'

And that's when it falls apart again: this marriage I thought we had *reassembled*.

I imagine sob stories have been doing the rounds. Hell! Who *wouldn't* believe them? Me here in my bachelor pad, pretending to work. Beautiful, blonde Becky at home, carrying the baby. Well if Becky's so good at sob stories, maybe she should write her own misery memoir. Since most of them are bags of hogwash, she'd be in good company. Could clean up. I could take time out. Retrain. Be that architect my mother always wanted me to be. Or, better still, write a book that doesn't have a cool-dude detective at its heart.

She's still up there, the Brown Woman, doing her slow-motion washing up. How many dishes can one woman use? Unless there's a wild dinner party going on in there and she's barred her guests from the kitchen. Somehow I doubt it. Though she does have more of a spring in her step now.

I was in the living room yesterday, standing by the window, sipping a mug of tea, looking up the street. It was the very edge of dusk, the lights had just come on, the street, wet from the afternoon rain, glistening – and even here, in the centre of this grimy city, there was more than a hint of magic – when, looking down, I see her rounding the corner, crossing the street. And she didn't look quite so brown somehow. In fact, she was wearing a *black* leather jacket. Nothing particularly smart. Hardly Burberry. Probably picked up from the charity shop a couple of streets away. In fact, I remembered seeing one just like it in the Cancer Care window last week. Had thought as I walked by, *You'd better get your act together, fella. Or else, forget Hugo Boss, bye-bye John Smedley; Cancer Care is around the corner. You may have a book contract, but, these days, most book contracts aren't worth the paper they're written on. So don't go assuming you are the exception.*

I know what they say about February, but this year it hasn't got to me in the way it so often does. I can already smell spring in the air.

I walked up to the park yesterday as dusk was falling. The snowdrops are out, crocuses still pushing through. I've begun to make a habit of it: walking around the park. It lifts me. Two days ago I thought I saw him there – in the half-light, it was hard to tell. Anyway, whoever he was, he smiled as we passed each other, and I heard myself say, 'Good evening.'

'And what a lovely one it is,' I heard him reply, as he continued towards the gate.

He's not exceptionally handsome. Just nice-looking, in an honest, trustworthy sort of way. I'm glad about that. I know it makes no sense, but I am.

I haven't seen him quite so much this week. There's been more to do at the library. We've become the main *hub* for this area. They tell us this as if we should be grateful, as if it's a reward for services rendered, but it just means we have to work a lot harder for the same money and, with a bit of luck, won't get sacked. Mustn't grumble. I need to keep this job for another decade or more, or else... Still, must *not* think about that. *Inch by inch, life's a cinch. Yard by yard, it's very hard.* I have to chivvy myself along. Remind myself to live in the moment. It helps. It's been my life's work, self-chivvying.

Lots of new things happening at The Hub – as we jokingly call our buzzing old workplace. We've a series of events coming up soon. I normally make a few preliminary phone calls, do some of the arranging, leave at the usual time, and that's that. But last week, as I was distributing the new periodicals, Freda comes up to me and says, 'Megan! Fancy doing a bit of hospitality for one or two of these upcoming events? I know it's not your thing, but who knows? You might enjoy it. And you get to hear the writers.'

'Why not?' I hear myself saying. 'Yes! OK.'

I thought, having agreed to it, I might find an excuse, might back out before time, as I once did. But, so far, it hasn't happened.

As winter's turned to spring the Brown Woman's become less brown. I swear her hair has a glint of autumnal redness about it.

We passed in the street again last week – well, passed on opposite sides of the street. I waved, smiled silently.

She did the same. She may've been coming back from the park. I was going up there, getting away from my desk, my computer. I've changed the setting for my emails: no more cheery little pings and red numbers flashing when Becky sends me another of her *I'm sorry* missives. I've got so I don't check my inbox for days on end. It's quite liberating! Unfortunately Duncan doesn't give up. Just gets on the phone.

'Hey there, mate' – chirpily at first, hoping the Mr Nice editor will get more out of me than Mr Nasty has to date – 'Gigi wants you to do a couple of gigs next month. Thinks that lovely profile of yours needs raising a bit. You up for it?'

The gap between books panning out to become what Duncan sees as a yawning void of three years, he's getting rather twitchy.

'Thought I was supposed to be keeping my nose *down*, Dunc; get the damn thing done?'

'Speaking of,' Duncan says, pretending he had no intention of 'speaking of', 'how is *The Damn Thing*?' Adding dryly, 'Good macho title. Like that. So far, so good.'

'Oh,' I say, 'you know; not exactly flowing but,' I lie, 'it's trickling along.'

'The Damn not *blocked*, then?' All chirpiness draining from his voice. 'Two or three chapters would be nice.'

'Do they have to be *nice* chapters?'

'Y'know – words, sentences; a few paragraphs on a few pages'll do fine. Electronic pages, you understand. Email me a doc ASAP. Thursday pm; i.e., before four. On second thoughts, make that three. I'm curling up by my Cheshire wood burner this weekend. Just me and my Kindle.'

Grant, darling, Becky writes, *can't we somehow work this thing out? I'm almost certain the baby's yours, not Harry's. Can't we just forget it ever happened? Because I almost have.*

Almost. Not once, but twice. *Almost.*

If you've managed to so completely fuck up your actions, Becky, *darling,* then do try not to fuck up your words too. *Almost* certain is not certain enough. Yet, I presume, you assume you have me over a barrel here; assume, if this baby's mine, I'll want it to have a good life, a family life. Even though you fucked that family up before it came into existence. You know something, Becks? I almost hate you.

My boy was born on May 10th, 1974, I having been shipped away to a distant relative in time to save the family honour. Oh, the disgrace of it!

I don't suppose it was meant as cruelty. But neither was much kindness shown. Though my father – in those last sad weeks before I was transported to Derbyshire, feeling branded, unclean – would, more frequently than usual, put one of his big, warm, hard-skinned workman's hands on my skinny shoulder and pat me gently as he passed by, saying nothing, my own pale hand reaching up to lightly brush the tips of his blackened fingernails before he whisked them away.

'It's for the best,' all my mother could say. 'For the best.'

If this is the best, I thought, *what, in heaven's name, would the worst be like?*

But, to my parents, the worst was inconceivable. And even if the shame of it could be tolerated, where was the money for another child? I might have had a brother or sister of my own had they been able to afford the luxury of children.

He was quite a long baby, his skin the colour of the drilled soil that warm, waterless spring. His father's skin had been much darker: humus rich, fertile, full of goodness – I thought. And maybe that was the case, since I have never been able to hate him. For what was there to hate? I suppose that had been part of the fascination, that difference: his drawling, relaxed voice, his coiled-sprung hair, the gleaming copper-nut beauty of his skin. I had no fear then. I was bursting into life. Wanting, wanting, wanting.

'*Megan!*' my outraged mother said. 'Whatever were you thinking of?'

I said nothing. Since she had never understood, never before enquired as to what I was thinking, why should she know now? Though if I had told her, I would have said, *Mother, at the time, I was thinking of absolutely nothing. Was, for one brief, beautiful hour, one warm, insect-buzzing, bird-twittering, cricket-chirping September afternoon, so at one with nature, with my body and with his, that nothing else concerned me, nothing else mattered. Nothing else at all.*

I saw my baby for fifteen minutes. A kind nurse allowed me to hold him. 'Against the rules, really,' she said, laying the child in my child's arms and leaving us alone together. I was not supposed 'to bond' with him, you see, since this would make the situation more painful for me.

Until that moment, I'd had no realisation that anyone was unduly concerned with my pain. I kissed his damp forehead, whispered his name – the name I had given him – and cried.

Soon I was shipped back to a place that was now more alien to me than ever. Some cobbled-together story was put about to cover my absence. Should anyone ask after my 'illness', I would nod and attempt a smile. Sometimes I would cry; this completing the picture of the vulnerable girl who had had a 'nervous breakdown'. Returning to school seen, by my mother, as too big a reward for my sins, nothing was said on that score. I was given a job in the nearby canning factory, where I spent the next year shelling peas and washing carrots, until, thirteen months later, I left the place the fortunate fondly call home.

Duncan has gone apeshit. So apeshit he feels compelled to call me from his Cheshire wood-burner-side.

'*Fireside* sounds so much cosier, don't you think, Dunc?' I say warmly, before Duncan hits me with his fiery rage. 'Perhaps I should've dropped off the hard copy? Then you could've chucked it in there.'

'And I bloody would've!' Duncan growls. 'What the *hell* is this about? What's happened to the original synopsis? And, more importantly, where's our bloody hero? Does Darius Armstrong come into this strange story at *any* point?'

'What do you reckon?'

'Grant, you *cannot* do this. You're bloody *contracted*!'

'Sorry, Dunc. Killed Darius off. It was him or me. Happened off the page. Got no control over what happens off the page. Anyway, since *I* gave birth to him, don't I have the right to write him out of my life?'

'Are you sure going off-piste like this is not more about your private life, about you and Becky, than any *real* desire to kill off DI Armstrong?'

'Certain, Duncan. Honest t'God. I'm feeling pretty sober about all that right now. I'm living like a monk, here in my little writing cell, and y'know what? I am actually *enjoying* writing. Enjoying it more than I have done in years. So, if you don't mind…?'

But Duncan's still grumbling on about me throwing the baby out with the bathwater. Speaking of which, if Becky finds out – and I wouldn't put it past Duncan to grass on me – she'll be on the phone soon, wanting to know where the money's coming from. Mortgage and rent for this place just about doable. But money for a baby? Then, come Monday afternoon, Gigi'll be breathing down my neck, pissed off with me for shuffling off the shelf she likes to keep me on. *Grant, sweetie*, she'll say, *you can't just abandon your readers like this.*

'Come on now, Grant,' Duncan is saying. 'Just *one* more. Put this worthy stuff aside for a few months, kill Darius off in a big, blockbusting final book. We can bring out the boxed set the following year, *then* you can move on.'

'Sorry, Dunc. The man's dead. D-E-A-D, *dead*. He is an ex-protagonist. He is as stiff as your favourite Kindle. He will not rise up, whatever inducements you throw at me.'

Thing is, this… *little death* has got me out of the hole I've been in for years. For the first time in a long time, I'm flying. Don't know what I'm doing, don't know where I'm going, don't need to – just yet. Just know I haven't written like this since way back. Know that, despite all the shit that's gone on in my life, I can still hack it – or rather, *not* hack it. I can sit in this room, looking out on those dreary grey walls, all those windows – most of them dark, most of the time, save for mine and the Brown Woman's – and not be in Grub Street. Can transport myself to another world. A world where craft takes over from the marketplace; a place where I'm starting to feel quite at home.

'Inducements are thin on the ground right now, Grant,' Duncan informs me, 'as you well know. Literary fiction only *really* sells if you make the Man Booker, land yourself a big prize. Is that what you're aiming at? Getting a gong before you hit forty?'

'Not aiming at anything, Dunc, old mate. Just want to write well. Want to write a novel caring about every word that's in it.'

'Well, we're going have to renegotiate your contract for that one! Trust you're aware this'll change things? And not necessarily for the better!' A thoughtful pause follows, in which I'm supposed to come to my senses. Then Duncan says, 'How's Becky doing, by the way?'

I ignore this blatant attempt at emotional blackmail. 'Renegotiate away, Duncan. Money's not everything, is it?'

'Isn't it?' Duncan says, putting down the phone.

It's been abnormally warm for early April. The other evening, my top sash pulled down, her casement opened wide, I hear cutlery clattering onto the draining board up there; hear, post-clatter, her radio on: a concert on 3, the music wafting down. Schubert, I think. I flick on the radio I keep on my desk but seldom listen to, and, after trying to work to it, stop and just listen. I must've been blasting it pretty loud, too, because, when I look up, I see her looking down. I raise my hand in a thumbs-up gesture, and she gives me a double thumbs-up back. And I find myself feeling extraordinarily content. It was one of those sublime moments when the moment itself feels quite perfect. I completely forgot how shitty I'd felt after Becky's call. Why *should* I be at the birth? Does she think if she gets me there, whatever the outcome, she'll have me? Life's got to be more than duty, more than responsibility. Where's the passion in that? And perhaps, I've begun to think, it's got to be more than knowing. Or more than *thinking* you know. You see, I'm getting to like *not* knowing. Getting quite fond of this intuitive approach to my work – to life in general.

She's not been in quite so much over the past few weeks, the Brown Woman. I'm glad she's got more of a life for herself. Though I always like it, come the evening, when I look up and see a light go on up there, see her making tea, cooking, washing something in that sink. Funny, that.

'Please, Grant. *Please* think it over,' Becky pleads.

'So! Have you invited Harry along to this… big opening, too?' I ask her. 'Have you covered all the angles?'

'*Jesus, Grant!* I *told* you, Harry's out of the picture.'

'Completely out or *almost* out?'

'You are so fucking…'

'*Pedantic*, I think you'll find the word is.'

And Becky hangs up.

Gigi felt the need to come round yesterday, to brief me re. my profile-raising gigs. 'Grant, whatever may or may not be going on in your head re. Darius—'

'Never fear, Gigi,' I say. 'Nothing re. Darius *is* going on in my head.'

'Whatever. Anyway… Just do this *one* incy-wincy thing for us, will you? *Please*, Grant, sweetie? Just make like Darius has taken a holiday or something. Keep the punters interested. Right? Do *not* go saying you've killed him off. Not yet, Grant. OK? Budgets are friggin tight, y'know. And *I* need my job, even if you don't need yours.'

I get the message and promise to be good.

There's quite a crowd at the library, quite a buzz. I start to get that tug-tugging feeling, that egoistic kick. See a few of my readers looking over to me, hear my name whispered behind one or two hands, and get quite a buzz myself.

I'm standing there, commanding my horned inner demons to back off, when this rather nice voice, soft but with a hint of huskiness, says, 'Would you care for a glass of wine?'

She's pretty slim – beneath that earth-brown coat, that Cancer Care leather jacket – is the Brown Woman. Close up, the face looking up at me looks a little younger than I'd thought. She's wearing a bit of make-up – all very subtle – a black top and a rather nice chunky necklace. And I don't know quite what to say to her, face to face, so I just nod, and she hands me a glass of red.

'I'm afraid I'm not a fan,' she says. 'I just work here.'

'Don't be afraid,' I say. 'Be proud. I'm sure you have much better taste.'

She doesn't assure me she has or has not, just says, 'I'm Megan, by the way.'

'Grant!' I say, holding out a hand.

'I think I already know that, don't I?' she says, indicating the poster on the wall. 'Unless… Is it a pseudonym?'

I shake my head.

After I've done my self-reverential spiel, signed a pile of books, sold a few, I notice she's still there, gathering up the glasses, collecting the bottles.

'Would you care for another?' she asks, holding up a half-empty bottle of red.

'Any chance of a quick cup of tea?' I say. 'Throat's a bit dry after all that blah-blah-blahing.'

She tells me how good my blah-blah-blahing was, and I find myself telling her what I shouldn't tell her about the death of Darius Armstrong. And then, after standing there for half an hour or more, after topping up my tea, each of us by now perched on a table amongst the dishevelled chairs, the shelves of books, she says, 'I had a child once, you see. His father came from Louisiana. He was taken away… my baby. Well, I was only a child myself. It was just… well… well, you reminded me… and I thought, I wondered…'

'When?' I ask. 'When was this?'

'He would've been – *will*, I hope, wherever he is, be – thirty-seven next month.'

'Me too!' I say. 'Except, for me, it's October.'

Her face flushing, she looks down. Then, looking up again, says, 'It wasn't that I thought you were… not that I even wanted you to be… it was just… I don't know.'

'I know,' I say. 'I know.'

23

'I know,' he said, 'I know', his face looking down into mine with such kindness, such understanding.

A few days later, I'm turning my key in the front door, when I hear his voice calling from across the street. 'Megan! I'm just off to the park. Fancy a walk?'

As we walk he tells me about his wife, about the baby due in two weeks' time.

'And you know what?' he says. 'Right now, in spite of what I've said to her, in spite of the anger I've felt towards Becky for lying to me back then, for putting me in this position now, I find myself hoping this baby *isn't* mine. Find myself – even though Becky swears she and Harry are through – wanting its skin to be as lily-white as Harry's. Wanting it to be Harry's. After all her lies, I find myself hoping my wife *is* lying to me now, because, deep down, whatever happens, I feel our marriage is over.'

I tell him he might feel differently when he sees the baby, might feel something for it – and for his wife again – whatever the colour of the child's skin. But he shakes his head and says he's 'had enough of being a performing seal'. Then, suddenly changing the subject, he says, 'Isn't "Death and the Maiden" sublime? Got myself a copy: Amadeus Quartet. *Beautiful!* Can't stop playing it,' shaking his head, smiling to himself. 'You know, if my mother was still around to hear me say that, she'd either be baffled or proud.'

'Maybe both?' I say.

We are approaching the café. He gestures over to the tables. I take a seat at one of them as he goes to get tea for us both. Then he comes back, sits down, and tells me the story of his life.

Bird Brains

Bird Brains

'It's their highly responsive MHV!' Aurelia said, adopting that high-flown tone of hers.

They were discussing the intelligence of birds. Aurelia had edged the conversation in that direction, maybe as a way of proving, if proof was needed, how very clever she was. Her PhD had been on avian cognition: *Thinking Psittacinae-Fashion*. She had spent two years in close communication with a rather bright parrot, and for a while student and 'guinea pig' were almost inseparable. Well, until Aurelia's dissertation was completed. But then, beneath those sleek Sloane Street clothes, that expensive salon-blonded hair, that purring cut-glass accent, there had always been a cut-throat masculinity about Aurie. 'She dumped the poor bugger when she met me,' her husband Frazer had joked, on more than one occasion, before going on to do his 'Who's a pretty girl, then?' party piece parrot impersonation.

'Their *what*?' Andrew questioned.

'Mediorostral hyperstriatum ventrale!' Said as if any fool with half a brain would know that.

'Well, torture me with a turkey baster for not knowing. Can't birds just have brains like you and me?'

'Forgive me, Andrew,' Aurelia's right hand drawing back her lustrous blonde hair to expose the forehead within which all that grey matter resided, 'but *my* brain and *your* brain are two quite different kettles of fish.'

'Ah!' Andrew said, topping up his wine glass. 'Explains those wretched seagulls dive-bombing me in Whitstable last summer, then.' Left forefinger tapping his temple. 'Must've completely emptied my rusty old kettle.'

There was a ripple of amused laughter around the table, though not, Helen noted, as she slid the sautéed courgettes into a dish, from Aurie herself. Aurelia had always taken herself far too seriously. But then, to get where she was in the competitive world of neurosurgery – a world dominated by preening men who took themselves very seriously indeed – she'd had to.

'If, as you say, Frazer,' Duncan said, while transferring the penultimate duck breast from pan to plate, 'parrots can only count to six, how come they can say *Pieces of eight*?'

Duncan had suggested it: 'A little dinner party come *le weekend*? *Ça va*?' A rare weekday morning, husband and wife together at the breakfast table, neither in a rush. 'Christen the kitchen!'

After a decade of aimless discussion, the dining-room wall had at last been demolished, creating, according to Duncan, 'an extremely convivial space'.

'I'll call a few' (*Please don't say it*, Helen had silently pleaded) 'chums, shall I?' And then, 'How's about my signature dish for mains? Don't worry. I'll take charge of the duck!'

Duncan was the sort of man who took charge of things. Helen, it transpired, had become the sort of woman who did the vegetables; the sort, her husband informed their assembled guests over an aperitif of champagne on the postage stamp patio of their pocket-sized Georgian terrace, who 'rustled up a very yummy pud'.

Public school boys had chums. Little boys brought up on *Janet and John* readers had chums. And Duncan, though he would have liked to have been the former – and had worked hard to give the impression he had been – was neither of these.

'Right, then!' he'd said. 'I'll give the usual suspects a buzz.'

And, although a closet fan of Gabriel Byrne, Helen wished that film had never been made, the number of times Duncan, and a whole line-up of men like Duncan, had hijacked the title. And *buzz*? Whoever said 'buzz' these days? Beekeepers, maybe? Except, if bees were on the decline, then beekeepers would surely follow – not to mention the manufacturers of their peculiar garb. Unless of course, seeing a gap in the market, with a slight revamp, they were made available to far-right racist groups. Now *they* were most likely on the up.

'Don't forget the ducks!' Duncan shouted as he flew downstairs that Friday morning. I mean, a man who led an uber-busy life as a cardiothoracic surgeon (a job offering up a steady supply of subordinated handmaidens) could not be expected to take charge of the shopping as well as the ducks. His live-in handmaiden was thus deployed to wade through a Waitrose awash with frustrated Friday-evening shoppers to source the dead, denuded birds.

And had not the ducks in question already been made oven-ready, Helen imagined, prior to quacking their last quack, the once-feathered trio might, at first sight of Duncan in masterful Master Chef mode, have plucked out their own feathers and performed their own ritual mastectomies, flipping their tender breasts into the pan to lay, breastlessly, down to die before Mr D. J. Threvithick BS, FRCS (Eng). Duncan sometimes had that effect on people: a way of subordinating them just by being Duncan. *Sometimes*, Helen thought – sometimes fondly, sometimes not – *Duncan has that effect on me.*

'Whole ducks, Helen!' had been Duncan's parting shot before slamming the front door.

It had become a habit: this surfeit of duck. One begun by the senior house officer, out to impress the young art therapist who would become his wife. Impress her not only with his cooking skills, but also with the surgical precision of his dissecting skills – not to mention, back in those single days, his shopping skills. Duncan wielding the knife that afternoon with ever-greater expertise, while commanding his wife check all the ingredients for his special-recipe marinade were available to him. Helen, searching the larder cupboard for runny honey, wishing her husband would sometimes 'take charge' of the ravioli or the risotto, or could occasionally 'rustle up' some sub-Eton-mess of a pud, resenting the gender-specific pigeonholing her husband's carnivorous nature had forced upon her.

'Cormorants can count to eight,' Frazer responded, ducking the parrot question. 'Some fishermen – China, I think it was; isn't it always China? – allegedly offered up every eighth fish as a reward and, do you know—?'

'Bollocks!' Andrew interjected. 'Don't believe a word of it. Not a single digit. Bloody birds were just hanging around for the damn fish. Who says they were *counting*?'

'But what about crows?' Duncan stepped in. 'I imagine a crow, should it need to, could count *way* beyond eight. Crows, jackdaws, all the corvids are as bright as their gimlet eyes. And they've pretty meaty forebrains, I believe. Isn't that so, Aurie?'

Aurelia nodded. 'Reckon, given the chance, they could run the whole damn country. At least get the economy moving.'

'Then,' Frazer said, slathering a roll with a similar volume of butter, 'at last we'd have something to *crow* about.'

'Hurry up with those potatoes, darling!' Duncan commanded, his knife incisively lacerating the final duck breast. 'I've just finished slicing Andrew's breast.'

'Oo-er.' Frazer's large, square hands protectively clamping his pink-shirted chest.

'Trouble with you surgeons,' Andrew said, 'is you don't know when to stop. I may be a tad porky, but I do *not* have boobs! Well, not on a par with yours, Aurie.'

Reaching for the vegetable dish, Aurelia raised a disdainful eyebrow.

'Watch it, Andrew!' Frazer instructed. 'Not your territory. Thought you would've learned by now.'

'Just comparing and contrasting. No offence, Aurie.'

Leaning back in her chair, the fingers of her left hand checking the whereabouts of her plunging neckline, Aurelia remained silent.

'Jesus, Andrew!' Helen put the dish of creamed potato down on the table before sitting down herself. 'You've got through half that bottle already. I hope you're not driving home?'

'Dunno. Thought I might boot old Dunc out and stay with you, Hel.'

It was happening again. That was the trouble with chums. Chums sometimes took advantage. Chums had a habit of pushing the boundaries of friendship.

'How could she, Hel? You wouldn't kick a gorgeous fella like me out, would you? I mean, that woman… you *know* how I love that woman. Love her to bits. Tell her that next time you see her, eh? To bloody bits.'

'Please, Andrew,' filling his empty water glass with water, 'do *try* to hold off until dessert or we'll all be in tears, and you will definitely be cabbing it home.'

Last time he had drained their whisky bottle dry in the night. Last time he had puked all over the stair carpet as they were hauling him upstairs. Last time Helen's bare feet had experienced an overly intimate encounter with her husband's oldest chum's urine – a large quantity of which was puddled about the bathroom floor.

'Remember last time?' Said more sharply than she'd intended. Andrew's vacant, bloated face gazed blankly back at her across the table. 'Well, you may have forgotten, but *I* most certainly have not.'

His puffy eyes brightening, he said, '*Do* remember you reminding me of it a couple of weeks later, though.'

'Just remembered!' Aurelia said, brightening herself, 'I was once quite close to a *Jack Dawe*. Briefly. Way back when. At med school.'

'Two-timing the parrot, were you?' Andrew chipped in.

A morsel of duck hovering near his mouth, Duncan said, 'Didn't realise your wife was such a bird fancier, Frazer.'

'Nice body,' Aurelia continued, 'but so-so brain. Made it through, somehow. Couldn't count for toffee, though. Three months into his proper job, the idiot left a clamp in a patient.'

'Just the one?' Andrew's familiar boozy-woozy smile spreading across his face.

Apprehensively eyeing his loaded fork, Farid wondered why so many middle-class Brits – and, come to that, almost all the carnivorous French – were so fond of undercooked meat; a love of bloody juices apparently adding a soupçon of sophistication. 'You see!' he said. 'Now, a cormorant would *not* have made that mistake.'

Everyone smiled. Including Helen.

Helen has such a lovely smile, Farid thought, admiring the glossy redness of her hair as it brushed the plum-coloured silk covering her shoulders.

'Is this duck *sushi*, Duncan?' Helen asked her husband. 'Thought you'd seen enough blood for one week.'

'Big ops?' Frazer asked.

'*Knackering!* Three of the buggers.' Turning to his wife, 'And I assure you, my sweet, this duck is perfectly cooked.'

'Just right,' Andrew professed between glugs of wine, of the meat he'd yet to taste. 'Something to get your teeth into.'

Finally doing just that.

Watching him masticating the undercooked flesh, Helen pictured Andrew collapsed on a flattened box, legs splayed, cardboard soaked in urine, spidery rivulets of pee meandering across the pavement. Still chewing, he was already topping up the half-drained wine glass, his glass of water left untouched.

'Shouldn't you hold off a bit on that, Andy?' Aurelia suggested.

'Give me one good reason why.'

'I'll give you three: Jules, Franci and George.'

His big, empty eyes welling, Andrew put down the glass.

Helen flashed Aurelia a piercing glance. OK. It was a good answer. It was the right answer to give. But Helen did not want Andrew sobbing at her dinner table again. Did not want his salty tears on her shoulder again, his winey drool on her new silk shirt. Did not want to mop his urine, wipe up his puke ever again. Did not care for, or about, a man who would do one stupid arsehole thing and then, when he was found out, proceed to do an even more stupid arsehole thing, while still expecting his friends to feel sorry for *him*.

As she reached for the water jug Helen's eyes met Farid's. *How kind they are*, she thought. *How feminine. His lashes are twice the length of mine.* And then, *It must be strange to wake up beside such a beautiful man.*

Turning to Andrew, Farid said, 'You know, there is life beyond alcohol, Andrew.'

'*Beyond?*' Frazer questioned. 'Since, Fari, you've never jumped on that particular wagon in order to get off it again, how the hell would *you* know?'

'True. But I have lived for forty-three years, thirty of them knowingly without the stuff, and twenty of them in this country – with all the alcoholic temptations implicit in that fact – without feeling I'm *missing out* on anything.'

'But you *are*, Fari, old man,' Duncan insisted. 'You decidedly are.'

'But he's not, Duncan,' Helen felt forced to say. 'He *decidedly* is not. And you know it. Booze is a trap. A prop. Dinner-party drinking around a table like this? Winos on a street corner? What's the difference? It's all addiction. It's all weakness.'

'Hey there, folks! Can we change the subject, please? I was just beginning to enjoy myself.'

'No you weren't, Andrew. You bloody weren't!' And, overcome with anger, Helen whisked the glass en route to Andrew's mouth from his hand, Shiraz splashing over his plate to mix with the pinky-red juices of the duck. 'You're just burying yourself. Drowning yourself in the damn stuff. It's so, *so fucking stupid*!' And standing up, her chair almost toppling as she did so, Helen grabbed the three bottles on the table and rushed over to the newly installed Butler's sink, the assembled diners, including Farid, watching in stunned silence as what remained of the rather expensive wine was poured down the drain.

Returning to the table, she raised her topped-up water glass in the air.

There were several seconds of silence, then, raising his glass of elderflower, Farid said, 'Cheers! Here's to Helen!'

—◦◦◦—

'That was *quite* a performance you gave us last night,' Duncan got around to saying on Sunday morning. 'Not like you at all.'

'No?'

They were clearing up the kitchen. Or, rather, Helen was clearing up the kitchen. Duncan, who had suggested they had 'better get up and tackle the bloody mess down there', was sitting at a table awash with unwashed glasses and stained coffee cups, the sports section of the newspaper in one hand, the mug he had just filled with coffee in the other. *As if I was a paid helper*, Helen thought as she loaded the dishwasher. Was Her-Wot-Does. Was *his* skivvy. Was not the other half of this relationship, the other name on the deeds of this fine Georgian three-up two-down box of a house, this money pot of a property which, she had recently found herself calculating, for some reason, if split down the middle could purchase two very decent flats in perfectly decent parts of London. Not *this* part, you understand, but still… a change was as good as a rest.

The rest of my life. The words wandering in and out of her head. *I will be forty-five come November. The rest of my life?*

Suddenly irritated by the back of her husband's neck, she said, 'Could you pour *me* one of those, please?' A small ridge of fat had collected there. Duncan had become a little fleshier of late. *Bulk* was how he'd described it – apparently with some pride. *Too much duck*, Helen thought.

Duncan had not spoken of her 'performance' until now. Frosty in the bathroom, he had managed a perfunctory peck on the cheek before switching off the light, and a cold 'Good morning' on waking. Although, immediately after this performance of hers, pulling a substandard bottle of red from the wine rack, he had chosen to crack a joke at Helen's expense. Not that anyone, other than Helen or Farid (should they have sampled it), would have noticed the wine's inferior quality. Even Aurelia, the designated driver – she who regularly operated on battered brains, on lives shattered by the idiocy of drink-driving – felt the need to accept another 'teensy-weensy glass'.

Helen, Duncan declared, had spoiled the evening. Had ruined his mood. All their moods. Had, in his opinion, made a molehill into a mountain, thus demeaning her recognition of the pile of trouble Andrew was in. Perhaps they were all in? All except for Farid. Farid who had neither drink problem nor spouse problem – nor child problem, Helen supposed.

It was often that way round: often Helen who made too much of something. Helen who took life too seriously. 'Lighten up, Hel!' Duncan would say, unconcerned as to why she might be feeling heavy.

'For heaven's sake, Duncan. It *happened*. OK. I couldn't stop myself. You and Frazer are his oldest friends. Aren't friends supposed to support each other? To *care* about each other? Surely friendship's about challenging actions, not simply accepting them? Friends don't just stand by and watch their best *chum* crash his entire life. A friend's got to be more than the good guy with deep pockets who buys the next round of drinks!'

'*Quite* a performance,' Duncan repeated, looking vaguely in her direction, but not looking her in the eye – and not really listening.

He was pretending to read the sports section. Folding the newspaper so aggressively it made sharp crackling sounds as she spoke. Then, tossing it on top of the mess on the table, he stood up. Helen did not turn round, but continued emptying the dishwasher, filling it from the dirty pile on the worktop.

'*God damn it*, Helen! There are places and times for challenging my friends.'

So they were *his* friends now, were they? Was that the way it would go? *This sofa's mine. That chair's yours.*

'And a civilised meal on a Saturday evening is *not* one of them. As if Andy hasn't got enough on his plate. What good did it do? Putting him in the spotlight like that.'

Pressing the start button, she turned to look at him. 'Christ almighty, Duncan. Hasn't Andrew been putting himself there for quite long enough?'

He was standing by their newly installed French doors, looking out into the garden. His back to her, he exuded resistance. Looked solid, impenetrable, but, at the same time, weak.

I could mend this, she thought; *mend you. Could bridge this widening fissure simply by walking up behind you and wrapping my arms around your broadening girth. I could take responsibility for spoiling your evening. Could say, 'There, there, promise I won't do it again. We're OK now, aren't we, Duncan?'* He would like that. Would like to feel her close, yet below him – beneath him – his overly paternal hand stroking the hair of his submissive little wife, tamed once more.

He was still standing there, sipping his coffee, staring out.

Taking in the clipped box 'clouds', the ubiquitous ivy, the darkness of the jasmine foliage, no longer lightened by its starry mass of flowers, Helen wished she had not given in to Duncan's desire for professional garden designers. How empty it looked. How colourless. How sterile. Not a garden for children. Just as well. How could it have worked? Her eyes drawn to the back of her husband's neck, she felt tears welling.

At twenty-five, his body spooned into hers, it had been the first thing she saw on waking: his soft, sandy hair, longer then, curling into his neck, tickling her nose as she willed him to wake, to make love to her.

'For heaven's sake, Duncan,' she said, breaking the poisonous silence, 'don't you *want* to save Andrew's life?'

'There you go again! Over-dramatising. A few drinks, for fuck's sake!'

'A few *months'* drinks. A bender that's lasted precisely…' She paused, counting the weeks, the months. 'Nineteen months! Christ knows how he holds down his job. And you're prepared to let him continue in this way?'

Putting his coffee mug down on the draining board, Duncan turned to look back at his wife. Helen searched for the kindness in her husband's face, the love she wanted to see there, hoping it might osmotically draw out her own, but saw only Farid's soft-eyed gaze. *Pathetic. Juvenile. Grow up, Helen.*

'Andy'll pull himself together, given time,' Duncan was saying, still waiting for her to go to him.

'Come *on*. Do you really think that? Can't men mother their friends as well as be their best Budweiser buddies? Can't men *grow up*?!'

He looked a tad hurt by that. She did not want to hurt him. But what else could she do?

'In fact, on the contrary, you seem happy being his supplier. Because that doesn't deprive *you* of anything, does it? Because *your* preferred tipple comes in bottles with chateaus on the labels, you can all be chums together. Which must be all right, since posh people live in chateaus. Posh people spend a fortune soaking those they love in expensive booze. It's low-life scumbags who use dirty syringes and bits of foil, and get high in back alleys, or purchase their preferred tipple from a hardware store that are the problem, not a six-pack of classy consultants sipping claret from crystal glassware!'

Did she love him or hate him? It had become as woolly, as uncertain as that.

She could see he'd had enough. He never liked her raising her voice. It was not what *nice* women did. Nice men? Well, that was a different matter. Nice men had to stand up for themselves. Nice men *should* stand up for their chums, for their women, too – if they were nice. Nice men should stand a round of drinks.

The fingers of his left hand combing angrily through his sandy-brown hair, Duncan said, 'Of course, when it comes right down to it, your performance was really for Farid's benefit. A way of *currying* favour, you could say.'

'*What?!*'

She hated his use of that word. Hated the way his lip curled when he said it. Hated the whiff of racism attached to it. At that moment, hated Duncan.

'Yes. You were putting yourself in the spotlight. You were playing to an audience of one.'

'I was *what*?'

'Your number-one fan.'

'*Jesus Christ!*'

She was so angry, she thought she might hit him. There were a few seconds of silence. Then the telephone rang.

Helen agreed to meet Jules in Cream Teaz. Countless Sunday afternoons had been whiled away there: first the two of them, the midwife and the art therapist; then, coupled up with their high-profile specialist partners, came the romantic foursome; then five come Georgiana, and six come Francine. *Will it soon be we two again?* Helen wondered, watching Jules ordering cakes at the counter. 'Maybe Duncan and Andy see us as safe bets,' she had suggested to Jules, on a similarly grey Sunday twenty years before. 'As good, supportive wife material. They know we're not quite in their league.'

Franci at a sleepover, and George sleeping in with Maxxi, Jules was free all afternoon.

'Don't you mind?' Helen asked her. 'I mean, George is barely fifteen.'

'Fifteen and a half now! Well, y'know, better the devil and all that.'

'And is Maxxi a bit of a devil?'

'Far from it! Picture the cutest choirboy, put him on the rack, stretch him to six foot one, add a smattering of pimples, dress him in black, and you have it! Not the greatest catch, in my opinion – not that I've said as much. More than my life's worth. Still,' Jules sighed as she topped up their teacups, 'George dotes on her Maxxi.'

'And precautions?'

'Sorted! Bed 'n' breakfast 'n' pill. All part of the parental service.'

Jules was amazing. A natural mother. No. It would never have worked.

'Y'know,' Jules was saying, 'I've even found myself wondering what it'd be like to start over myself.'

Jules professed to having turned a corner, to having seen the future and found herself intrigued, not frightened by it.

'But sex?' she went on. 'Sex with a stranger? Exposing this!' Hands searching for her waistline. Then, fingers returning to break off another piece of cake, 'Perhaps I should stick to the book club for company and slices of lemon drizzle for comfort?' Wiping the crumbs from her lips, she said, 'How is he?'

'Not bad,' Helen said, not wanting to dampen her friend's spirits. Then, picturing Andrew staggering to Farid's car, 'Well, not so good, actually. It'll take time, Jules. Anyway, I'm to tell you, he still loves you.'

Lemony fingers scraping back her straw-coloured hair, Jules sighed. 'Trouble is, he's a *helluva* lot of work. The girls... well, at least they behave, more or less, like adults. And they've been so supportive, so sensible through this. I need a grown-up for a partner, not a stressed-out boy-dad in need of a mum. I can't, Hel, I *won't* allow him back the way he is. Andy's gotta do the work. And do it fast! Then maybe...' Looking down at her plate. 'Oh, I don't know.' She crumbled off another mouthful of cake. 'So! How's the lovely Farid these days? I do miss him dropping by. Such a sweet guy. He and Annie still going strong?'

'Afraid not.'

What a lie. When Duncan told her there were to be six, not seven diners on Saturday night she'd felt a rush of pleasure; had not been in the least bit afraid. Or was she?

'Gosh! Annie doesn't know when she's well off.'

'Actually, I think it was Farid who did the dumping.'

'*Why?* They looked so good together. Such a beautiful couple.'

'Farid Manduri!' he'd announced.

Not Dr Manduri, but *Farid* Manduri. And then, when he'd called the department to ask how his patient was progressing, simply, 'It's Farid from Haematology', as if he was some lowly technician.

Eight years ago, Helen thought. *My chum then. Mine.*

They kept bumping into each other at lunchtimes. That third time (by then, their patients overlapping, Farid had also met Duncan), Farid had talked of his childhood in Pakistan, of visits to his cousins in the once-beautiful, *still*-beautiful Swat valley. Helen had pointed out the bitter irony of its name, imagining it crammed with children swotting for their exams. Boys *and* girls! And Farid had spoken of benevolent rulers who had developed a network of libraries and educational institutions there. 'Maybe,' he'd said, 'hoping for just that.' And then, 'My favourite cousin's daughter was shot while walking to her school. They missed Salma's brain – one assumes they were aiming at that. Scary things, where I come from, women's brains.'

She knew then. Just knew.

'But they got her in the neck. Miraculously, the bullets – there was more than one – missed her spine. She has a voice, of sorts. But will never sing as she used to.'

Tears welling in Helen's eyes, Farid had produced a tissue from his pocket. 'I'm so sorry to have upset you,' he'd said, holding it out to her.

'What pampered lives we lead,' Helen finally managed to say. 'What selfish, pampered lives.'

'Nonsense! We are born where we are born. If, as I believe, we have but one life, better to be comfortable and content in it, than miserable. Do *not* feel guilty for your good life, Helen. And do not let my sad stories ruin your good life.'

But my life is already ruined, she'd thought.

Returning home, she found Duncan in their newly painted kitchen-diner salting the duck legs: confit of duck was, understandably, his second signature dish. He did not look up, but did say, 'Hello, you,' in a friendly tone.

'Hello,' she replied, a hand brushing his shoulder as she squeezed past him to open the window – did men need less oxygen than women, do you suppose? 'I'll just go up and put on something sloppy.'

'How's dear old Jules?' he asked, sprinkling the rest of the salt, pressing down the lid of the container and shaking it as he turned to her.

'Very good, actually. Best I've seen in a long while.'

'She won't want him back, then?'

'Probably not. Maybe? Who knows?'

He slipped the salted duck into the fridge and pulled out a carton of eggs. 'By the way, Farid called an hour or so ago.'

'Oh.'

'Said to say thanks for your contributions to the *delicious* meal. Turns out Andy stayed with him last night. Well, Fari insisted he stay. Says he hadn't the heart to leave him at the flat in that state.'

Helen said Farid had almost too much heart. Duncan agreed.

'Did Andrew puke on Fari's carpet, piss on Fari's bathroom floor?'

Duncan said he didn't think so. Or if he had, Farid had been courteous enough not to mention it. 'But Andrew *did* cry on his shoulder. Last night and this morning. In a terrible state, apparently. Rock bottom. So rock bottom that, thanks to Fari's gentle, persuasive tongue, Andy's agreed to go to AA. Even checked online. Found his nearest group. What's more, his teetotal mentor has volunteered to get him there on Thursday evening. So, my princess, your wish has come true!'

'Wasn't it your wish too?'

'I guess. Yep. Sure it was.'

She was right, he said. But then, she was almost always right. Which could be particularly annoying, *particularly* for a man.

Putting the carton of eggs on the table, he slipped an arm around her waist. She felt his hand stroking her hair in that paternal way.

'How's about I whip up a cheese soufflé omelette for a light supper?' He hadn't done one of those for months and months. 'That, a spot of salad, and a glass of apple juice should do us, eh?'

'Lovely.' And, releasing herself from his grasp, she walked into the hall.

Frazer had once told them how Aurie's grieving 'guinea pig' had mourned the loss of his mistress. 'Poor bugger called her name every morning for weeks,' Frazer had said, before reprising his parrot impersonation: '*Aurie! Aurie! Aurie!*'

'For fuck's sake, Frazer!' Aurelia had snapped. Then, more softly, 'The *poor bugger's* name, as you well know, was Ton-Ton. Dear Ton-Ton,' she'd repeated in barely a whisper.

Helen thought she had seen a glint of moisture in Aurelia's faraway gaze.

Would I be like Ton-Ton? Helen asked herself. *Would I mourn my loss?*

'Omelette in fifteen!' Duncan called up to her.

'Great!' she called back, pulling on her comfy velour loungers.

She could hear him down there, whistling while he worked: a clear, melodious tune, if a tad high-pitched for a man, and a little too wavering for the sort of man Duncan was, the sort who took charge of things.

A Blonde Woman

You think you won't forget, but you do. You make promises to yourself – and to them. You promise never to forget them. But you do. Those early black days become painful weeks, bearable months, until, looking back, you realise you've not thought of them for days on end. Then the years start clocking up, tick-tock, tick-tock, until, out of the blue, forcing their way into your unfaithful memory, they come to you. While you might still recall a birthday, an anniversary, some other special occasion you've continued to mark on the calendar that first year or two, knowing there was no cause for celebration, no need to send a card, yet feeling not to mark it would be to somehow write them off. Then, decades later – more than three decades in my case – when trying to resuscitate them in your consciousness, you find their face, or the totality of that face, eludes you, and, try as you might, you cannot remember that other important date in their life – the one you chose not to mark on the calendar year after year – and you find yourself searching for their death certificate, to remind yourself of the day your father died.

UL451167. Entry 179. Date of death: October 23rd, 1974. Cause of death: myocardial infarction. My mother's usually bold, free-flowing signature reduced to a shaky, uncertain scrawl in the bottom right-hand corner.

I was in Fife at the time. In my last year at the University of St Andrews. Applied economics. God knows why.

It was eleven months ago when I found that crumpled death certificate in the desk drawer, when I smoothed it flat with the flat of my hand and slipped it into a protective plastic sleeve, reminding myself that such documents – those to which a lifetime of memories are attached – must be preserved. Treasured.

It was May 8th, 2008: the day of Flora's operation.

My bothersome presence by my wife's empty bed more hindrance than help, the hospital staff had suggested I go home. 'Get a good night's sleep!' the nurse said. 'Come back in the morning. She'll be wide awake by then.'

Duly evicted, I found myself travelling home on the same crowded commuter train I frequently took in what now felt like my former life. Felt myself a pale-faced alien amongst the jostling, repugnant bodies of the living: those able to chat, laugh, swig their cans of booze, eat their foul-smelling, life-taking takeaways without a care in the world. As if life was a breeze, an easy ride, a certainty. While all I wanted was to be back at Flora's bedside, waiting to see her living, breathing body safely returned to it. Going back to the empty house seemed pointless to me. Felt like a trial run for a life without my wife.

Supper that night was a bowl of cornflakes. I remember peeling a banana to add to the bowl. Remember how the sweet, overripe smell of it put me off the notion; remember finding it there on the worktop next morning, brown and shrivelled, already rotting.

I drank two or three large whiskies that evening: a drink I seldom touch. And, putting the certificate safely away in the box containing our wills, went in search of the photograph albums, overcome with an urgent need, not just to remind myself of my father's life, but, more importantly, to reacquaint myself with the pictorial history of my life with Flora. Desperate to fix our past firmly in my head. Terrified there might not be a future to photograph.

It took me a while to find the albums. Flora would have located them in an instant.

'I wish I'd met him,' Flora had dutifully pronounced on first seeing a photograph of my father.

It was a family group: my four- or five-year-old self standing between my parents, my small, chubby hand held up to my father's surprisingly bony one, caught in a blur of affection. At least, that was how Flora saw it. Though, since my mother's hand could clearly be seen gripping my right hand, I suspected that my father, seeing no need to perform this double parental duty, had been *withdrawing* his hand from mine as the camera's lens came down.

'He was a good father,' my mother informed Flora at the time. 'Wasn't he, Aidan?'

'He was,' I dutifully answered. Not knowing if this was the truth or a lie.

'And here we are in Paris!' my mother pronounced, turning the page, pleased to have this opportunity to talk about her dead husband.

Five years had gone by since his death, and, fool that I was, I no doubt considered enough mourning time to have passed, rarely making reference to my father in my mother's presence, since he no longer had any reference in my life.

How cruel the young can sometimes be.

'What other women have you loved?' Flora asked me within minutes of my first declaring my love for her. Asked insistently, unromantically, as if about to demand an inventory. I half-expected her to grab a pen, wave it in front of my nose, and say, *Go on, then! Write them down! I want names, dates, addresses! Then that'll be an end of it. You've got me now.*

And who but a fool would want more than that?

'There was one woman I once had a particular obsession with,' I told her.

She looked intrigued and, I was pleased to see, a little worried.

'*La Joconde!*' my father announced in his badly accented French, a hand gesticulating in her direction, as if he himself had placed her there. '*Magnifique! N'est-ce pas?*'

And for once he and I were in complete agreement.

He was a teacher. Classics and history in the classroom, and whatever else he considered a worthy subject for study out of it. Renaissance art a particular fascination of his. And as a consequence, thanks to my father, I became a rather unfortunate sort of boy: the sort who at the tender age of fourteen became fascinated by a woman some 450 years older than himself, returning from that summer holiday with her picture in my breast pocket, and keeping the *Mona Lisa* between the pages of my empty diary for a full year.

Revisiting the Louvre four years later – by then looking upon real live girls, girls of more or less my own age, as better prospects for a fully consummated love – though not as yet having summoned the courage to touch one of them – I must admit, a little of her holiday magic remained.

My father had set himself up as our educator: me and my accommodating mother. Though my mother was far less accepting than was I of the lengths our intellectual tour guide might go to in order to stiffen the flabby sinews of our lazy, lackadaisical minds. Left to her own devices my mother wanted nothing more than to stretch out her body on a sunny beach, or to slump down in a shaded café to watch the world go by.

'The *real* world!' she protested, recalling our mind-refining summer trips shortly after his death. 'Oh, the sheer boredom of it,' gazing out of the sitting-room window as the sun went down, 'but I'd give anything to be in a stuffy old museum standing beside him now.' Cupping her face in her hands, crying again.

'Why do these places always make me think I'm losing my sight?' she once said as we traipsed through yet another 'stuffy old museum', while outside, in the 'real world', the sun shone down.

'On the contrary,' my father rebuked, looking reproachfully over his shoulder to his reluctant students, '*these places*,' his arms stretching up, long fingers curving heavenwards, 'help us *all* to see in the dark.' Pausing to give full weight to his next sentence. '*If* we can but look.'

Shrugging her shoulders, glancing in my direction, my mother sighed, then, hooking her arm in mine, we two trooped dutifully on behind our tutor: my *good father*, her *fine husband*, the man whose praises were sung at a cheerful, if tearful, funeral. The perfect funeral, many said. And why would they not? Since, several years before his sudden departure from this life, in case his allotted span was as stingy as it proved to be, the subject of that funeral had drawn up clear and detailed guidelines to ensure the proceedings ran as smoothly as they did. Right down to the reading he assumed his son, his only child, would give: *Death is one of two things. Either it is annihilation, and the dead have no consciousness of anything; or, as we are told, it is really a change: a migration of the soul from this place to another.*

Socrates 470–399 BC, he had written after those lines, a teacher to the very end.

This bit of philosophic wisdom coming back to me soon after Flora was diagnosed. I wishing it had not, seeing its return to my flagging memory as a bad omen.

My father was a barometer of the time: a man who did what was expected of him; a father with great expectations for a son who would have preferred a different childhood. For, whether as a result of my parents' disjunctive certainties or my own woolly nature, I grew to adulthood a sheep in wolf's clothing, a soft-edged man in the hard-edged world of corporate fat cats, not quite knowing how he got there, yet not having the claws, or claws sharp enough, to scratch his way out.

This innate 'woolliness' perhaps partly explains my childhood love of *La Joconde*. The *Mona Lisa*'s questionable gender, back then, coming as no surprise to me, since I had seen far prettier boys at boarding school. Although, examining the bald beauty of her face now, I see Leonardo's subject could only have been a woman. What man would suffer the self-mutilating torture of plucking his eyebrows, perhaps eye*lashes*, in the name of beauty, for the sake of art?

I myself have always straddled that vacant void between the sexes. Not that I have ever questioned my gender, ever wished I'd been born a woman. Far too great a burden to bear. It's just that I have sometimes wished I had *not* been born a man.

By and large, I've led a pretty simple life: good education, goodish degree, OK job. Rising through the ranks to a certain level: not too low, not too high. Never CEO material. Not dynamic enough. Never cared enough. Reliable, that's me. A sticker. Married to Flora for thirty years. Three children: two boys, one girl. Same dog for sixteen, recently died. One grandchild, a girl, recently born.

A man with an aversion to pubs. 'Coming to the pub, Aidan?' the guys at work used to say – because they thought they should. 'They do a very decent pint, y'know.' *What in heaven's name is a decent pint? I would ask myself. Is there an in*decent *one? Does it pour itself sexily into a curvy glass? Does it slide down your throat as pole dancer to pole? Does it give good head?*

Neither am I a joke-telling, backslapping sort of man, like my brother-in-law Robert, whose back I did slap three Christmases ago, when, full of seasonal cheer, too much claret and his own self-importance, he managed to choke on a pistachio. And, although dying to kill the unfunny punchline he was about to deliver, I felt forced to punch a bony fist between his well-padded shoulder blades, sending the half-masticated nut halfway across the room. 'Cheers, mate!' Robert said, before finishing the godawful 'joke', his embarrassed audience laughing more with relief, now that the joke-teller's face had returned from puce to its usual ruddy pink, than from genuine amusement.

To add to my catalogue of unmanly attributes, I profess to having little knowledge or interest in what goes on under the bonnet of my fuel-efficient car. There's an engine in there, somewhere, that occasionally needs diesel, oil, the windscreen washer filling up. Anything else? I call Gary at the garage.

Sport: ditto. I possess a schoolboy horror of rugby, loathe soccer, and simply hearing the word 'cricket' makes me yawn. Though I do have a basic grasp of tennis – to watch, not to play. I like the sound of it on TV: the thwack of the rackets, the back-and-forth bounce of the ball, the gasps and groans of the players, the oohs and ahs of the centre court crowd. This, and an occasional sight of the scoreboard, is enough for me. I could do without the commentary. Unless of course it's Flora's. Unless Flora is lying there on the sofa, the green fleecy blanket pulled up to her neck, despite it being sunny outside, her lovely head resting on the brick-coloured velvet of the cushion, almost the same colour as her hair used to be.

A strangely happy time: those weeks when I took work home, setting up my office on the long refectory table in our open-plan living area.

'Aidan!' Flora said. 'Why ever don't you use the study? Surely the sound of Wimbledon will put you off your stroke?'

It did. But what did I care? I wanted to look up and see her there. Wanted never to leave her again. I even began to wish she might stay that way: alive, but incapacitated, always on the sofa, a permanent excuse for me to remain at home.

Flora gave up work to have our children. That was the deal, as she saw it. 'No half measures!' she said. Though she herself had been marked out as a high-flyer, was going places before she met me. Little Leo arrived two years after we met, Beatrice four years later, and young Benedict seven years after Beatrice. All three children benefiting from Flora's full-on commitment.

I hated leaving the house each morning when Leo and Beatrice were small. Especially Monday mornings. I'd get that same gut-wrenching feeling, that same sense of injustice I used to feel at the start of a new school term, my grey commuter suit as imprisoning as the maroon uniform in which, stiff and uncomfortable, I would sit in the back of the shiny maroon Daimler, looking up at the back of my father's head, slicked-down hair precision-trimmed above stiff, sparkling white shirt collar, the pink bulge of his thickening neck sandwiched between.

In teacher mode before we'd even hit the road, he would quiz me on whatever homework I had been forced to complete that holiday. While I, conscious only of the minutes ticking by, of the distance between myself and home lengthening, myself and school shortening, would tell myself I was too old to feel this way: too old to want to fling my arms around my mother's neck and say, *Can't we go back home, Mum? Can't I go to Bickersfield Comp like everyone else?* But no. Even though my father had done well for himself without the torture of boarding school, I must have the education he'd not had, 'but *should* have had!' I must suffer for his sake.

I can see Flora's red-gold hair haloed about her head.

It was a June morning. A Monday. Flora's pale hand was unbuttoning her white shirt, offering a milk-engorged breast to new-to-the-world Beatrice. While on the floor, using the space between the chair's legs and his mother's, three-year-old Leo was *choo-chooing* his wooden train back and forth.

'Bye-bye, Daddy!' Leo called out, as I came down the stairs.

I walked over to tousle his golden mop, to kiss Flora's pale neck, her lovely hair, to put my hand on Beatrice's bumfluff head. 'I can't bear to leave you,' I said. 'It's utter madness!'

'Go!' Flora's soft fingertips running down my freshly shaved jawline. 'We'll still be here when you get back. *We* are going nowhere', as Beatrice's gummy mouth gurgled up a surplus of watery milk.

I wiped Bea's chin with the knuckle of my index finger, lifting it to my lips. 'Yum!' I said.

'*Go on!*' Flora commanded. 'The sooner you're gone, the sooner you'll be back.'

That was some comfort, I supposed.

Halfway to the station I had to pull the car over. Couldn't see for tears. Nearly missed the damn train. Wished I had. That 'important' meeting didn't matter. All that Keynesian bollocks didn't matter. Holding your brand-new baby on a June morning, that mattered.

By the time Benedict arrived on the scene I'd more or less succumbed to my commuter lifestyle. Our children grew. Hamsters were demanded, a dog and two cats purchased. One cat later flattened. One hamster 'mistakenly' (we lied to our children) mutilated by our marmalade mog, prior to her own judicial flattening.

'Will she manage to have another life, do you think?' nine-year-old Leo enquired of Mitzy as I slid the spade under her flattened, oozing guts.

'I doubt it somehow, don't you?' I said.

Leo shrugged. 'Thought not!' he said nonchalantly. 'That nine lives stuff is all bollocks, isn't it?'

'Think I'd prefer "rubbish", "not true" or… um…'

'Bollocks?' Leo repeated, dribbling his football back up the drive.

When Benedict was two, Fritz, our Welsh springer-collie cross, after a sudden short illness, passed the way of all furry flesh. This bothering our toddler not one jot, upsetting Leo enough to put him off baked beans for a month, and devastating Beatrice, who wore black from head to toe for five weeks and, in the no-half-measures way of our daughter, a black armband for four months.

And, suddenly, before we knew it, Leo was off to Edinburgh University.

'He'll probably end up living in Scotland,' his mother mourned. 'We'll never see him.'

He did choose to live in Scotland. But we see him quite a lot.

While Mummy's girl Beatrice, on the other hand, like me, a stay-at-home from birth, opted for UCL, and continued to live at home until, two years into her linguistics degree, she announced she was moving out to move in with one of her lecturers.

'What's all the fuss?' our beloved daughter complained when I complained. 'He's only *fifteen* years older than me. We're practically the same generation!'

Although despairing inwardly, Flora knew better than to convey her despair to Beatrice, who, two years later, the 'young' man in question landing himself a professorship in the Language and Humanities Department of Humboldt University, upped sticks and moved with him to Berlin.

'I suppose it's not much further than Edinburgh, really,' Flora said, trying to smile.

One of the dubious 'benefits' of Flora's diagnosis has been Bea coming home more frequently than her previous, dutiful three trips a year.

'Are you going away, Daddy?'

I was in the hall, zipped-up lounge suit over one shoulder, overnight bag at my feet, leaving later than usual, since I would be staying later than usual.

'No,' I told my seven-year-old daughter, who sat cross-legged on the kitchen floor, pawing through a large box of decorations, 'just to work as usual. And then to the Christmas party later on.'

'*Ooh!* Can I come?'

'But not a very good party. No cake, no trifle, and *no* Father Christmas bringing us presents!'

'That's no party at all!' Beatrice said disdainfully, her attention returning to the responsible job of picking out what *she* considered the perfect ornaments to hang on the tree.

'Not much of one,' I agreed, not wanting to go to it either.

So far, Bea had picked out several lurid pink baubles, three white-winged angels, one with only one wing, and four pink mice, all freckled a dubious shade of green.

'*Sweetheart!*' Flora said, picking all four up by their tails in one mouldy bunch. 'We can't use *these*! However did they get in there?'

'Look after Mummy for me until the morning!' I instructed Leo.

'Always do!' my son grunted from several rungs up the ladder, from where he was attempting to hang the first of many home-made paper chains, too engrossed to turn his head. 'See ya, Dad! Watch out you don't step on our chains!' Not even bothering to look back as I pussyfooted to the front door, feeling an interloper, feeling one parent surplus to requirements.

Having binned the mice and checked on two-month-old Benedict in his carrycot on the sofa, Flora followed me to the front door.

'Now you have fun!' she said, hooking an arm around my neck. 'Let your hair down. A *little*.'

And she kissed me, brusquely, on the lips, in the way she might kiss Bea or Leo, before shooing me out onto the drive.

'I should be home before eleven tomorrow.'

'No need to rush! Have a good sleep. Make the most of not having a crying baby to wake you. And enjoy a decent breakfast without having to cook it yourself!'

Now if Flora had said, *Stay with us. Cancel the damn hotel room. Come home at the usual time*; or, better still, *Don't go at all*, I would have turned round in an instant. But there she was, waving me away, closing the front door before the car had even swung out into the road.

Twenty-four hours later, back in the bosom of my family, I wondered how little it might have taken to keep me the pure, unsullied man I was that morning. As little as a puff of air? As little, or as much, as Flora blowing a kiss through that closing crack of door?

My wife over the worst of the chemo, I returned to my daily commute. Took to wandering around the National Gallery at lunchtime, finding a worshipful solace there.

I would drift aimlessly from room to room, sometimes looking at the paintings, sometimes not. Sometimes gazing blankly at whatever hung before me, thinking of Flora, sometimes looking with great intensity at a single painting, and thinking what my father might have said about it, while doing my best *not* to think of Flora. Though she was never far away. And soon I found her, hiding around a corner. Except she had hair again: long strawberry-blonde hair, trailing over shoulders far meatier than those my wife now possessed. And she had eyebrows and eyelashes – and breasts! Much of her right breast exposed, the left partially covered by the material of her untied blouse, artfully slipped down over those meaty shoulders. Or maybe aggressively pulled down by the painter himself. 'Artistic licence!' Palma Vecchio might have said – or the Italian equivalent – his hands smelling of turpentine, green and yellow pigment collected under his fingernails, the pad of an oily thumb circling the model's nipple before, loosening the tie some more, he traced the curve of her breast beneath the thin white muslin, leaving the blue ribbon to echo it. 'All for the sake of art, you understand!' he might have lied.

Was she paid to be his sitter? Or was *she* his payment? Her subdued expression suggests this might have been the case. The goddess not worshipped but tamed. This Flora no white-winged angel but a courtesan.

'But, Aidan,' Flora's fingers on the buttons of her hospital-white nightgown, 'it won't seem quite so bad if you face it.'

'Not yet,' I said. 'Not quite yet.'

Though my youngest son, our baby boy – he who, eighteen years before, had suckled at that breast, had grown strong on its milk – could bear to face it, could bear to ask his mother if she would allow him to see the place where his small, unthinking head once rested, the soft maternal breast that had cushioned it now gone.

Gazing at *A Blonde Woman*, those other breasts – enhanced, grotesque, obscene – reared up in my memory, the scarlet-taloned fingers shimmying down the sparkly, barely there dress to reveal her 'treasure trove', her prized possessions pushed into a deep valley in which I might bury myself. Getting off on her own hideous beauty, her terrible tackiness, those talons tugging at my belt, fumbling with my fly.

'*No!*' I screamed through the red wine haze, stumbling out into the cold car park.

'Well, thanks very much!' she spat as I pulled up my zip. 'Go *fuck* yourself!'

Searching for the exit, I turned to see her spilling out of the rear car door, one stiletto-heeled shoe on her foot, the other in her hand, her hooker's dress barely more than a scrumpled 'belt' of sequins around her bum and thighs, and, shivering, tried to remember where I was in relation to my hotel.

Back in the hotel room I found several blonde hairs on my lounge suit – more on the trousers than on the jacket – and felt sick.

'What happened to that lie-in?' Flora said when I wandered in at 9.30 that morning. 'That cooked breakfast? You're *way* too early!'

'Too much wine!' I groaned, holding my forehead.

'Not quite up to baby-minding while I do the supermarket run, then?'

'I'd like nothing better,' I said, going to wash my hands at the sink.

'A litre of coffee? Or a gallon of water?'

'Both!'

My parents had a painter in the house. One who had revamped the guest room, transformed the hall from gloomy grey to apple green and was, I was told, putting a fresh 'lick' over the kitchen. This man the reason I, and not my mother, was sitting in the passenger seat beside my father as I returned home for the Easter holiday.

'He's overrun, of course,' my father said. 'Should have finished the day before yesterday. But a nice chap all the same. A lot going on up top!' He tapped his own balding temple to knowledge. 'Could have done better for himself, I'd say. Had he tried.'

'Did you?' I asked him.

'Did I what?'

'Say. Did you say that to him?'

I somehow knew my father's response.

'I most certainly did! It's never too late!' I told him. 'There are evening classes in a myriad of subjects. There are Open University degrees on anything you like! There's a world of opportunity awaiting minds up to the job!'

And I began to wonder if my mother had stayed at home in order to ensure this *nice chap* did not, as his parting shot, give the kitchen the Pollock treatment.

But when we walked through the apple-bright hall to the half-licked kitchen, there he was, sitting at the table, a mug of tea in his hand, his newspaper propped against the teapot.

'Your wife'll be back in two ticks,' he told my father. 'Run out of milk. Thanks to yours truly, no doubt. Hello there, son! Good to be home, I bet.'

My gaze magnetically drawn to the newspaper, I assured him it most certainly was, both wanting to look, to take a closer look, and not knowing *where* to look, feeling an uncomfortable boy-man, my body tingling, my face hot. Acutely aware that this was an important part of my education, but also aware that the subject was one my father considered unworthy of study. Fascinated, yet tainted by that fascination. While knowing other boys of the same age found this a far easier subject to absorb than did I.

Observing my flushed cheeks, the direction of my gaze, my father shook his head and without a word whipped the tabloid from before the startled decorator's eyes.

'I'm sorry, Tom. You may sit at my table. You may drink my tea. You may use up my milk. I will not complain. But you cannot, I will *not* allow you to profane this kitchen with that pornographic rag masquerading as a *newspaper*!' And, scrunching it into a crumpled ball, my father took it outside and threw it into the dustbin. 'Here!' he said, returning to pull *The Times* from his briefcase and plonking it before the bemused, stuttering Tom.

'I didn't… I mean… your good wife… yer see, she never said… I'm…'

'My wife can be more accommodating in these matters than can I, Tom.'

'Well, anyways,' poor befuddled Tom, taking a final swig of tea, said as he stood up, 'I'd better be getting on or I'll *never* be done.'

'Take it home with you!' my father instructed, folding the newspaper into a neat, portable size and holding it out to him like some mind-improving baton. 'You might get a taste for it.'

Nodding, Tom slipped the newspaper into the capacious back pocket of his overalls, my father giving him a crusading smile of approval. Although Tom and I both knew that my father's favourite broadsheet would be in Tom's dustbin before sunset, or, if not, unread cat litter by dawn.

———

My father's attitude to pornography could be judged only by his singularly definitive view of it, using Renaissance art as his marker: Veronese's *Allegory of Love* was 'a fine work', Bonnard's *The Indolent Woman* 'a slapdash bit of impressionistic porn', Titian's *Venus of Urbino* 'a thing of beauty' and, as far as my father was concerned, a joy forever; while Leighton's *The Bath of Psyche* (and on this I might agree) was 'a top-shelf bit of tat!' And a great favourite of my father's, Tintoretto's *The Woman Who Discovers the Bosom*, showed, he said, 'great sensitivity', whereas the single, 'prurient' breast Lucian Freud required Kitty expose in *Girl with a White Dog* demonstrated, my father said, 'the artist's lack of respect for his wife's body'.

'But, Dad…' I would protest, to little effect.

'OK?' Flora says.

'OK,' I answer.

She is wearing her golden-yellow robe (very like the one the first Mrs Freud wore when sitting for her faithless husband). The collar is pulled up around her neck, where her red-gold hair once fell, a few strands of white beginning to mingle through it, the red-gold replaced by a darker hue: Flora's naked scalp now stubbled chestnut brown, with not a single spike of white. 'There has to be some compensation for all this,' Flora declared, when I'd examined every inch to confirm this to be the case.

She takes my hand between her own.

'You're cold,' she says, rubbing my hand warm.

Then, slipping it beneath the soft fabric, she leads it down, sliding it over her still-bony ribcage. 'I've put on two whole pounds!'

'Wonderful!' I say, as my hand is drawn up to that flat absence, that awful nothingness, that blight of everything, the phantom that has made me afraid of the dark and the light, of everything that moves, that does not move – or might never move again. Has made me wake each morning fearing I might find her dead. Or if not this morning, tomorrow morning, a morning six months hence. Six years?

'Life's a very dangerous place to be, Aidan,' my wise wife has said. 'We live it day by day, as best we can. Apart from this wretched cancer, I'm as strong as an ox. You know I rarely catch a cold.'

Just like Flora to accentuate the positive for my sake, to be as strong as an ox because she has a pussyfooted husband, a fourth child, dependent on her, terrified of a life without her.

She withdraws her hand, leaving mine alone. I can feel her heart beating beneath it. I press the flat of my palm against the flatness of her pulled-together skin, spread out my fingers, feeling each rib bone, tracing the ridges of the scar with my fingertips.

'It's quite discreet,' I say.

'Not bad at all, is it?'

'Can I?' I untie the loosely tied belt of her golden-yellow robe.

'Thought you'd never ask.'

And I begin to cry.

'*Hey!* The worst is over. Think positively! My T-cells are going great guns. I'm popping the drugs. And I have *you*!'

'What good am I? What good have *I* been?'

'You've been who you are,' she says, cupping my face in her hands, her clear green eyes looking into mine. 'You've been Aidan: the man to whom I've entrusted my life.'

'It's a shame he never met you.'

'Your father?'

I nod.

She says, 'He was about my age when he died, wasn't he?'

'He was *exactly* the age you are now. And he would've been amazed his spineless son had managed to strike gold.'

She smiles. '*You* have never been spineless. And I'm no golden girl. Copper, maybe?' A hand going up to brush her head. 'Or *was*!'

'My goddess, then.'

'Please God, not that.'

But there she sits on our bed, one knee tucked under her, one bare foot brushing the sage-green carpet, her golden-yellow gown open to reveal the single breast of my brave Flora.

'You know, you needn't put that nightdress on tonight – not if you're doing it for me.'

'It's for me too. I'll wait until after the reconstruction. Goodbye, lopsided boobs. Hello, lopsided bum. Still, too much down there anyway, don't you think? Were you, *are* you a tit or a bum man? I can't recall.'

'I'm a Flora man,' I say. 'Always was, always will be. Whatever shape she's in.'

And Flora holds up her arms as I slip the fine white cotton gown over her convict's stubble.

Reflections

S he notices it more and more now: sees the stark reality of her ageing face staring back at her in that defiant, worn-down way. *Mirror, mirror on the wall, who is the* least *fair of them all?*

She particularly notices it now that Marco has moved to this bigger, brighter salon. Three years ago, when he was tucked away in the mews, she could still look upon her fifty-five-year-old self with a degree of admiration; could note the prominence of her cheekbones, if not her chin, the relative smoothness of the skin beneath her eyes. Of course, the lighting there had helped.

Although the room itself was rather gloomy (the mews salon was long and skinny, with barely any frontage on the mews itself), each individual mirror had been lit from behind: four etched squares on either side of the glass, through which eight small bulbs flatteringly glowed. So that within two months – between her last trim at the mews and her first in the square – Lauren saw herself age by several years.

'Why didn't you bring your lovely mirrors with you?' she'd asked Marco. Their squareness, the etched squares running down, would've looked just right here.

Marco's was now Marco's on the Square. Indicating the floor-to-ceiling glass frontage onto the pavement, the abundant natural light, Marco had mentioned the need for energy efficiency. While Lauren, eyeing Marco's colourist, perched on a stool by the gleaming stainless-steel counter, swinging her summer-bare, freshly coloured legs, had wondered if sacking Jules might be a better place to start.

Several small shops had once flourished in the square. In her teens, before leaving home, and in her twenties, on her infrequent visits back there, Lauren recalls a guitar maker's, a crammed-to-the-gunnels art shop, a picture framer's conveniently next door, and a dusty hardware store which, had you the time to wait as they searched amongst the chaos, most likely had whatever it was you wanted. There had been a second-hand bookshop too: opposite The Fox and Grapes, a pub since 1789 – until two years ago.

All flourished while the twice-weekly market was held in the square. Many were still doing well when, under some Health and Safety edict, the number of stalls was reduced, and Lauren, with two small children, married to David, returned to live in a nearby village. Although within months of her return the market was restricted to Thursdays only.

The final nail in the coffin, the killer stroke for the *old* square, was the decision to move what was left of the market to a small car park, no longer needed by the large supermarket close by, in whose name a swathe of wild buddleia-strewn wasteland (inhabited, it was said, by feral children with ASBOs), had recently been tarmacked. The same feral children with ASBOs, Lauren supposed, who now used the empty, moonlit space to play dodgems with whatever beat-up cars they could lay their hands on – or the not-so-beat-up ones they *could* beat up.

Soon the few remaining shops were reclaimed as homes, but not by those who worked in the town. Until, property prices on the rise again, the square was designated for a facelift, the crumbling, north-facing Georgian terrace gutted and The Northgate, an elegant five-star hotel, opened its doors to those discerning, well-heeled types who believed they alone had discovered this stylish weekend getaway. Opposite The Northgate, Mortens art gallery soon replaced the guitar maker, the art shop *and* the picture framer's. Lauren had met its owners, Richard and Zelda Morten, at its glitzy grand opening. Lauren was still married to David then. As, surprisingly, was Zelda to Richard; and, even more surprisingly, was still. Since, according to Marco, Richard had 'jumped ship' years ago, or, rather, had jumped Alessandro: a Michelin-starred chef at La Pêche D'Or, ten miles up the coast. Zelda, Marco alleged, had spent so much money 'rolling back the years' she would have been better off '*buying* a Picasso, rather than starting to look like one!'

Lauren, fifty-three at the time, taking in Zelda's forty-something face, sixty-something neck, seventy-something hands, vowed never to reclaim her own youth in such a way.

'Urgh!' She'd shivered as they drove home that evening. 'Those oriental eyes. That tight mouth.'

'Whose?' David had innocently questioned. And, when Lauren told him, 'Oh. Can't say I noticed. She looked pretty good to me. Anyway, *you'll* not be needing any nips 'n' tucks 'n' bull's semen, or whatever it is some women have syringed into themselves, will you?'

Lauren squirmed at the very idea.

'You've a naturally youthful face.' He had taken his hand off the steering wheel to squeeze her thigh. '*You*, my dear,' he'd said, 'will grow old gracefully.'

She had been wearing a new pair of tights: opaque, but shiny. Black. *He must find them sexy*, she'd thought. Though afterwards, looking back, she realised it had already begun, and felt a fool. Why had she not noticed the change in him? Those little things: the 'my dear' said like that – like she was his mother-in-law, or even his mother! – instead of his usual 'darling'; the fact that, had she cared to, had she dared to note it, his usual 'darling' had become quite *un*usual of late. Noted that his squeeze had been more playful than sexy, more calculating: the index finger and opposing thumb clasped about her leg like calipers checking for cellulite; his palm not firm against her sometimes-bare thigh, sometimes pushing up under her skirt. Though, come to think of it, he'd not done that for some time either. So that, on reflection, the squeeze she had mistakenly interpreted as the beginning of something had, in fact, signalled the end of something.

'Hmm...' Marco runs a strand of Lauren's lacklustre locks through his fingers, lets out a despairing sigh, shakes his head. 'Too busy to condition? Or just too lazy?'

Disgraced, Lauren lowers her eyes and confesses to being neither – which may, of course, be part of the problem. Actually, she confesses to Marco, as she might to her doctor, hoping for a cure, I have been feeling rather lethargic lately. Wants to say, *I've felt a bit out on a limb, a little lost. You see,*

Marco, my mind's not my own these days. At least it's not the mind I wish to own. And, what's more, my body's becoming someone else's.

Marco rubs her hair between his fingers and thumb. She feels it pull at her scalp, hears the sound of its brittle dryness rustling in her ear, like straw. Turning from her, Marco lets it fall. Bits of 'straw' stick out above her left ear. She smooths them back with her palm. Her hair does not feel smooth.

'OK, Jules. I'll finish off Fleur! Janet is *still* waitin for her roots to be done.'

Then, looking at her reflection in the mirror, lifting Lauren's shoulder-length hair from her neck, Marco's hands clamp onto her scalp, his splayed fingers combing back through it, fanning hair out on either side of her head. *I look as if I've had a shock*, she thinks.

'Lifeless!' Marco pronounces.

That's me! she thinks.

'Want a coffee while I finish off Fleur?'

Lauren shakes her lifeless head as Marco sidesteps over to Fleur, who, in Lauren's eyes, looks quite finished off as she is.

Reflected in the large mirror they both share, Fleur is a picture, a rose stripped of all briars: a Fleur stripped of almost all her clothes, since, in the if-you've-goddit-flaunt-it way of the young these days, much of Fleur's smooth golden flesh is on view.

Looking askance, Lauren watches Marco, hairdryer in one hand, fingers of the other running through Fleur's long, lustrous mop. Which, as if by magic, triples in volume. Watches the care he takes in grooming this unabashed beauty (who would look beautiful if she doused her head in a bucket of muddy water and let it dry in the sunshine); watches and thinks, *Why can't you do that for* me, *Marco? I need it much more than Fleur does.* Lauren can barely bear to look, and yet finds her eyes drawn back to the image of slutty perfection she sees beside her in the mirror.

It has returned. It bubbles up inside, a head of steam slowly building. Lauren keeps having to switch it off before it boils over. Before she explodes. *She* should be saving energy, conserving the little she has.

'Ah!' Marco has found two of Fleur's silky hairs still out of place. Snip, snip. 'Perfection!'

Eyeing Fleur's reflection, Marco runs his fingers through the Pre-Raphaelite locks one last time. Does he swoon with delight at the sight of Fleur, Lauren wonders, or at the sight of his own work?

On first meeting Marco, Lauren assumed him to be gay: his hairstyle at the time (a Tintin quiff, plus the hint of a kiss-curl where sideburns should be); the overdose of cologne; the sexy swagger of his skinny hips; plus the earring *and* the bracelet… Well? What was a girl supposed to think? But four months later Marco had mentioned he was flat-hunting.

'For a bigger place?' Lauren had suggested, picturing a minimalist white kitchen, black silk sheets, a Bang & Olufsen stereo.

''Fraid not,' he'd said. 'Smaller! The wife's divorcing me. Says I'm married to my work.'

And Lauren wished she had not gone into *quite* so much detail about her recent smear test.

Regarding herself in the mirror, Fleur turns her perfect profile this way and that, flicks the heavy weight of her silky hair over her silky shoulders, inhales, exposing more of the firm golden orbs exposed by her purple top, and looks, let's face it, dead chuffed with what she sees. A squeeze of glosser, slicked between Marco's palms, glides over the gleaming maple, and Lauren turns away, looks out into the square, thinks: *It really* doesn't *help, being exposed like this.*

Gone are the days when her own flesh could be given such a public airing. Lauren has begun to see the benefits of the burka – even a *need* for it. But not, on the other hand, for the hijab. You have to be quite a beauty to pull that one off; the face 'spotlighted' like that. As Lauren feels spotlighted now: sitting by the window, the sun streaming in, passers-by looking in, as if Marco's customers were part of some interactive art installation. Or were for sale! Now, if that *were* the case, Fleur would've been snapped up before she sat down. Whereas poor, badly thatched, rejected wife, rejected mother Lauren would have been thrown onto the bargains table, been the last to go. 'But, Lauren,' her friends have insisted, 'Jonno and Jodie are grown-ups. What do you expect?' *More*, Lauren thinks. *I expected more than this.*

Marco's on the Square being sandwiched between a wine bar on one side and a coffee shop on the other doesn't help either. Lauren tries not to make lunchtime appointments – particularly in summertime. She cannot tolerate having a wine-quaffing audience on one side and a lunch-munching one on the other. Cannot bear being 'on show'. Or, while on show, discovering she has a hole in her tights, or is still wearing her comfortable old shoes with the run-down heels – *and* there is mud on them.

Sunshine is flooding in now. It highlights the fuzz on her face. *When did it creep there? I look like a mouldy old peach*, she thinks, wanting to cry, right there in the window, in full view, like a child.

'*Now!*' Marco says. 'What are we going to do here?' Said despairingly. Even her hairdresser is tired of her now. Is bored by her very existence.

'Vitamins?' Lauren suggests meekly.

'Hmm?' Marco shakes his head.

'Extra C or E or D or something?'

'Uh-uh. Keep it simple. Just eat well. More fish 'n' greens. Less caffeine. Stay off the alcohol!'

'Oh.'

So there is no once-a-day answer.

She had hoped HRT might do it. Had chosen not to read the latest scare stories in the newspapers. But if her breasts still looked like two empty sacks she herself had no desire to touch, barely dared expose to her GP, herself a woman, let alone to… Oh no. *No.* Forget that. What *was* the point? And as for her skin? In this light Lauren sees wrinkles she never knew existed. *Well, my sight is still reassuringly good*, she tells herself. *I should at least be pleased about that.*

'A wax-pac, I think,' Marco says. 'Don't look so worried. I'm not gonna scalp you with it. It's just a penetrating moisturiser. Got an extra twenty minutes?'

She says she has. Just.

'*Jules!* Warm up a sachet of DP Max, will ya?'

The perverse thing is, since another man has shown interest in her, Lauren has become angry with David all over again. Or, more precisely, become angry with the thirty-something woman David divorced Lauren to be with. Lauren finds it hard to say the woman's name. To even think it. She still prefers 'The Woman' or 'That Woman', which seems an improvement on 'The Slut', 'The Selfish Cow' or the bog-standard 'Bloody Bitch'. She wishes she could be more original. But creativity, Lauren has discovered, requires a certain level of contentment to sustain it.

And a certain level of contentment had begun to seep back into her life: her anger diminishing, grief in remission, lapping slowly away, in the way the tide pulls back with each surge of surf, until a swathe of smooth, sea-soaked sand lies exposed, flat and untroubled, waiting for a bare footprint to make its mark.

Eight months ago she had joined an art club. Had begun to pursue a lifelong desire to see if she could paint. Not wishy-washy watercolours or soft-edged pastels. No. Big, brash, brutal oils: expressionistic landscapes or townscapes, barely discernible as such. Anything, as long as it was not sweet, not tamed, not controlled. She has a gallery of them in her head.

Her initial rush of enthusiasm was at first clouded by the fact that, apart from one acne-chinned young man of twenty-something and a slightly unhinged forty-something woman with a Tourettian sniff, most of the club's members were older than Lauren. It seemed so unfair: David running off with his younger model, while she, observing the preponderance of grey-haired heads bent over their easels, feeling old before her time, was sitting there painting a much *older* model. And a woman to boot!

But then the painting took over. And Lauren even considered letting it take over the house – or part of it.

The possibility of downsizing to boost her hopelessly small pension pot had flitted through Lauren's mind. For what was the point of living in a four-bedroom house if your two children returned to it so infrequently – and so briefly? Then, crashing through this last-tranche-of-life scenario, had come the thought of bashing her children's two light, bright, unused bedrooms into one large, light-filled studio. If Jonno and Jodie could be selfish, if Jonno and Jodie's father could be selfish, then why not their mother?

It was soon after this optimistic thought crossed her mind that the tide had turned, and any movement, forward or back – even picking up a paintbrush, let alone dipping it into paint – seemed to require such an effort, Lauren returning to packet pasta and Pot Noodles (if that), and drinking *way* too much red wine.

At first she blamed Glen.

Glen was not handsome, like David, but neither was he unattractive. At first she had found his lilting Perthshire accent and gentle diffidence rather irritating. But she soon came to realise that his quiet shyness was a by-product of his attraction to her. *A little too high*, she'd found herself thinking on first seeing the shock of salt-and-pepper hair standing to attention above his easel. *He should get it trimmed. Nice and thick, though. He'll never go bald.* Such thoughts not implying any particular interest on her part, you understand, merely observations. And yet, the awareness that Glen found her attractive added, in Lauren's eyes, to his own attraction. As did the fact that this man was patently not the sort of man to go sniffing after a woman half his age.

'Rinse off Lauren, please, Jules. Roxanne's doin your 12.15 highlights. How long does it take to buy a coupla packets of decaf around here?!'

Lauren looks down at her watch. Only twenty-five minutes to lunch. She has booked at the wine bar. Marco will have to get a move on. But then, he never takes long over her. 'The usual,' he'll say. 'Suits you. Why change?'

Though recently Lauren has hoped Marco might suggest something radical: a brave coup de maître. She herself has not felt up to it. The responsibility is too great.

Marco asks, 'How's the old painting goin?'

Lauren tells him it's going nowhere. Tells him she thinks she's been kidding herself. Thinks she might have been wasting her time.

'Doesn't have to *mean* anything, does it?' Marco says. 'Just so long as you're enjoying doin it.'

That *had* been the plan.

'I wasn't bad at drawing at school meself. Did I tell ya that? Not much cop at paintin, though. Never got beyond those paint-a-number kits me mum used to buy me. Maybe it was those bloody paint-a-number kits that put me off the art lark altogether.'

At first Lauren had imagined Marco to be part of a large Italian family, pictured his parents running a sandwich bar, a coffee chain, an ice-cream emporium; his siblings all mucking in, all part of one noisy team, save for Marco, the oddball, daring to escape all that mamma-papà love. And so, from time to time, she would drop the occasional Italian word or phrase into their conversations, hoping for, almost expecting, a complimentary remark on her accent (which she knew to be good), although, at the same time (not being exactly fluent in the language), somewhat relieved when Marco did *not* babble back to her in Italian.

Months later Marco had mentioned an elderly mother, 'Peckham born and bred', and a father who had 'buggered off' before Marco was three years old, Lauren discovering that for the first nineteen years of his life Marco had been Mickey Spinks. '*Pettinarsi*,' he told her; 'something t'do with hair, I believe. Forgotten exactly what it means. Yeah. Changed 'em. Changed 'em both to *Marco Pettinarsi!*'

On that particularly enlightening visit to the mews salon, Lauren had spent so much time talking to Marco/Mickey she had barely glanced in the mirror he'd flashed about her head. When she got home, rather wishing she had done so. He had taken too much off at the back, giving her dipping sides; 'bangs', an American might call them. *Bang! Bang!* Even a short bob forced to carry a shotgun in case it got scalped by Injuns. 'Looks good!' David had said when she walked in, not really looking at all.

Had her husband's disinterest in her gone back that far? Had he *ever* loved her?

For a short while, after that haircut, Lauren considered not returning to Marco's. She would find another hairdresser, one who practised under his own name. But then she thought of poor little Mickey Spinks, growing up with paint-a-number kits, but no dad.

'What d'ya reckon to that water-lily fella?' Marco asks her. 'Monet?'

'That's the one! Not bad, his stuff. Wouldn't mind one of them on me wall. Soothin.'

Lauren admired Mickey Spinks. Admired the way he must have looked in the mirror and made a conscious decision *not* to be Mickey Spinks, had decided to make his own mark, be his own Marco.

'Marco?' she'd once asked him. 'Have you ever thought of looking for your father?'

Marco's fiery nostrils flared. '*Fuck* that! If someone doesn't want to love you, that's it as far as I'm concerned. I'm not crawlin back to them, twenty-five years after they left *me* crawlin around on the floor.'

Lauren recalls the resolve she'd seen written on her hairdresser's face when he'd said this. She could learn a lot from Marco.

Marco is combing through her damp hair. Now's the time. Keeping it there, brushing her shoulders, doesn't make her any more feminine. Did not make her feminine enough for David, who ran off with an Audrey Hepburn-cropped 'boy'. Well, that was how she looked from a distance, all legs and shoulders, and no breasts, and Lauren had no wish to get any closer. The 'boy', the cow, the bitch, the love of David's life (Yes! He had dared to tell Lauren that) had become chubbier of late. Or so Daddy's girl, Jodie, said.

'Cut it off!' she says.

'What?'

'Shorter.'

'An inch or two?'

'No. *Really* short.' Adding, 'Do you think my neck can take it?'

'Sure it can. Your neck's fine.'

His scissors glinting in the sunlight, Marco sets to work with renewed vigour, and for the first time in months – perhaps years – seems fully concentrated on the task in hand, silently lopping off her newly waxed hair.

It is dry now. Marco is cutting into the feathery fronds fringing her forehead – exposing more of it while, at the same time, managing to make her look a little younger – when Lauren sees a flash of red drive by.

Marco is squeezing a slick of finisher into his palms – he has not done that for quite a while – when Lauren glimpses Jonno's red Mini backing into the one remaining parking space outside Mortens. Lucky Jonno. And on time, surprisingly.

Lunch in town had been Lauren's idea. A deliberate ploy to spend more time with her son, while avoiding the painful wait at home, hoping to hear the sound of his car on the gravel, yet expecting, almost as a matter of course, to hear the sound of the telephone, hear of roadworks or traffic jams, some excuse for Jonno still being several miles away. And this weekend, what joy! Jonno has promised to stay until Sunday evening. He, at least, is feeling empathetic. That element of his character did *not* come from his father.

Should she ask him? Jonno would not bring it up himself.

A shame Jodie has inherited her father's ruthless streak. Blurting it out on the telephone like that, without a thought. Lauren had hoped her daughter's favourite parent deserting the family home for a woman not much older than Jodie herself might bring mother and daughter closer. But no.

Marco runs his fingers through Lauren's feathery crop, while Lauren studies her son's reflection, caught in the mirror; watches him take his wallet from his jacket pocket, neatly fold the jacket (lining outermost), lay it in the boot, lock the car and turn to look over towards Marco's. She will never be able to forget David as long as his son remains loyal to his mother. Jonno is more roughly hewn than David, but, from a distance, crossing the street, barely looking each way, moving with the confident swagger of his father, he looks so like the man she met thirty-three years ago. And there he is on the other side of the glass, silently waving, as Marco makes his finishing touches.

And already she feels lighter. Not just her head; her body, too. Could she fly now, do you suppose? Could she take off?

Jonno gives his mother's new look the thumbs-up. Lauren holds up a hand, spreads three fingers, mouths, *Three minutes!*

'Grown into a nice-looking young man, your son. Handsome.'

'Takes after his father.'

'Don't put yourself down! He has your kind eyes.'

She should be kinder to those around her, and to herself – and to Glen too, perhaps. To have rejected him twice over. She might invite his opinion on her new painting; the one she should have finished by now? And it was peevish of her to blame Jodie for loving her own father. Had Lauren not been so… yes, jealous *is* the right word, of her daughter's visits to David, then Jodie might have come home to her more often.

Marco's fingers ripple through her wavy crop. It feels good, being touched like this, being cared for – being liberated of all that hair! A final tweak of the fringe and the towel is whipped from Lauren's shoulders, the mirror held this way, that way, this way again.

'Pleased?'

'*Really* pleased.'

'That's what I like to hear. Enjoy your lunch! But, if you're a purist about free range, organic stuff, *don't* eat the chicken. Whatever it may *say* on the menu, I saw the crate they came in out the back yesterday.'

She *will* ask Jonno. Will look the present in the face. What else can she do? Hungry or not, she will eat her starter (the starters are good there), be waiting for her main course (the service is *not* so good there), take an extra gulp of wine and say, *So! Tell me. Is it a boy or a girl?* And, if she can go on, if she can manage it, *Have they decided on a name yet?* It's a start, she supposes. A new beginning – of sorts.

'This style'll need a little bit more attention, y'know, Lauren,' Marco is saying as he reaches for her jacket. 'Come back in five; six weeks at the outside. Perhaps we'll work a few more highlights through it next time? That'll lift it even more. Remember that when you book: the extra time.'

Marco is holding out Lauren's jacket, waiting for her arms to slip into it. Has she been transformed to that extent? She shakes her lightened head, thanks him, but takes the jacket and slips it over one arm, saying, 'Just look at that sunshine!' before walking out into the square.

Jonno is sitting at an umbrellaed table, scanning the menu. He looks up as she approaches. Lauren remains standing, waiting for his verbal approval. But Jonno is looking past her, looking across the square.

He says, 'When I was a little, did you or, perhaps,' he hesitates, as if he dare not mention him, 'perhaps it was Dad... Did he or you ever take me into a guitar shop that used to be over there? I have this vague memory...'

'The *bookshop*! I was always dragging you into the bookshop. You always *wanted* to go into the guitar shop.'

Isn't that often the way of things? Lauren thinks, sitting down and picking up the menu. *To want the thing you can't have, the thing you imagine you want; to paint a picture of it in your mind, an abstraction of something that has never really existed.*

The chicken breast with *a farce of black olives, porcini and pesto* is the first thing to jump off the menu. Stuff where it came from. Life is a farce. Rules are made to be broken.

'Like the new look, by the way,' Jonno says. 'Makes you look younger.'

The sun is shining on her face. She feels its heat on her peach-fuzzed cheek, on the crow's feet around her eyes, on her newly exposed fifty-something neck. It feels good.

'I feel like having a glass of very good champagne,' she says.

'Make that two!' Jonno says. 'As long as they're both on me.'

This is the life. She will have dessert too!

Body Language

When she was pregnant, when she was eight months gone, he told her she looked like the letter D. 'Capital!' he added, in a tone that suggested she should be comforted by this fact. 'Not lower case.'

'But what about my long neck?' she said. 'What about my legs? My head?'

'Your head's always all over the place,' he told her. 'Here today, gone tomorrow. In the clouds one minute, in a black hole of despair the next.'

Thus reducing her to nothing more than a ditzy baby carrier: a ditzy baby carrier resembling the letter D.

'And anyway,' he went on, 'you've often admitted your legs are not your best feature; you said as much only the other day.'

Had she? Didn't he mean the other month? It had been weeks and weeks since she had seen her legs. Perhaps she no longer had legs? Perhaps she just rolled along like a ball? A big fat beach ball about to go pop!

'And my arms!' she said. 'What about my arms?' Watching him folding his newspaper, laying it on the table, smiling that irritating smile of his – well, more of an irritating smirk – apparently finding the notion of his wife as a letter rather amusing.

Had he become a secret drinker, she wondered? But it was barely two o'clock. And it was Sunday. And, as far as she knew, he had not been out of the house. A house that, aside from the dregs of a stale Merlot, in the fridge now for more than a week, was an alcohol-free zone.

'Lunch?' he suggested. 'I'm hungry. What've we got?'

She shrugged.

Why should *she*, a boring, bored old consonant with no arms and a here-today-gone-tomorrow head know what *they* had got? Anyway, a capital letter was not capable of getting lunch together.

'Hmm.' He was surveying the contents of the fridge. 'Pâté? Toast? Cof… fee… Oops! *Sorry!* You're still off the C-word, aren't you? Can't bear the sound, let alone the taste.'

So why say it out loud like that, then? Did he *want* her to throw up?! He was bored with it all, she knew. Bored, bored, bored. Bored with her looking like the letter D. Bored with her differing fads and fancies. Bored by the fact that she did not fancy him. While he, he said, still fancied her. But how could he? She looked like a capital letter. She looked like a big fat D. Now if he'd compared her to a curvy, sexy S, she might understand.

The truth was, he just needed sex. She could be anyone. Any*thing*. She could be any letter of the F-ing alphabet and he'd still want to put his fertile, baby-producing protuberance in there. Come to think of it, an O was what he really needed. A gigantic capital O. A massive hole in which to relieve himself. Where was *her* relief? Where was her Mother's Pride? Another month of this and she…

She sighed. 'Tea, please,' she said. 'I'd much prefer tea.'

'Thought you were off tea too?'

'It comes and it goes,' she said.

Did she mean her desire for that particular beverage, or her head? Or perhaps her legs? Her now-you-see-them-now-you-don't legs, hidden from view, sitting here on the sofa, by this massive bump that appeared to be part of her own body – her once-lithe, once-lean body. 'And cheese and pickle!' she added.

'Sandwich?'

'No. Just cheese and pickle.'

'Oh.'

He was taking a knife from the drawer in order to slice the Cheddar.

'*No!* Not sliced. Chunks! Chunks of cheese. And not rough chunks,' she insisted, 'cubes. Neat cubes of cheese, please.'

His turn to sigh. Was she all right? She was getting worse, for sure.

'And the pickle?' he asked her. 'Do you want that cubed as well?'

What a stupid question! What a wind-up. He must think she'd *totally* flipped.

'No, silly. Dolloped! Two humungous dollops.' Watching him moving about their galley kitchen. How could *she* get lunch? She could barely get in there now. If this baby didn't come soon she might end up dropping it in that damn apology for a kitchen. Might find herself jammed between the pull-out larder cupboard and the bloody fridge-freezer, her waters leaking out over the faux quarried millstone floor. That kitchen was made for skinny types like him. Was made for Is or Ts, not Ds.

'Dolloped,' she added, 'in the small blue bowl.'

He turned to look at her. His face wore that familiar bemused expression. She who had become a never-ending source of wonder and amusement to him. It was as if he had forgotten who she was. Who she used to be. *Me. Myself. The independent individual I was back in those S-for-sexy, S-for-single days.*

She said, 'With the mustard spoon!'

'With or without mustard?'

He wasn't serious, was he? Why ever would she want mustard?

'Of *course* without mustard! Whoever eats cheese and mustard?'

'Well,' he said, flicking on the kettle, 'I'm having a good old-fashioned sandwich. If that's all right with you?'

Of course it was all right. Why shouldn't it be all right? And why ask for her approval? Moreover, why ask like that? Sarcastically. Ironically. Haughtily. He who would never, *could* never look like a letter D. Not even after gorging his skinny self on a bucketload of Cheddar cheese sandwiches. Standing there, so taut, so sinewy. So spare. So uninhibitedly male. So fucking wombless. The lucky sod!

She stretched out one leg. There was a foot down there… somewhere. Ah! There it was. She stared at the black leather pump, waggling it from side to side, remembering the seven-year-old girl who had wanted to be a ballet dancer. Her! Mrs Blobby. A ballet dancer? Imagine it! That skinny child who had dreamed of being in the spotlight, dreamed of being a prima ballerina. None of that corps de ballet cygnet stuff for her. Oh no. *She* would be a swan. *The* Swan. She would shine. Had wanted to shine so very, very much.

But had she ever wanted to be a mother? Why do so many silly women want to be mothers? Anybody can be a mother. It takes determination, discipline, dedication to be a dancer. And was this the right thing for her to be doing? Doing now? This mother thing? She who often felt herself too young to be a mother, too old to be a mother, too exhausted, too fat to be a mother. Too late! The job was done. Her alphabet-obsessed partner's alpha-male sperm had seen to that. She was an overweight consonant who in three weeks' time would divest herself of a child: a child created with half the A-C-T-G of her DNA and half of his. Their lovechild. Or was that believing in fantasies? Believing in the A-is-for-apple, B-is-for-baby, C-is-for-Cinderella world of fairy stories? Oh, for a magic wand to wave her back to skinniness. Oh, to be single. Oh, *not* to be the carrier of another life. It had become such a burden, you see. And not just a burden before the event; a burden for so, so long after it.

'For madam!' He put the tray down on the coffee table beside her. 'Thought you might want some bread.'

He had cut the bread into cubes too. Had assembled them in an incomplete pyramid in the small terracotta dish. She hadn't wanted bread, but, seeing it arranged like that, popped a cube into her mouth and smiled up at him.

This was love, she supposed.

It would be OK, she told herself. It *would* be OK. As long as the baby was OK.

She was in great shape, he told her, *really* great shape. He congratulated her on managing to get her figure back in such a short time. 'Especially,' he commented, 'after the size you were.'

'We'll have to do a C-section… Mrs… er…' the obstetrician had mumbled, searching for her name on the notes. 'Mr… um… The anaesthetist will be along to see you shortly.'

A Caesar baby, she'd thought; *what a relief!* A weight of responsibility had been lifted from her. No huffing and puffing. No panting. No 'Push down! Push down *hard*!' Now she would not tear, would not split, would not scream; she was certain she would have screamed the place down. For how could three or four kilos of anything – of offal, even, let alone of a wriggling, fully formed baby with arms and legs – come out of such a narrow orifice? Nor would needle and thread be pulled through that part of her anatomy that surely was not meant to be pierced in such a way – at least not by needles that she would be aware of. Though there would be an abdominal scar. She would not be able to wear a bikini for years. And by the time she could, she might be too old for bikinis. 'Thank you so much, Doctor,' she'd said.

Her husband told her she looked like her old self. Whoever that was?

'Apart from your breasts,' he said, smiling in a smug, smirky sort of way. He liked her bigger breasts, he said. Though she did not. Nor did she want him to touch them. Why would he want to? They were so big, so swollen, so taut, so tight. They were not her breasts at all. They were no longer sources of sensory pleasure – for him or her. For her *with* him. They had become food factories: overinflated dummies with which to silence her overfed baby.

By now he had expected her to be pregnant with lust, to be ready to deliver herself up to him. She knew this. Could see it in his sad, doe-eyed looks. But she could not face it. Could barely face the word 'S-E-X'. Could not say it. It felt redundant to her now. For wasn't this what it had been for? Wasn't this what it was all about? To produce this baby, this new life? Job done, then. And after all, after this, they surely did not want another.

'I'm… I'm… sorry,' she would say, turning from him.

And he would sigh.

Or he would say, 'But it's not as if you've had an… E… E-P-Z…'

'*Episiotomy!*' she'd snap back. Surely he ought to be able to pronounce the damn word by now, was familiar enough with it, the number of times she had been forced to repeat it? 'But I *do* have stitches,' she would remind him.

'But not down there!' he would remind her – as if she didn't know.

What was this all about? Why had they become so prissy? So uptight. So unlike who they had been: those two lovers who'd had sex in a public park, sex in a cinema, sex on the top deck of the all-night bus, but who now could not manage to have sex behind closed curtains, lights off, in their own double-glazed, fully insulated bedroom. Could not manage it, and could not manage to talk about not managing it, about *how* to manage it.

Had he really been the one who had been fool enough to want to be a parent? Want to live in a sexless zone full of garishly coloured plastic crap that squeaked and rattled and rolled, and that before their child was old enough for swimming lessons might well be swirling around some Pacific trash vortex waiting for a poor unsuspecting gannet to gobble it up, to be throttled by a multicoloured death rattle?

Should he complain about their lack of sex, lack of money; should he remark on how seldom they went out, how little time they had to talk; should he say how he wished things could be different, better, how they used to be? Then she would shrug and say, 'Well, it's down to you, matey. You were the one who wanted to be a daddy, desperate as you were to pass on your A-plus genes. You wanted this more than I did. Remember?'

He couldn't say he did remember. It was all such a long time ago. Though misty memories of their BC sex life (their life Before Conception, as he thought of it now) still haunted him, taunted him. Memories of sweaty Sundays when they barely got out of bed. Them? Him and her? Like that?! Surely not. Now they hardly slept. And *he* had wanted *this*? Why in God's name would any man want this? Want a squawking, red-faced, forever complaining baby getting all the attention? He couldn't get a look-in now. And if he should want to talk about you-know-what… Well… forget that. The only S-word she ever mentioned was of the hyphenated Z-Z-Z variety, complaining that she never got enough of it. Well, he knew all about *not* getting enough, didn't he?

And why were they avoiding touching? Or talking about touching. Touching those intimate parts of her anatomy, those unmentionable places *down there*. Talking about those words beginning with V and C. Not to mention the F- and C-words. Could those two not be brought back on the agenda? Might they not be an alternative route to non-penetrative satisfaction?

'Are you OK?' he would ask her.

'Fine,' she would say, in that blank, empty way of hers, yawning, picking up the child and silencing it with her breast.

At first he'd thought it beautiful. At first he was convinced this was the most glorious scene in the world. Biblical, you might say: the two people he loved most bound together as one, day after day, week after week, month after month. But now, well, to be honest, it almost repelled him, physically repelled him. Those swollen breasts of hers: breasts that no longer belonged to him, her darkened areola being thrust into the baby's demanding pink mouth; this cuckoo child she continued to feed come what may, whom he knew to be an impostor.

Most days it made sense: this devotion of hers. How much she had to give to this squirming, squiggling little thing that had come from her and just one of the millions and millions of his squiggling sperm. Sperm that no longer swam for their lives, fighting for survival inside her, but died, she supposed, inside him. Or didn't. Who knows? She didn't ask. She did not want to know.

She herself did not miss that part of it – not really. For now she felt herself to be quite a different being. Which was both good and bad.

And yet, every so often, there would come a moment, moments, even a whole hour, when to look at him, to look at the man who had helped make this child, would almost break her heart. And her heart would open up to him as it used to. Just her heart. Nothing else.

Sex had been so good with him – in her memory, at least – so complete in itself, she could not absorb the fact that this baby had come from it. Had come from it and had also destroyed it. She longed for that feeling again, longed for the completeness of being with him, the completeness and yet the separateness. A separateness she would never have again. No. There was no way back to that lost world. Not now this child was in it: this dependent creature who had hijacked her life, whom she would defend with her life.

When he's a bit bigger, he thought, *when he's a boy, when he's no longer a baby, when he stops hanging on to his mother's breasts, his mother's hands, her skirts, her legs, perhaps then I'll be able to get a look-in.* Then *I'll make him mine.* It felt like that to him, felt like he was staking his claim. *It'll be my turn then. See how she feels about that.*

He imagined it would begin with a ball of some description. A beach ball, perhaps? They would be on holiday somewhere: a beach, most likely, hence the ball. His wife would be stretched out on a colourful towel. Their child, *her* child, would be sitting beside her, Buddha-like, beneath a sun-shielding parasol. There would be a large rainbow-coloured beach ball close by. It would be almost as big as the mound that had once contained their fully formed baby. And he would put down his novel (how many Philip Roths can one man read without becoming a closet misogynist?) and gently pat the striped orb, causing it to roll towards his son. En route it might nudge his wife's tanned thigh – her taut abdomen still hidden beneath a one-piece bathing costume. Stirring, a hand instinctively stretching out to touch her child's fat little toes, she would feel them slipping away from her grasp, and, opening her eyes, would prop herself up on one elbow, exposing her breasts – sadly returned to those of the puny boy/girl he'd been crazy about – and turn to see her beaming baby (the baby who was becoming a boy) push at the ball with his outstretched palms, sending it straight back to his father, father and son all sunshine and delight. And it would be as if it had suddenly come to him, come to his very own boy in a flash, come in that moment, that one movement: *Yes!* the look would say. *This man I've seen coming and going about the house, passing me with a scowl, a nod, a wink, a wave, an occasional smile, a tousle of my hair, might be someone worth knowing. Might, just might be my father.*

Yes, some day, some day soon, a beach ball would seal the deal. Other balls would no doubt follow. By six it would be a football. By ten a tennis ball. By fifteen a golf ball? Perhaps not. But it would come to pass. They were both boys after all.

He put down his newspaper. *There are worse places for a man to be than this*, he thought, watching his wife prise the child's greedy mouth from her right nipple and reattach it to her left.

'Lunch for us too?' he suggested, rising from the sofa.

'Why not!' she said. 'Give me five minutes. What've we got?'

For better or worse, he thought. In many ways life was worse, and yet, at the same time, it was a whole lot better. There had been times when he had wished he'd not wanted this. But she had been right: he had – no doubt one sex-filled weekend – been the first to bring up the subject of parenting. *Why?* he had often asked himself. For fear of losing the freewheeling, single-minded woman he had fallen in love with? Or, so in love with the freewheeling, single-minded woman, he'd had, as she had put it, a 'desperate urge' to merge his body, his mind, with hers? 'Have my baby?' The words slipping out so easily – more easily than the baby.

And here they were now. All three of them.

He said, 'I'll make us a sandwich, eh? Tea?'

'Coffee, please! What I *really* need is a double espresso. Wake me up.'

His hand lingered to stroke her thick, soft hair. A few strands of white were already hiding amongst the gold. They were not there a year ago.

'Right, then!' he said, going over to the kitchen. 'I'll make you an extra-strong Americano.'

This was love, he supposed, or something like it.

A Life

I don't remember putting down the telephone, don't remember going there, but, afterwards, I must have returned to the shed. Must have run in from the garden, thinking it might be you, and then, somehow, got myself back there again. Because hours later that was where I found myself: slumped against the bags of peat-free compost I'd dragged in there, that fine, blue-skied Sunday morning. Found myself looking down at my legs, splayed out before me like some scrawny rag doll's – a scrawny rag doll with all its stuffing knocked out.

The clouds that had multiplied as the day had lengthened, their cumulating gloom layering one upon the other – as if they knew before me how dark this day would become – had, by late afternoon, blanketed the hopeful morning sun from view, and continued to blanket the moon, their brief parting allowing its light to fall on my face, beckoning my eyes heavenward. And stretching my neck, grown stiff in its rag-doll flop between my knees, I looked up and asked, *Why am I here?* Why *am I still in the shed?* Then it hit me. And while the moon continued to illuminate the shed's contents – convinced, as I was, that its previous owners, having left a jumble sale's worth of junk about the house, and a car boot's in the garage, must have left something I might find a use for now – I searched in the half-light for a substance to keep me fallen amongst the bags of compost on the dusty floor, soon to become dust myself. But I found nothing. And since I myself am an organic gardener (one who relies entirely on thrushes and toads to slaughter her slugs for her), I realised the shed contained nothing more ferocious than a bantam's scratchings of poultry pellets, half a bottle of dilute washing-up liquid, and a jar of old coffee grains. None of which was capable of transporting me to the next world – or at least helping me get the hell out of this one. And surfacing from the shed – the moon showing its disapproval of my use of its light by retreating behind a cloud – I walked back to the open kitchen door and, without light, felt my way to bed.

I must have slept, since I woke early to another clear, bright morning, my bedroom flooded with harsh spring sunshine, and, half-blinded by the light, questioned why I was still clothed, why the blinds were not pulled down, why I felt so exhausted.

Dragging my leaden limbs downstairs, feeling taxed by this everyday action, my mind still did not fully comprehend what my body already knew. Even after noticing someone's footprints had trailed earth across the kitchen floor, still it did not sink in. Had a burglar crept in to rob me of my most precious possessions, I asked myself?

Not until my dazed head turned to gaze down the long, skinny, partially cultivated garden, not until I observed the shed door was still open, not until then, did I remember those earthy footprints were my own, and that this was not any autumn dawn; this was *my* new dawn. You were dead. And this was the beginning of the first day of a life without you. And, if I chose to carry on living that life, from now on, every day would feel a little like this one: the pain receding over time, an acceptance of loss overlaying it, a muscular survival fighting its way to the fore. Better days would surely come. Days in which I would come to believe in some form of 'recovery'. But this wound, this bleeding hole at the heart of me, would always be there. This chronic, daily ache would become a part of me, I and it so close as to be inseparable, so close I would come to fear its passing.

So many days without you, for better, for worse: blue-skied and empty; cloudy and empty; raining buckets, and empty.

'Christ! What a godawful day! Jesus, I hate this damn entrance, don't you? When I began working here there was a straightforward swing door anyone with an ounce of strength could push open.'

We waited to shuffle into a vacant section as the door slowly revolved, a few people spilling out, shaking their dripping umbrellas over the marble floor, others unsheathing those still damp from their lunchtime excursions.

'Now we have this Tardis-like monstrosity. What's the bloody point of it? Can it teleport us to another world, do you think? I swear less people pass through this damn thing than went through the old door in the same amount of time!'

By now we were outside, protected from the downpour by the entrance awning, teetering on the edge of Waterworld, you staring out at the teeming rain and at what, until that moment, had been about the grimmest day I could remember; I eyeing the drooping bus queue across the street, huddled beneath the limited shelter the bus stop afforded them. While others, exposed to the uncaring elements, gazed mournfully through the grey curtain of gloom, praying for salvation in the form of a bus. For a few seconds there was silence – save for the sound of billions of raindrops refracted off limestone. You, I assume, contemplating an umbrellaless rush into the breach; I remaining there because you remained there.

'Bad day?' I said.

You turned to look back at me. I noticed a few white hairs in your sideburns, one or two flecking your right temple. You were almost forty-four.

'Pretty shitty.' And then you smiled, your wide mouth revealing surprisingly white teeth. 'Hell no! Not really. I complain too much. It's becoming a bit of a habit. I'm becoming a miserable old sod. This weather doesn't help.'

You stepped beyond the awning. Within its bony cage, my heart, as if it had a mind to break through the bars containing it and handcuff you to one of them, panicked as I fumbled for something to say to keep you near me. Your left arm was in the air, two fingers of your right hand at your mouth. You let out a long, shrill whistle. And there at the foot of the rain-drenched steps was a cab.

'Here!' you said, offering me your briefcase as an umbrella. 'Use this!'

And, holding it over my head, down the drenched steps I ran, hesitating at the cab door.

'Don't worry!' you said. 'This is on me. Anyway, think I'll charge it. Company can't complain; the number of hours I've put in recently. My wi…' You paused, but I had already seen the ring. 'Anyway, enough of my groaning. Where exactly do you live?'

'Beechwood Gardens. Not far from Tufnell Park tube.'

We swung into Gray's Inn Road, London, grey and slippery as a seal sliding past us in the evening light. Or maybe *not* Beechwood Gardens. Maybe Timbuktu? Maybe Outer Mongolia? Outer Space! Somewhere far, far away. Somewhere where we could stay like this, warm and dry and waiting to get there, for days, for weeks, for months – forever – the world going on as before, my world turned upside down, my centre of gravity changed in a moment.

'But, Rosie, you must know you'll never have a life with him; a home with him. They almost never leave their wives – whatever they tell you. They stay where they're looked after, where they're most comfortable. Men are boys at heart. Life, a glorified Scalextric game. No wonder we're in such a bloody mess. Look at the city! Look at the world! Look, Rosie, I know it's all fine and dandy now, and I'll admit, seeing you yesterday, you positively glowed with… well… I suppose it's love, and I really don't want to put a damper on your happiness – it's been quite a while since…

'Anyway! Just remember, Rosie; most of them can't cut off from Mummy's apron strings. In spite of their macho demonstrations of derring-do, out there in the big warring world, take it from me: when it comes to relationships with that complex species that is woman, the path of least resistance is the path most often taken by most men. *Especially* the married kind!'

'Hi, Rosie. Is this a good time? I don't wish to pry… Yes. I know it's none of my business… Yes. I did have lunch with Esther yesterday… Sweetheart, is this a good idea? I mean, after all you went through, you, of all people, deserve a full life. Not one full of snatched phone calls and afternoon sex. Not one in which you'll never need a super-king-size bed! One in which you'll sleep alone night after night, year after year. It's just not worth it. If you're as hooked on this guy as Esther seems to think, then take it from me, that's how it'll pan out. You, Rosie, are better than that. And, let's face it, there are better men out there than that. Nice guys who care about their wives – care about the women who will *become* their wives.

'I know I shouldn't bring it up after all this time, and you've always said you're fine… It's just… I've been wondering… Look, I know it's not your thing, but, as you know, it has changed my life. Consider the C-words: "counselling" and "closure". In my opinion, you can't put the cart before the horse. If you do, you'll never really move on… I'm simply putting it out there, Rosie. Take it on board, eh? Mull it over… No. Don't worry. Mum's the word. And I've sworn Esther to secrecy.'

'Quit now, Rosie! Quit while you're young enough to find someone else… Yeah… OK. Yeah, I bumped into Esther yesterday... OK. OK. Yes, you're right: Esther *did* call me. By the way, did she tell you she's pregnant again? Anyway. Thought it seemed a good time to pass a little secret of mine on to you. Although you've only ever known me as a happily married woman, and although I may not seem the type, I've got form in this area too... No! Not the baby thing. The unavailable man thing. Haven't talked about it. Nothing to boast about, in my opinion. Let's just say I know what it's like. Been there, done that, got the scars! Because there *will* be scars, Rosie. Almost always *our* scars. The selfish buggers usually get away without a scratch. Well, my bugger is all behind me now. Oh dear! Didn't mean to put it quite like that. Never did quite... Let's not go there. Is it illegal? Anyways. Get out now! In my experience it's downhill after those first few head-in-the-clouds months. Pretty soon you'll be nothing more than an unpaid call girl. And, however glowing you feel right now, that ain't pretty.

'Oh! And before I go, one little word: *children*. I know you're only thirty-two. But if you leave it much longer, you'll not just be saying goodbye to motherhood, you'll be saying goodbye to grandmotherhood, too. I don't wish to sound brutal. But it needs to be said. Because if this thing is as serious as Esther fears it is, *you*, my girl, will be saying hello to a rather lonely life. Time's precious. Don't waste it on the bastard! Think about it. *Please.*'

What was there to think about? I was where I belonged. I'd come home.

Home, the home of my childhood, by then had become a distant place I seldom returned to.

'Heavens, no!' she had said. 'It's just a nasty cold. He's taken to his bed just so as I'll pamper him, that's all. He'll be up and about in twenty-four hours. Stay with that young fella of yours.'

She was relieved that, at last, I had a 'young fella' to stay with. Pleased I no longer returned, weekend after weekend. 'Have a nice weekend!' Glad to be rid of me.

My mother had a face like stone: smooth, pale, unmoving. She and I were born to stultify one another, to rub each other up the wrong way. Left side by side for long enough, I swear we would have ground each other to dust. We shared one thing only: our love for the man who was her husband, my father. Aside from this, we were closer to being strangers than mother and daughter.

Even now, should I wish to conjure them, I can picture some of the mothers I considered more acceptable in that role than my own. I would catch sight of them stepping onto a bus, sitting on the train, queuing at the supermarket. Would see one, and think, *If only I could swap* my *mother for* that *mother, I'm sure Dad and me would be better off.* It was a phase. I was eight or nine, or ten. My chosen matresfamilias were invariably slightly overweight, somewhat dishevelled creatures, with scrubbed-clean faces and unkempt hair. Women who looked, to my discerning child's eye, both busy and relaxed, looked the kind of women a child could go up to and ask to be their mother. And although these 'mothers-to-be' might not be in the position to take up my suggestion, they looked the sort who would bend down to wrap their arms around me and thank me for suggesting it, and they would smell of fried eggs and washing powder and squidgy love. Not perfume.

She had wanted a boy, you see. I, her firstborn, coming into the world without the external accoutrements to qualify me as such; she choosing to stop at this first hurdle for fear of squeezing out another specimen as ill endowed as me.

'Really, Rose' (she seldom called me Rosie), 'you can be such a boy sometimes!' I standing before her indifferent gaze with mud on my dress/a cut on my knee/a graze on my elbow. In her eyes, girls were supposed to be flawless, delicate creatures, their clothes and skin especially designed to repel such boyish substances as mud and blood. '*Such* a boy!' Said harshly. Said as a rebuke for my singular inability to be one. Or, perhaps, in the hope that, if said often enough, her useless daughter might go the whole hog and transmogrify into a real live boy-child. A boy-child who would worship his beloved mother. Would not adore his father quite as much as this muddy, bloody girl-child of hers.

My father's face, on the other hand, was as soft and malleable as flesh-coloured plasticine; the two of us together, it became a mobile, play dough sort of face: one eyebrow raised, another lowered over his twinkling eyes, his wide mouth smiling, cheeks rippling, brow wrinkled in a feigned frown. Though he seldom scolded me; a genuine frown bringing a mere, 'Tut, tut, Rosie. You can do better than that.' Or else, 'I expected more of you, Rosie.' This, the height of his anger.

Although, back around the tea table with my mother, my father might, momentarily, adopt his wife's stony look. Once, fearing his plasticine face lost to me forever, I waved an index finger near his chomping cheek, to see if it would sink in or be rebuffed by the pumice-stone grey of his afternoon stubble. 'Rosie!' he said, putting another slice of bread and butter on my side plate. 'What are you doing? Concentrate on finishing that salmon!' While, signifying her approval of his firmness, my mother's manicured fingertips reached out to stroke the black hairs creeping from beneath his white shirt cuff to fleck the backs of his large hands. She had her man back. He was her possession now. My father had put away his boy-self for the day, leaving me to sigh and shuffle, to kick hard at the chair leg with my heel, willing his playdough face back to me.

The 'nasty cold' was pneumonia. By Monday evening my father was dead.

'How was I to know?' my mother said. Yes, he'd had a bit of a temperature. Yes, he'd complained of a few aches and pains. But how was she to know?

'Because you were there!' I screamed. 'Because you were with him! Because you *should* have known!'

He was sixty-two.

By the time I reached my childhood home, my mother, she who loved pristine tidiness, had already arranged for my father to be whisked away.

My last sight of him was in the funeral parlour; more a room full of coffins – empty, I assumed. An attempt had been made to curtain them off: on one side by a not-quite-long-enough claret velvet curtain, and on the other by a length of green brocade. A sickly scent of lilies, in two over-elaborate vases, filled the room.

My warm fingers touched his stone-cold cheek. I wanted my play dough father back again. Wanted to push my thumbs and index fingers into the corners of his mouth and lift it into that warm smile of recognition I would never see again. *Hello, Rosie*, I silently mouthed. *Lovely to see you, sweetheart*, I heard him say, before falling to my knees, my forehead against the oak, soon to be turned to ash.

Then came an arm around my shoulder, strong, sweet tea served in a fine bone china cup, and a vague awareness of both the appropriateness and inappropriateness of bone vis-à-vis china clay. And, while a far steadier hand than my own guided the gold-lipped cup safely back to its saucer, it occurred to me that Goddard & Burnley's investment in such an expensive tea service may not have been a wise one.

My 'young fella', the man some later believed capable of breaking my heart (I not disabusing them of this ludicrous notion), accompanied me to my father's funeral. The lover without whom I would have been at home with my father. Would have seen him alive. Would, at the very least, have insisted on the doctor coming round. Would have called an ambulance. Would *not* have been three hundred miles away playing at this new game of love – or, rather, of sex. Would not have been feigning enjoyment of fellatio. Would not have been faking orgasms – not that I knew what a real one was like. Would not have been playing at foreplay with a man who was knee-high to a boy. Should not have imagined myself 'in love' with that boy-man. Should never have let the word 'love' pass my lips in relation to him.

Though, afterwards, his manhood was such that he managed to prop me up for a few months. Or gave the appearance of propping me up. I imagine he hung around because he felt obliged to. Would have appeared a bit of a rat had he not.

Back then I had no shed in which to grieve. Though the bathroom in the flat he and I shared was conducive enough to grief. Its walls were funeral-parlour claret, its roller blind a dark jade green. I would pull it down, light the tea light in its black marble cup and lie, motionless, in the steamy heat, waiting for the walls to 'cry'; in Waterworld, where I belonged.

'Rosie!' my boy-man would shout, banging on the door. 'You had a bath this morning! *I* need a shave. I've an early start tomorrow. *Talk* to me, for fuck's sake!'

But I couldn't talk to him. I no longer had anything to say to him. To anyone. I wished I had never imagined myself in love with him. *Glad you're home, sweetheart*, my dead father's grey plasticine mouth said.

But my 'young fella' was there, supporting me, at the graveside, letting my head lean on his shoulder. Letting my mother lean on him too, her arm linked in his, her hat and hairstyle preventing her from taking full advantage of the muscular breadth of his other shoulder.

Afterwards, she told me what a fine-looking young fella he was. How pleased she was for me. Though I saw nothing to be pleased about.

My mother shed a wifely tear in the church, the lone damp trail running down her immaculately powdered cheek – buffed that day from stony white to powder pink. She dabbed it with her pristine, lace-trimmed handkerchief, her carmine widow's lips set in a suitably sombre line (one drawn with what must have been a very steady hand), her hair perfectly arranged beneath a veiled beanie – bought, I noted, especially for the occasion. Watching her kissing all and sundry at the wake, my boy-man thought her a 'rather lovely lady'. By then, I doubt he thought the same of me: my blusher-free skin grown pale, my hair lank and dishevelled, my eyes shadowed only by twelve tearful days, by eleven sleepless, sexless nights. I was done with faking it.

'Rosie. How much longer? This is unhealthy.'

I was glad when he went. I could crack up in peace.

'How *are* things, Rosie? Shall I come round? Called you yesterday… Yes. Yesterday evening… Yeah. Thought you'd be in. Where were you?'

'Rosie. About this Pilates class… Come on, sweetheart. It'd do you good! Do us *both* good! We could have coffee afterwards. Make it a regular thing.

'When was the last time you saw anyone outside of work, Rosie? No. Not listening! I'll be round tomorrow. At seven… Uh-uh! *Tomorrow!* We'll go for a pizza… I don't bloody care if you don't like bloody pizza!'

I spent a lot of time in the shed. Tidied it up. Put an old beanbag in the corner. Sat there most evenings – whatever the weather. The house felt too warm, too comfortable, too much like a home I should feel comfortable in, that first bitter season without you. It could not be right, now you were dead, to feel warm in there.

I would layer up, pull on my boots, take a pot of tea – biscuits, if I was in an eating mood – and sit there in the dark for hours; and, should it deign to look down on me, look up at the moon, talk to it, to you, and to my father – and cry, of course.

'A life together!'

Those first few years, my friends would continue to remind me of what I was missing, hoping I would give up, and eventually join them in the righteousness of holy matrimony.

'A *proper* life!' one or other or all of them would say.

But I thought I was leading 'a proper life'. Two notches on the bedpost seemed to me quite a record in the properness-of-life stakes. The life I led was a good life. I had no regrets about that life. No false promises were given; no impossible demands made to give me that *proper life*. Not that, at the outset, I didn't voice them to myself. But as the years went by an unspoken thought ran between us: *This is how it will be from now on*, it said. *What else can we do?*

'A life?' I would shrug, with an exasperated sigh. 'I *am* living a life!'

But I was only thinking of life itself. I was not thinking of life's end.

'Rosie?' Esther's voice unusually quiet, strangely restrained. 'Can I pop over? Yes, right now... No... Yes. Things are fine... Yes. Dan's fine. *We're* fine... No. It's nothing like that... No! It's not about me. It's about you... No. I promise. No! No more "self-righteous stuff about marriage". Never again.' Said in almost a whisper. 'Never. You see, it's more... Rosie, it'd be easier if I just came round.'

I felt sick. Felt I had inhaled a funeral parlour of lilies. Felt my insides wilt.

'Rosie, please don't make me tell you... the telephone's not...'

Felt weightless and heavy, felt my world spin.

'Leave you alone tonight? How can I, Rosie? You need someone... Rosie, please... OK. OK. I'll be round first thing in the morning.'

A neighbour of Esther's had seen it in a local newspaper; barely that: a freebie pushed through the door every Friday. Put it aside for cat litter. Flicked through it that Sunday morning – casually, no doubt, a mug of coffee in her hand – and there, smiling that broad, white-toothed smile, looking far less than your sixty years – looking as if you might live for at least another thirty – was your face: the sort of face that draws you to it; and below your face, your name.

'I'm so, *so* sorry.' Esther's arms enveloping me. Esther's voice a cracked whisper in my ear. It had been a slip of the tongue, she said. She had been wrong to gossip about a man she had never met, to a woman neither you nor I knew. She would never forgive herself.

'Please do forgive yourself, Esther,' I said. 'I'm glad it happened this way. Glad it came from you.'

I'd had lunch with you ten days before. Six days before we'd had one of our marathon telephone conversations: 'Forget about evergreen shrubs!' you'd said in that bossy tone of yours. 'Forget about all that creating "rooms" nonsense. Plant a tree slap bang in the middle. A tree that bears fruit. Plant a plum tree! I *adore* plums!'

You were scheduled to come round that Tuesday evening to continue our discussion on the pros of plums and the cons of apples – at least, your pros, your cons.

'But the garden's too narrow!' I protested.

'Bollocks!' you said. 'See you Tuesday.'

Your last words to me.

He had been walking his dog, the short piece said. Though it did not say if you had been walking alone with your dog, walking with your wife and your dog, or walking with your son and maybe your daughter, perhaps visiting with your grandchild, and your dog. It just said, *He died suddenly, while walking his dog*, and that *he was a man with a ready smile, much loved by family, friends and all who knew him* – including his dog Shrek, no doubt.

'Happy anniversary!'

Fifteen years. I had known you for fifteen years. It was two weeks after moving into this house.

'What are you doing?' I had turned my back on the remaining unpacked boxes and was sitting on the floor, leaning up against one of them, reading the Sunday paper. 'Where are you?' For a moment hoping, praying you might say, *Surprise! I'm only two streets away. Be with you in three minutes.* But that wasn't your style. Dates were arranged, time dedicated to our being together. Sundays were rare. Though rarely did you renege on a promise made.

'Supper on Wednesday? Luigi's? Six-thirty OK? Think I'll book. *Shrek!* Come back here! Bloody dog's gone apeshit across the field. Six-thirty, then. Love you.'

It was autumn, of course.

I slipped on my jacket and drifted up the road to the nearby park. Just inside the gate a park keeper was sweeping up the leaf-fall that had carpeted the path. As I approached him a scatty cocker spaniel, chocolate ears flapping, chocolate-dipped tail whirling, hared past me, scattering the swept leaves.

'Shrek! Come here!' I said out loud.

'Bit of a handful you've got there,' the park keeper said, looking over to where the dog, now reunited with its male owner, was jumping up and down, tail wagging furiously.

'Haven't I just,' I said, the puzzled park keeper shaking his head as I turned to take the path in the opposite direction.

The plum tree has shed its leaves. It is its third anniversary and our nineteenth. It's a Sanctus Hubertus. I chose it for its name alone – my plum adviser not available to specify his choice. Its fruits are purple-blue, their flesh golden yellow and as sweet as honey. Sometimes, a bough laden with plums, I see your long arm reaching up to pluck a fruit, see your head turning as you flash your white-toothed smile in my direction before biting into the juicy flesh. *Bless you*, I say. *Bless you always*, blowing a kiss through the air.

At first I thought I must find out. Must know more. Must go to kneel by a gravestone, touch a marble plaque on the family tomb. Must have, as your family must have, should they wish to go there, a place of pilgrimage, a place where I might go at least once. But then I thought, what would be the point of that? You and I shared a life. Had a life together: in the first flat I owned, in this house, in restaurants, in wine bars, in parks and cinemas. So many places where we were happy in that life. And trees are life itself. This tree is for you. *Is* you. Is what you wanted to see standing there if you were standing beside me now, looking down my long, skinny, cultivated garden with the sage-green shed at its end, Sanctus Hubertus now stripped of its leaves, its bony canopy – already filling more than half the garden's width – fingering the pink autumn dusk. There! Another leaf drifts slowly down. The last leaf of autumn. Now it is completely bare. Until spring. Until it comes back to life again.

Ah! Raindrops. Raindrops on the windowpane. How I do love the rain.

Black and White

I am watching the pianist's hands racing across the keys, envying their delicacy, their strength. We are in the cheapest seats: those, on some other occasion, the choir might have taken up. Louise bought the tickets. And I, not wishing to disenfranchise her, resisting my instinctive desire to contribute to an upgrade, accepted her kind offer. The programme being one entirely devoted to Brahms, Louise knew this was an offer I could not refuse – since I adore Brahms and rather like Louise.

It's during the tumultuous second movement, the stormy scherzo quite carrying me away, that, out of the blue, that enigmatic smile, that brooding look flashes across my mind; and I see the long, pale neck; the square, almost manly jaw; the broad, high-cheekboned face above the trademark black roll-neck. See Monika as clearly as if she were sitting beside me now.

This inner vision must have produced an external reaction, because, at that selfsame moment, I feel Louise's tentative fingertips brushing the back of my hand, resting, or I thought resting, on my left thigh, and I turn to see her questioning blues eyes looking into my murky grey ones. I smile reassuringly, before returning my gaze to the magical hands. But, disturbed by my inner vision, the music is no longer a part of me; now it washes over me.

It's not until the soloist is taking his final bow, and the jubilant applause, though greatly diminished, not completely died away, that, beyond the orchestra, in the main body of the audience, in the middle of the middle row of the most expensive seats, I see two people rising a little earlier than is considered de rigueur on these occasions – especially after such a brilliant performance. Find my eyes following them as they move to the end of the row.

The brown blob of a man is nothing special: medium height, broad of body, bald of pate, big of paunch. But the woman? Well, the woman looks to me to be the sort of woman who should not 'belong' to such a man. She has style, poise, sophistication. Her bobbed hair, grey to the extent of being almost white, still has life in it, still swings as she walks. She is dressed entirely in black: a slim tube of fabric, thinning to gauze on the sleeves, her pale arms visible beneath. Her legs are opaquely black, her feet clad in high-heeled ankle boots. I note the broad shoulders, the sway of the slim hips, as my gaze follows her ascending the stairs to the exit, and a voice inside me says, *Monika. I swear to God that woman is Monika.*

'That was quite something, wasn't it?' Louise is slipping on her coat and bending to gather up her capacious brown bag from the floor. 'You're still there, aren't you? Takes a while to come down from something like that, doesn't it?'

Louise has a tendency, a habit bordering on a linguistic affectation, by way of the soft upward lilt of her voice, to turn almost everything she says into a question. 'A sign of insecurity,' my daughter Phoebe informs me. 'But then,' she adds, 'who wouldn't feel insecure going out with *you*?'

'Louise and I are just good friends,' I have informed my daughter.

'In your ballpark, Dad,' my daughter insists. 'No one else's.'

'Shall we go?' Louise says, waiting for me to make a move.

'Let's,' I say, leading the way.

Knowing some form of sustenance must be factored into the evening, yet not wishing to find myself in the position of rejecting or, dare I say, *accepting* an invitation to supper at Louise's place, I had suggested pizza and a glass of wine at a nearby pizzeria. 'Least I could do,' I'd said.

To date, pre-theatre or concert drinks, the odd casual café snack, and a couple of communal get-togethers at friends' houses has been as far as it's gone on that score. The thought of a candlelit dinner à deux in Louise's neat but uninspiring maisonette somehow bringing me out in a cold sweat – psychologically, you understand, not physically. And yet, as I say, I really do like Louise. Like her a lot. The only problem being, Louise seems to like me a helluva lot more.

'So! When am I gonna meet this "nice woman" of yours?' my pushy daughter – she of the cupcake tea parties in Clapham, the hen-night brouhahas in Barcelona; even, God save us all, a white wedding weekend in Guadalupe, 'hard-up' generation – asked me, yet again, last week.

'Louise is not *my* "nice woman". Louise is her *own* woman,' I assured my daughter.

'Yeah. Right,' my daughter responded, slathering cold cream over her overly rouged cheeks and reaching for another tissue. 'Is that so?'

We were in a glorified cupboard, aka 'the dressing room' of Kensal Rise Community Centre, Phoebs having rolled out the first of four 'drunken' performances (the whisky on these occasions merely apple juice) as Martha in *Who's Afraid of Virginia Woolf?* The ambitious, overly hysterical performance put on by The Mad Rams: the am-dram group my commanding daughter has herded together and anagrammatically named. So don't go telling me that lower second in English my chip-off-the-old-block scraped by on hasn't been worth every penny of the overdraft *I'm* paying off.

'Indeed it *is* so, daughter dear,' I replied. 'Louise and I come from a far less conventional generation than your own.'

'Well,' Phoebe said, sweeping her face with a Wet One, 'in that case, why'd you marry Mum?'

'Because she was there,' I said. 'Because she asked me.'

'You old romantic, you. So? When?'

'When what?'

'When *Louise*?!'

'Some day soon. What's the rush?'

'You are *sixty-two*, Dad. *That's* the rush. Men on the shelf,' she fingered a loose button on my jacket, 'they get kinda dusty, y'know… You'd better get that fixed before you lose it somewhere.'

'*I'd* better? Or *Louise'd* better?'

'Jeez, Dad. What century are you in?'

———

'William has potential,' Mrs Eviss, my piano teacher, once told my mother; their conversation having taken place in the hardware store that morning, where my mother had come upon Mrs Eviss purchasing beeswax polish with which to feed her burr walnut piano.

'Yes,' my mother went on, joyfully reiterating Mrs Eviss's lukewarm assertion as she popped a couple of slices of Hovis into the toaster, 'Mrs Eviss said, "If he can apply himself, young William has a *good deal* of potential."'

It was 1962. I was twelve years old.

The only problem being, I could apply myself to nothing in particular.

For I was not drawn to the piano as bee is to honey. I was drawn only to the *idea* of being drawn to the piano, to some romantic notion of commitment. I was not drawn to the long courtship, the slow, patient conquering, the week-upon-week, month-upon-month, year-upon-year journey from finger-aching scales on Mrs Eviss's Boyd upright, to polished adagios on a glossy concert-hall Steinway grand. Yet my mother, a woman able to see potential where there was none (after all, she married my father), actually believed *I* had potential. And so, for several months, I believed it, too.

But there was insubstantiality about me. I had recognised this lack, this void at the heart of me, from an early age. Felt myself a will-o'-the-wisp sort of boy, knowing this was quite the wrong sort of boy to be. 'Fairy!' the rock-solid, thick-as-shit boys masquerading as men chorused as

I walked by, as they pushed me over, as they rubbed my will-o'-the-wisp nose in the dirt. While I, like some feather-light winged seed, wished only to be blown away, to be deposited on some desolate, unpopulated shore free of punching boys who grew into punching men, men who became fathers.

'That was *really* lovely, William,' my mother would say, ignoring my muddled notes, my lack of phrasing, my hopeless pacing, continuing to see potential where there was none. 'You're doing so well.'

The bubble burst six months later, when, returning from my weekly lesson with Mrs Eviss, closing the back door behind me, I heard my father's booming voice ricocheting off the walls of our small kitchen. 'It's a bloody waste of good money, Elsie. And you know it!' He must have heard me coming in, but carried on all the same. 'You know damn well that boy can't stick at anything for long. Let alone some namby-pamby, Tinker Bell sonata. Why'd you encourage him? A performing flea's got more talent, more discipline than he has!'

From then on my mother lost heart and I lost confidence – as well as the limited enthusiasm I'd managed to summon up. Four months later my piano lessons with Mrs Eviss came to an end – no doubt much to Mrs Eviss's relief. As did my fantasy adult life as a concert pianist, and I began to wonder what use I was to the world.

Monika rescued me.

The idea that the sort of woman Monika so obviously was could see potential in the sort of man I so obviously was quite blew me away.

'I was wondering… would it be OK… wondered if I could invite someone for Sunday lunch?'

It was the spring of 1969. I'd known Monika for seven months.

'A girlfriend, you mean?' my mother said, all smiles.

'A girl. Yes. A friend.'

My father, making a great to-do about turning the pages of his newspaper, peered over it, one bushy eyebrow sarcastically raised. 'My, oh my,' he said. 'So the boy's managed it at last. I was beginning to wonder about you, lad.'

I said nothing, wishing I had not said this much – wishing I had a different father.

'Can't she come down with you, Friday night?' my mother said. 'There's the spare room. University girl, is she?'

'Absolutely!' I said. 'But she'll drive over. She has her own car, you see. We'll go back together.'

'Well,' my mother said, looking a little crestfallen, '*next* time then, eh?'

'Hope so,' I said, bringing the smile back to her face.

My pushy daughter tells me I am in denial. It seems we blokes get our 'fingers burned', then become 'scared shitless' to dip our 'toes in the water'.

'Once bitten, and all that,' my budding psychoanalyst, she who dropped psychology after a mere seven weeks, proclaimed.

I – wondering how many mixed metaphors a dusty, loose-buttoned, on-the-shelf dad with a double first in English could take – put forward the notion that women rather like men who actually *like* women. 'If, daughter dear,' I said, 'you'd stuck at psychology a bit longer, you might have discovered Freud's pretty passé these days. Not *everything* comes down to sex, you know.'

'You think?' Phoebs questioned, unconvinced.

You see, when you get right down to the nitty-gritty, to the nucleic acid sequencing of life, my daughter has more of her mother's genes than her father's. Phoebe and I share the same straight, fair hair, the same dubious grey eyes, but the rest...?

'But *why*?' I asked my wife. 'Why do it, Joanna?'

'Because,' Joanna declared, '*it* was there.'

Its name was Ed. Ed, the tooled-up one-man-band of a builder who'd taken a *helluva* time to build our small extension – soon to be renamed by one or two people, previously known as friends, as... yes, you've guessed it, and I refuse to repeat it.

Five days earlier I had left It slow-motion tiling the roof of our small extension, returning to find the job at last completed. In fact, as my car swung into the drive, I remember admiring the softly undulating terracotta roof, while delighting in the fact that, for the first time in six sweat-smelling months, there was no sign of It's muscly torso on my premises.

'It meant nothing, really,' Joanna insisted.

It was the 'really' that did it. I sometimes think if Joanna had said, *It meant nothing, William*, or, *William, it* really *meant nothing*, things might have run differently; I might have accepted this It was a one-off. Or, rather, a six-nights-and-five-days-off. But, 'It meant nothing, *really*' to me suggested that, to Joanna, it *really* meant something.

'You know,' Joanna said, casually flicking on the kettle, as if tea for two was all we needed to clear this little *nothing* thing up, 'it was just one of those things.'

'Oh. *Was* it? Well, this *nothing* thing sure as hell means *something* to me.' And, for the first time in my life, I took a stand. 'Up with this I will not put,' I declared.

'Up yours!' or words, and actions, to that effect my soon-to-be-ex-wife retorted. And within eighteen months the decree nisi became absolute.

Phoebe – a budding young woman of fourteen at the time, conveniently tucked away at boarding school – chose to forgive her wayward mother; or, rather, her wayward mother's version of events. 'Can't *you*, Dad?' she pleaded, six months down the line. 'I mean, it *was* just one of those things.'

'Let's put it this way, sweetheart,' I replied. 'If it was, then I'd much rather your mother had taken off somewhere on her *"gossamer wings"* than bonked a bloody tiler under my own bloody roof!'

'Sorry?'

'No. *I'm* sorry, Phoebs. I'm really not suited to today's forgive-and-forget take on marriage. I don't like to let you down like this, but your mother's let me down and I can't whitewash that away.'

'But she won't do it again, Dad.'

'Did she say that?'

'Yes… Well, no… not exactly. I just *know* she won't.'

'Well, she won't do it to me again, Phoebs. *I* know that.'

'I'm growing quite fond of your Johannes,' Louise says as we descend the stairs to the foyer.

'*A little wisp of a scherzo* is how "my" Johannes described that second movement. Which, to me, sounds a rather derogatory comment for such a fine piece, suggesting something lightweight, flimsy. Inconsequential.'

I hear my voice reverberating in my head, am aware of Louise's honey-skinned face looking up at me, but, inside, my stomach is churning, my heart thumping in my chest. We are walking straight towards them through the foyer – there must have already been a queue for the cloakroom. The brown blob is holding a creamy-white coat out to her, its shimmering scarlet lining exposed. Her black back is turned toward me. At the foot of the stairs I hesitate.

'Really?' Louise's questioning voice is saying. 'You see, to me, the word "wisp" suggests something fine, something delicate. Something magical.'

I watch the brown blob – a most unlikely toreador – whirl the red lining before her, watch her gauzy arms slip into it. Watch her wrap the pale fabric around her black body. See her tie the belt, loosely, around her slim waist. See the youthful bob swinging as she turns, her face a blur of grey.

'Someone you know?'

'Hmm? Sorry?'

'The people you're staring at. Do you know them?'

Is the jaw still square? The neck still long? Is there mellowed beauty in that sixty-something face? *Is* that woman Monika?

At first the 'red-blooded man' my father professed himself to be appeared equally enamoured of my girlfriend's beauty, of the quiet politeness she had, so far, displayed.

I had given Monika fair warning of the shyness of my mother, the smallness of the house, the bigness of my father. Had told her of the sense I'd had throughout childhood of being no more than an irritating insect, an annoying pest to be swatted should I buzz too near him. I did not tell her I *had* been swatted, since, by the time I reached my teens, the 'swatting' had ceased, and it seemed to me to be a betrayal of the red-blooded man whose genes ran in my own 'lily-livered' veins.

Monika had been unusually quiet until that moment, she and I both more than a little uncomfortable in the claustrophobic setting of the rarely used dining room: not much bigger than the table we four sat around. Unused to seeing her in restrained mode, I found myself becoming abnormally jovial, boasting about my girlfriend's intellectual achievements, as an abnormally bashful Monika attempted to change the subject by complimenting my mother on the lightness of her 'battah' puddings.

'Yorkshires, you mean, love. Oh, anybody can make a good Yorkshire.'

'I don't zink—' Monika said.

'You don't *think* what?' my father said abruptly.

'I don't zink every person can make such puddings.'

She had said so little until then that my father, entranced as he'd been by her beauty, had barely noticed Monika's accent.

'Where're you from, exactly, Monika?' he asked, putting down his loaded fork.

'Munich!' she answered. 'From Germany.'

'Ah!' he said, and I held my breath. 'So *we* win the bloody war, and you Germans end up not only taking up places at our very best universities, but *somehow* managing to afford a bloody car my own son hasn't the spare cash for into the bargain! Perhaps we should've lost. What d'you reckon, Monika?'

'*Frank!*' my mother said, not knowing what else to say, a hand reaching out to touch Monika's black shoulder.

Her pale face darkening, Monika looked down to her plate. For several seconds no one spoke. Then, rising from her chair, Monika said, 'I am so sorry, Mrs Bennett. But, I zink, if I do not have an apology, I will go now. You see, I have become quite uncomfortable in this situation.'

'No!' My mother stood up. 'Oh, love, *please* don't do that. You mustn't mind him. He's all bluster.'

Monika looked down at the small woman standing beside her. 'I should have liked very much to taste your apple pie, Mrs Bennett, and I so much thank you for your kindness, but my appetite is not as it was.' Then, turning to me, 'William?'

I looked up at her, but remained seated.

This affair no longer his concern, my father, tackling the last slice of beef on his plate, looked across the table to me, as if to say, *Don't do it, lad. Or she'll be jackbooting you about for the rest of your life.*

And for a moment, for too long, I hesitated. I did not demand that my father, the man I had cursed with a vengeance, had professed hatred for, apologise to the woman to whom I had declared everlasting love, but simply stretched out a hand to touch Monika's fingertips and said, 'Come on, Monika. Sit down a minute. Let's sort this out, shall we? You were only joking, weren't you, Dad?'

His mouth stuffed full of the last piece of batter pudding and gravy on his plate, my father raised a quizzical eyebrow and said nothing.

'I am so sorry,' Monika repeated, a hand on my mother's arm. Then, turning, she opened the door to the hall. 'Goodbye then, William.'

'I'm... Monika... *Wait a sec!* Sorry, Mum.' And, my lips brushing my mother's dampening cheek, I trailed Monika to the front door.

We survived for three more months, but not as before. For the woman who had made a man of me had witnessed, in that one short visit to the house in which I grew up, the wilting of my manhood. I was far too woolly, way too sheepish, for someone as clear-cut, as strong, as certain as Monika. And however much I professed my love for her, however firm and thrusting my lovemaking, in Monika's eyes, that love had itself become a construction, a man-made means to an end; the man she thought she knew now an impotent abstraction, a flimsy, insubstantial will-o'-the-wisp.

Moving towards them through the foyer, for a moment, the creamy-white jacket wrapped about her, she and I walk barely an arm's length apart. Then, veering left towards the North Exit, our paths cross, and for a split second I catch sight of her face. *Is it Monika? It may be? It may not be. Does it matter? It was all so long ago.*

'William?'

Louise's hand is resting on my upper arm.

'So! You didn't know them, then?'

'Sorry. For a moment I was miles away. No. I thought it was someone from way back. My mistake. *Right!* Now, that pizza place is only a few minutes away.' And I stride toward the South Exit.

'How's your daughter's new play going?' Louise asks.

'It's *gone*, actually. The four-night run ended on Saturday. I should've asked you along.'

'Why should you? I don't suppose young people are particularly interested in their parents' lives. Anyway, I have a strange relationship, or should I say a *strained* relationship with that play.'

'Well, it is a play about a very strange, strained relationship. *George doesn't like it when the conversation moves to muscle…*'

'What's that?'

'A rough approximation of one of Phoebe's, aka *Martha's*, killer lines. One, I imagine, Joanna greatly enjoyed.'

'Oh.' Louise looks down to the menu. 'Did Joanna go too?'

'*Too*, in the sense that Joanna also saw the play. Not *two*, in the sense that my ex-wife and I saw the play as a twosome. That will never happen. Ours was a clean break. A Domestos-doused divorce. Expensive, but *very* hygienic. As long as, as far as Phoebe's concerned, I've paid up, everything's fine and dandy – well, dandy-ish. No. Joanna went on Priority Parenting Night, i.e. Saturday: the night with the last-night party attached. I, though frequently second in line for most things, on this occasion, had the dubious pleasure of seeing the Rams', dare I say it, rather *ram*shackle first night.'

'The first time I saw it – well, the *only* time I saw it – was two weeks after Jeff told me he was in love with Lindy. It seemed a shame to waste both tickets, and I wasn't up to asking a friend to share my gloomy company. Kathleen Turner was quite ferocious. *Brilliant!*'

'Not better than my daughter, surely?'

Louise smiles. 'Boy, was it a raw experience. Quite…'

'Cathartic?'

'Something like that.'

As she picks up the menu her salt-and-pepper hair falls forward to curtain her face. Mostly chestnut brown, or mostly white, I wonder? And I wonder why I've not wondered this before.

'This is such a nice place,' she says, still scanning the menu. 'Have you been here before?'

'A couple of times. With Phoebs.'

'Are we *really* hungry, William, or just snacking?'

'We are absolutely famished. We are stuffing ourselves silly and glugging like there's no tomorrow. My treat. Remember?'

Her eyes meet mine and I think how pretty she looks in the candle's soft glow. Think, in her gentle, low-key way, how pretty Louise must have been at nineteen, at twenty-nine, at thirty-eight – at fifty! – and, for a moment, regret not knowing her then, regret not having had those years in which to know her.

'And don't forget,' I say, looking over to it myself, 'today's specials are on the board. Over there.'

A hand pushing the hair from her face, she leans forward. '*If* you can read it?' she says, and we both squint at the grainy chalk writing on the ill-lit blackboard.

Red Fox Morning

I t was on the morning she walked to the store that Zoe saw the fox.

'*Walk* to the store?!' the middle-aged woman who had introduced herself as Maime ('An' y'know somethin': I *always* get the blame') said, aghast at this potential act of idiocy. 'Are you *crazy*, hun? How the hellaya gonna bring back yer groceries if you walk there? Didn't Lorrie and Chas leave the car keys?'

'I'd prefer to walk,' Zoe said. 'I *like* to walk,' she insisted, as Maime, shrugging her meaty, blameless shoulders, rolled her unexercised haunches over the flat expanse of grass to the mailbox of 275 Gardenville Drive, pausing to look up at the sky and say, 'Hey. Whatsabettin' it's rainin' in little old England, right now? Just look at that blue. Ain't it somethin' else?!'

The word 'store' had brought to mind the village shop Zoe's grandfather used to take her to: small, friendly, a counter at one end, a few iced cakes dismally displayed beneath a plastic cover, a bacon slicer, only two sorts of cheese. Brought back memories of illicit trips made there: the aroma of aniseed twists, pear drops and fizz balls (sweets forbidden by her mother) being shaken from their dusty jars. Brought back the feeling of her tobacco-wafting grandfather's nicotine-stained fingers wrapped around her own, the bag of naughtiness stashed in his pocket (he refused to let her suck on a sweet while walking), the path across the field to his bungalow always so much longer on the way back.

Turning left at the end of Gardenville Drive, as Maime had instructed, Zoe was following the straight, paved path that ran beside the straight, tarmacked highway, the morning heat more fierce than she'd expected, the traffic fumes obliterating her sweet-smelling memories, when a voice called out, 'Hey there, little lady, you wanna ride?'

If she had wanted a ride, would she be walking along this path, eyes straight ahead, hitching thumbs firmly in her pockets? She scowled at the jowly face hanging from the truck window and wished she had not. His lascivious eyes were on her legs. She pulled her sunglasses down from her head. 'I most certainly do not!' she snapped, her shaded eyes on the path. So it's hot. So you wear shorts. Did walking along a path close to a road automatically turn a woman into a streetwalker around here? At *nine* in the morning? Were there twenty-four-hour kerb-crawlers as well as twenty-four-hour everything else?

Maime had been right. Zoe could only blame herself. She should throw in the towel and drive everywhere. Go native, like Tariq. Who, for reasons best known to himself, had leapt out of bed at seven o'clock to drive to the leisure complex. 'For a spot of weights and a swim,' he'd said.

'But *why*?' Zoe had asked him. 'You're never up before 7.30. Not even on a workday.'

And why had *she* decided to walk to this damn store? They were supposed to be on holiday, yet, within days of arriving in this soulless place, were falling into some kind of *Revolutionary Road* stereotypes; regressive roles they rarely took up at home. Perhaps later on she should fix cocktails for Tariq. Should she, before she fixed dinner, go to a beauty salon to fix her nails, her hair?

Reaching the store, bamboozled by the aisles of bottles, the rows of cans, the Himalayan ranges of cartons, the mountains of vegetables, the stacks of fruit, all supersized, shiny, surrounded by this sterile plenty, Zoe felt all desire to cook, or even to eat, drain from her body. *Even the apples look as if they've had facelifts*, she thought, picking one up and seeing her own drooping expression reflected in it. The empty trolley a Zimmer-frame prop to support her exhausted, overstimulated senses, she meandered 'drunkenly' about the store's vastness, feeling empty, hungry only for home. *Help!* she wanted to cry out like a despairing child lost in a monster maze. *Help!* And, abandoning her search for the Tabasco and the naan bread she had come especially for, she tossed a cardboard box of what turned out to be cardboard masquerading as tacos into the trolley, grabbed a couple of bottles of iced tea – why, she could not say – and rushed from the store's air-conditioned chill into the stifling blue morning.

'Hi there, hon. Say, you're lookin kinda hot.'

She had almost reached the turn-off for Gardenville Drive when the car – the stretched-out sort: aggressive tail fins, half limo, half space rocket – slowed down alongside her.

'It's cooler in here, y'know, babe.'

His dark retro hair was grease-slicked, his gleaming teeth whiter than his whiter-than-white shirt – washed for him, no doubt, by some cute little lady.

'I can take you *any* place you wanna go. Places you never been before: the light or the dark side of life. Whaddaya say?'

She could smell his sickly aftershave: tequila and lime cordial, with a splash of toilet cleaner. Increasing her pace, Zoe walked on. While, uttering mild profanities, he continued to cruise beside her, until, 'OK, *Mizz Frigidaire!*' he snapped as he accelerated. 'Your fuckin loss!' Turning back to shout, 'One tip, little lady… Get those legs shaved sometime soon. *Big* turn-off', before speeding away.

'Let's just try it,' Tariq had said. 'What's to lose? Three weeks. A longer, cheaper holiday. It's a win-win, if you ask me.' A house swap, he said, would give them 'a taste of real American life'. Zoe suggested they had tasted quite a bit of it, night after night, on TV. 'But there is another Baltimore, Zo,' Tariq insisted. 'A place where ordinary, decent, hard-working people live ordinary, decent, hard-working lives. It's not just a TV drama. It's a vibrant city.'

Tariq's company had a branch there, a branch with plans to expand. Brandon Holdings, Baltimore, had weekly videoconferences with Brandon Holdings, Tunbridge Wells. Conferences during which, according to Tariq, the Baltimore branch only ever drank bottled water, with not a single start-the-day line of coke in sight. 'Not even a can of the stuff!' he'd added with a wry smile, going on to point out that it was invariably the TW branch that got themselves tanked up on triple hits of caffeine. There was talk of promotion over there, he said, if you dared take the plunge.

'But if it's just talk…?' Zoe had murmured.

'You've gotta be prepared, Zo,' he'd said. 'You've gotta have your feet on the starting block.'

My feet? she'd thought. *My starting block?*

'And who knows?' he'd added, filling the coffee pot and putting it on the hob. 'You might find a better job too! I mean, it hasn't exactly been an easy ride, has it?'

Did he really expect her to throw in the towel after all she'd built up? Go back to a nine-to-five lifestyle? Correction! To 7.30 breakfast meetings, snatched fast-food lunches, to working their bollocks off fifty weeks of the year until they both keeled over with coronaries?!

Tariq said Zoe possessed a rather warped view of American life. She should, he suggested, before writing off an entire city, and this opportunity, at least find out what it was like.

'I'm self-employed, Tariq,' she'd said. 'Remember! I *like* freelancing. I can't start over just like that.'

He had turned to look out of the window. Appeared distracted by something in the far distance. 'On the other hand,' he'd said softly, fingers nervously drumming the draining board, 'we could start a family.'

'What?! For want of something to do while *you* make it big in the US of A, you mean?'

'No,' he'd replied, turning away from her, 'for want of a child.' Zoe had noticed a muscle twitching near the corner of his mouth as he did so. The sun going down beyond the wood was purple-tinged, melancholic.

He had boxed her in. He had pigeonholed her.

'When are you going to start a family?' people asked. As if it was as easy as starting a car – a stretch limo. As easy as firing a rocket to the moon. Automatic. A done deal. You get together, you get married, you *start* a family. *That's what it's all about!* The *Hokey Cokey*. The *real* McCoy. The meaning of life.

'There are still risk-takers over there, y'know, Zo,' Tariq had said, turning to lift the coffee pot from the stove; 'forceful guys who can fight their way out of trouble. They get by, they prosper, because they go out there and grab life by the throat.'

'Don't you mean *by the balls*?' she'd said, watching him overfill the cup, coffee spilling into the saucer.

Walking forlornly along Gardenville Drive, dripping with sweat, Zoe wanted nothing more than to call home, the home now inhabited by Lorrie and Chas McQuade, and announce their imminent return to 7 Church Walk.

'We are *so* looking forward to seeing England, you would not believe!' the McQuades had said. Or rather Lorrie McQuade had said; Chas McQuade, looking somewhat woebegone, peering over his wife's shoulder, a long, bony hand smoothing back the wayward strand of greying hair that no longer wished to be teased across his thinning pate, appeared to be 'looking forward' to very little. Observing his strained expression, it occurred to Zoe that she and Chas might well be in the same boat.

'Do you Skype?' Lorrie McQuade had chirpily asked towards the end of that first phone call. 'It'd be nice for us all to get together, face ta face. An you get ta see a bitta this place. See if it's ta your liken'. Skype's so damned dinky, don't you think?'

'I guess,' Zoe said, transatlantically.

Somehow, despite her protests, it had got this far. 'Three weeks of our life, Zo? Just to find out. It'll be fun!'

'No,' she told Lorrie, 'we... *I* don't. But my husband does – at work. I'll speak to him about it later.'

And, keen as he was to 'meet with the McQuades', Tariq had set it up that evening.

'Meet *with*?' Zoe questioned.

'What?' Tariq said.

Stop! a voice inside Zoe's head had cried out every step along the way to 275 Gardenville Drive. *No*, it said, *I do not want to see the McQuades' kitchen, their enormous fridge-freezer with its in-door ice dispenser. I do not need to know about their 'bathroom' without a bath but* with *a toilet, their wet room with its high-speed, water-consuming shower, but* without *a toilet. And I definitely do not need to* meet with *Bo-Bo and Snuff.* Had Lorrie and Chas hoped she and Tariq might fall in love with the snub-nosed miniature monsters and offer to dog-sit them, too, thereby saving the McQuades a fortune at their local Creature Comforts holiday spa? Bo-Bo and Snuff should get themselves facelifts while they were there. Not to mention nose jobs. Make themselves more adorable to future house-swapping suckers.

'The tiles over there,' Lorrie's immaculately manicured hand indicating their presence, 'are brand new... well, installed last fall. Aquamarine and peach. Real snazzy, don't you think? The guy did such a neat job. Didn't he, Chas?'

Nodding, with a silent wave to the screen, Chas, already losing interest in these Skype shenanigans, had backed out of the screen's view, thereby exposing more of the 'neat job'.

'Bathroom call!' Lorrie discreetly declared behind the immaculately manicured hand she'd raised to her colour-matched lips.

Could nothing be a surprise any more, or a disappointment, thought Zoe, as Lorrie insisted they 'hook up' next day 'to take a peek at the family room' ('Of course the family's gone now'), or Chas's den ('I guess *my* den's the kitchen'). Perhaps those cookies, perfectly positioned on the counter, *were* freshly baked, Zoe had thought? Pretty soon there would be Skype smells: pixel and peanut brownies. Microsoft freshly ground coffee grains. Manly megabyte aftershaves.

In sight of 275 Gardenville Drive, Zoe saw the front door was open, the screen door pulled over; Tariq was back from the leisure complex. Reaching the straight path to the door (were curved paths forbidden around here?), she could hear him whistling in the aquamarine-and-peach-tiled kitchen.

She stood for a moment, taking in the expansive double garage, the paucity of garden, and thought again of her grandfather's compact little bungalow, its small cottage garden crammed with flowers and shrubs, a haven of life. She could almost taste a fizz ball, hear bees buzzing in the lavender and hyssop of her memory. *Life!* she thought. *Where's the life here?* There was nothing but sun-dried grass and a few tall, straight trees dotted here and there. No shrubs. No hedges. Not even a picket fence. Her mournful gaze took in the long line of low, close-boarded houses, their double garages and carports, their short straight paths meeting the long straight path, running parallel to the long straight road, in 310 perfect ninety-degree angles. If only there was a breeze. Something to bend the motionless trees.

It was then she saw it: a large red fox. Like Zoe and the trees it stood motionless, its coat burning bright against the bleached grass. For a few fleeting, feral seconds their eyes met, then, turning from her, it slunk away through the trees. And, instinctively, Zoe wanted to follow it, wanted to go where she too might live in a den, might forage for food, might never see the inside of a supermarket again.

'Zo!' Tariq sighed as Zoe slumped on a stool at the breakfast bar. 'I said we'd drop by the store on our way back from the harbour!' His fingers brushed her flushed cheek. 'Didn't you get yourself any breakfast? No coffee, even?'

She shook her head.

'No wonder you look knackered. I'll get us some brunch. Then we can freshen up before we go.'

He seemed so energised, so at ease, so at home in this place that it made Zoe want to cry.

'Did you not put on any sunscreen?' he asked, putting three bagels in the microwave. 'Your nose looks kinda pink.'

No, she told him, she hadn't. Hadn't thought. She told him about the size of the melons, the smoothness of the 'Botoxed' apples. She told him about the ugliness of the kerb-crawlers, the friendliness of Maime, but as for the fox... well, she told him nothing about the fox. And yet it had been the fox, that brief moment of reality, that had made it all worthwhile.

The girl appeared early one morning, eight days later.

The previous week they had gone to Betterton beach for the day, and to Chesapeake Bay for the afternoon. 'Under an hour!' Tariq triumphantly announced. 'Not bad, eh? The places you can get to around here.'

And it wasn't at all bad, really. It was almost like being on holiday.

They had driven to Washington. Had seen the White House, the Jefferson Memorial and the Lincoln Memorial. Had gazed up at it feeling so small as to be almost insignificant. 'I wonder,' Zoe had questioned, 'now he's President, if, standing here right now, Obama would feel as we do?'

'Hope so,' Tariq had replied. 'A dose of humility is what the world – the rich world, at least – needs.'

'The let's-pretend-we're-rich world, you mean,' she'd said.

'Maybe?' Tariq replied.

'So, what about all that going out there and "grabbing life by the throat"?' she'd asked him. 'Would Abe approve of that, do you think?'

'Maybe?' he repeated. 'He looks too good to be true, doesn't he. Perhaps, made of marble, we'd all look that noble?'

Hooked on his early-morning swim, if not the workout, Tariq had already driven off to the leisure complex. Rising with him, Zoe had made coffee and taken it, and the novel she had almost finished reading, out to the porch. But, unable to concentrate, dropping the book to the boarded floor, had found herself just sitting there, looking out across the yard, wondering if the fox might come by again.

The mug, half full of cold coffee, was still at her feet when the battered old estate wagon slowed down and swung into the drive, and a girl, who looked barely old enough, or big enough, to drive it, got out. Peering over the car's roof, she cast a questioning look in Zoe's direction before, bending to scoop a child almost half her size from the back seat, she emerged to walk towards the house.

'Is Grandmaw insida there?' she asked.

Her mouse-brown hair was brutally scraped into a motley collection of multicoloured bands, the resulting scruffy tail fanning out on top of her head. Lank strands, escaping their confinement, hung about her neck, her cheeks, and down over her forehead, partially imprisoning the weary, dark-ringed eyes behind their greasy bars. Probably still in her teens, the girl possessed the world-weariness of a woman four times her age. An oversized T-shirt, a man's, hung halfway down her skinny, jean-clad thighs, the frayed edges hacked off at irregular lengths above pale, meatless calves.

'No,' Zoe said, shaking her head, 'I'm afraid she's not. That is, Mrs McQuade's not.'

And, as if losing the strength to hold on to him, to hold on to anything, the girl let the child drop to the porch floor, exposing the pregnant curve beneath her khaki T-shirt, and the words *PROUD ARMY DAD* emblazoned across it in scarlet capitals.

'So where *is* Grandmaw? Where the friggin hell's my grandmaw? I *gotta* see her, y'see.'

The child, who was barely two years old, had by now bum-shuffled his way over to the screen door and begun banging his small fists against the wire mesh.

'Quit that, Ethan!' the girl snapped. '*Quit it, I say!*' Then, turning back to glare at Zoe, 'What's happened to Grandmaw? She OK? Who the hell are ya, anyway?' Then, softening, her voice beginning to crack, 'I gotta see my grandfolks! I jus' *gotta!*' Before, knees buckling, she collapsed to the porch steps and, cupping her head in her hands, let out a wailing, animal cry.

Hearing it, the child stopped his banging and crawled over to rest his head against his mother's back and support her tears with his own.

Joining them on the step, not knowing whether to comfort mother or child, Zoe somehow managed to wrap her arms around both of them.

Quietening, the girl said, 'Grandmaw's not gotten sick, has she? Grandpaw's not... *Jesus!* Not Grandpaw too!' And she began to cry again.

'No. They're fine. They're *both* fine. They're on holiday, that's all.'

Hearing this, the girl began to wipe her tears with the heel of her palm.

'We've house-swapped, you see. They're in England.'

'*England?!* Oh, Jesus Christ!' Her sobs resuming.

Calm once more, her child silenced by scrambled egg and muffins, and surprisingly accepting of Zoe's lap, the girl, whose name was Kaylee – who had wanted nothing more than a mug of black coffee – felt able to talk.

'I bin drivin all night, y'see. An most of the day before. I din't wanna call. Din't know what I'd say if I did. Jus wannid to see Grandmaw and Grandpaw. Jus needed to talk to someone who cared about us. *Really* cared.'

'Your mother's not close by?'

'My maw's not close by anyone but herself. She din't much care for me. Paw cared for me – way back. But she din't much care for Paw either, so he din't hang around.'

They had found his body, she said; the father of her children, the *PROUD ARMY DAD*. She would not say in what state his body had been found – 'It's too damn ugly' – and she had no wish 't'go upsettin a total stranger'. Most likely, she would not tell her grandmother, since the shock 'might be one shock too many. Same goes for Grandpaw.'

The sergeant who'd brought her the news did not want to tell the whole story either. And many times since knowing it, Kaylee had wished she had not 'prised the pain of it outta him. But then,' she said, with a world-weary shrug, as if trying to reassure Zoe as well as herself, 'folks are more than their goddamn bodies, ain't they? We all of us got souls. We all of us got somethin in us a friggin sight bigger 'n' better than skin an bone. Otherwise, why the hellawe here?' Then she began to cry again.

This time Ethan, chomping on a muffin, observed his distraught mother with the detached interest of someone becoming well used to the sight.

'Poor little fella,' Kaylee said, surfacing from her sobs, 'he was *so* damn hungry. I jus kept drivin, y'see. Jus wannid to get here. Get to some place that felt t'me like home.'

'Shall *I* call them for you?' Zoe said. 'Or text them? They needn't know why until you see them – if that's what you want. I'll just say *we* need to get back: a family reason? Work? Say you happened by.'

Kaylee had pulled her hair from the ponytail bands and begun layering them, one by one, round her skinny wrist in a tatty, rainbow-coloured bangle. She pulled another band over her bony knuckles. 'Thanks, lady, but naw, I gotta do it. I'll tell them somethin to get them here. Then… God, I wish t'hell they *was* here. Sorry, ma'am. Din't mean to sound ungrateful.'

'Look,' Zoe said, 'why don't you go upstairs and rest for a bit? Your grandparents will be sleeping for a few hours yet themselves.'

Kaylee opened her arms. 'Com'on, Ethan. Come with Mommy.'

Ethan's eyes looked up, but his hands remained firmly clasped around the feeder cup of milk.

'Ethan'll be fine with me for a bit. And if he's not, I'm sure he'll soon let you know.'

'He sure as hell will,' Kaylee said, dragging her exhausted body across the room. 'He *always* does.'

When Tariq saw Zoe sitting on the porch, a sleeping child in her arms, he stopped, right there on the path, in much the same place Zoe had stopped when she saw the fox. Then, without a word, he came up the steps and bent to gently kiss the top of her head. Zoe thought his eyes looked a little moist. Or perhaps the moisture was in her own eyes?

The McQuades could not get a direct flight back until the day after tomorrow. They would cross over. Zoe and Tariq agreed it would not be right to be there when they returned. This was family time, after all.

They left 275 Gardenville Drive at 10.30 that morning – the McQuades were due in at Baltimore Washington International at five in the afternoon. Kaylee was sitting on the porch, Ethan at her feet.

'Don't you folks be worrying about me, now. I'm swell. Like I say, this place was home t'me, ten years back. An I'm gonna be at that airport in good time, waitin on them. I'll jus sit here awhile. You get goin.'

The proud army dad's name, strangely enough, was Brandon.

'He'd have been twenty-three, come fall. I used t'come visit Grandmaw and Grandpaw, back then, mainly cos Brandon lived close by.' They were sweethearts, she said, right from the start, her voice swelling with pride, tears welling, a bony hand tousling Ethan's floppy blond hair. 'Tha's how this little guy came into our fucked-up ol' world when I was sweet sixteen.'

Tariq was wheeling the cases down the path. 'The taxi's cutting it a bit fine.'

And suddenly Zoe did not want to leave, wanted to stay on the porch with Kaylee. She sat down beside her. Kaylee said, 'There used to be this old red fox prowlin about the place, back when Brandon and I was kids.

An, one summer, it went an had some kids of its own. We'd sit here on this old porch, swingin our legs, eatin Grandmaw's peanut cookies, watchin out for it. Then one mornin, jus like this one, she brings 'em to us. All three of em rollin an jumpin about the yard, right under our noses.' She smiled to herself. 'We'd left a trail of crunched-up cookies, which might've had somethin t'do with it. Ol' Maw Fox was standin right over there, in the shade of that tree, watchin over em. Then, time's up! She comes an rounds em up. An we watch em skippin away. Brand 'n' me, we felt *so* happy, y'know. Felt privileged this wild creature had showed em to the to of us. I never forgot it. Nor ever will, now. Brand's little boy's hand in mine, Brand's soft girl's lips on my cheek.'

Her fingertips caressing the selfsame spot, Kaylee stared towards the trees.

Zoe said, 'Y'know, *I* saw a red fox, soon after we arrived here: the third day, in fact.'

'What date'd that be?'

Passing by with the hand luggage, Tariq said, 'We arrived on June 25th!'

Zoe said, 'Then I would've seen it on June 28th!'

'Yeah? That was the very same day they brought my Brandon back. Reckon Brand's soul's found its way into that ol' fox. I'm gonna keep a lookout for it now.'

Maime's car was emerging from her garage as the taxi pulled up on the road. Seeing the luggage on the path, her round brown face leaned out of the window. 'What's happ'nin? You folks goin home so soon?'

'Something urgent's come up,' Tariq said.

Standing up, Zoe looked down at Kaylee, her clean hair hanging in straight, soft curtains down her cheeks. *What a child she looks*, she thought, kissing her goodbye and joining Tariq on the path.

'Lord save us!' Maime cried out, seeing the girl on the porch. 'Ain't that young Kaylee? *My oh my!* After *all* this time. An' you *still* look just a kid.'

Kaylee assured Maime that she had done a lot of growing up since then. 'I'll come by t'see yer later tomorrer, Mrs Spacey. If that's OK with you? After I spent a bitta time with Grandmaw and Grandpaw.'

'Look forward to it, sweetheart. Look forward to it.' And, wishing Zoe and Tariq a safe journey, Maime drove off down the long, straight road.

Within seconds their taxi was following her, turning left along the Boulevard, joining the freeway, driving past the store.

'Hope Kaylee'll be OK,' Zoe said.

'That kid's older and wiser and *tougher* than she looks.'

'She's had to be. Twenty-two is way too young to die. And to die like that…'

'Any age,' Tariq said, the corner of his mouth twitching, 'any age below eighty-something is way too young to die.'

'You still miss her a lot, don't you?'

'Yep. Miss her not being in this world with me. Miss her not knowing her daughter-in-law. Not knowing her flighty son found happiness when he found you.'

'Am I really worth finding?'

'Sure you're worth finding.' He stroked her cheek with the back of his hand. She had always loved the way he did that: the knuckle of his index finger curving down to gently brush her lower lip. Then, leaning forward, he said, 'Hey there, mate. Can you step on it a bit, please? We've got a flight to catch.'

'A flight home, is it?'

'Sure thing,' Tariq answered. 'A flight home.'

The Homecoming

Tuesday evenin' and we're eating chicken and mushroom pie with glazed carrots an' purple sprouting. The pastry's home-made! Mum says she's given up on fast fixes, shortcuts to a decent bit of shortcrust. Which means, these days, after working all week and shoppin' half of Saturday, she spends most of Sunday sloggin' away to fill the freezer fit to bust. Chilli con carne, vegetable lasagne, fish pie, cauliflower cheese – you name it, my mum's cooked it.

I brought my best mate Keesha home for tea last Thursday. Thought it'd be a bit of a treat for her. Keesh needed cheerin' up. But I could see it was tough for her: sitting at this table, all shiny waxcloth, sparkling glasses – paper napkins, even! Like something out of a fairy tale for Keesh.

We was having lemon chicken with chickpeas an rice.

'I thought peas were s'posed to be green!' Keesh says, spikin' a chickpea on her fork an givin it the once-over, before tucking in like she hadn't eaten for days, that sad look on her face. Got me thinking inviting Keesh back might've made matters worse; the contrast an all that. Seeing how civilised Mum and me are these days.

'Fancy some goosegog mousse, Za?' Mum says, goin over to the freezer to rifle through the loaded plastic bags and foil containers: it's chock-a-bloc in there. 'I know it's in here somewhere.'

'All right then,' I say. 'If you wanna get rid.'

Meanwhile half of her shortcrust is going soggy in the gravy.

'But, hey,' I say to her, 'you've not finished yet. What about those carrots? That purple sproutin? Brain food, you tell me.'

'You have it then, Za,' she says. 'You've more up there to nurture than I have.'

There she goes. Puttin herself down again.

I watch her toss a couple of her scrummy sunflower loaves to one side as she reaches to the back of the freezer, pick up a bit of her purple sproutin with me fingers, and think, *That woman's wasted on me.* Think, *That woman's wasted, period.*

Now that it's got a bit warmer she's thrown over her old fleeces, comfy trainer trousers and scruffy Uggs for a pair of capri pants and an old grandad vest top. Though her shoulder blades still poke out something rotten, that skinny bum of hers barely fills those pants, and I reckon those ankle bones are as knobbly as me grandad's.

'Jeez, Mum,' I said to her back then, 'aren't you raining on *my* parade? Shouldn't *I* be the screwed-up anorexic teenager in this house?'

'Finish this, will ya, Za?' she'd said, picking up a quarter of the apple she'd been nibbling at for the last ten minutes, lookin at it like *it* was about to bite her.

Still, we've come a little way since then. There's been a few ounces of progress.

Here we are! Mum's waving the turquoise Tupperware at me. 'It'll be ready in a jiff!' she says, sitting it on the radiator before sitting down herself. 'Have you heard how things are with Suze? Has Keesha said?'

Suze is Keesh's mum. Nice enough woman. But if my mum thinks *her* brain's not got much goin for it, God knows what she thinks of Suze's grey matter. Still, Suze is ever so kind. That's her trouble. It's weird, cos when I first met Keesh's mum (before I discovered what life was really like in that household), Suze struck me as being a bit of a doormat. Had *Welcome* written all over her, if y'know what I mean – and not in a good way.

'Much the same, I s'pose,' I tell Mum. 'Keesh's clammed up on me. She don't wanna talk about it.'

'Your mum not waiting at the gate today?' I says to Keesh.

She'd do that, would Suze: wait for Keesh by the school gates, on her way home from her job at B&Q. Like Keesh was some kid of six or seven, not thirteen goin' on twenty-one.

It was two weeks ago. We'd just finished our *Girls and Violence* class. A new thing on the curriculum. Just the girls, this time. The boys were havin a separate *Boys and Violence* session. Then we were all s'posed to get back together for the last two sessions. Bash it out, you might say. By then it's all s'posed to be peace 'n' love 'n' understandin' between us. Well, that's the theory.

Keesh an me was in the cloakroom. I'm babbling on about how much better it'd be for us girls if the boys *always* had separate classes, an the both of us are taking an age to get our shit together. I'm sortin me books in a spacey sorta way, and Keesh is just standing there like she don't wanna go home, when, ever so quietly, I hear her say, 'No, she's not, not today. Mum… Mum's…' And she sorta stops.

And because Keesh is being so slow, I'm like I am in double maths, i.e. *not* paying attention (which I should, cos I'm crap at maths), an I start banging on about this new band I copped on YouTube: Erasmus Takes a Jump, they're called. 'They are *piss-good*, Keesh,' I tell her, 'Ace! *Above* ace. They are out there in the stratosphere of megastardom. They are gonna be as big as The Beatles were! *Bigger!*'

But Keesh isn't listening. And when I turn round she's looking down at the floor and saying – not in an angry way, but in a sad, wistful sort of way, like life's a shithole we're thrown into and there's no escaping it until we fall into another shithole: one that's dark an empty an never-flippin-ending – 'Zara, please, *please* do stop banging on about some dipstick boys wanking off on their guitars.'

And I know this is serious because Keesh always calls me Za. So I don't get to tell her that Zac P, ETAJ's lead singer-songwriter, is the spit of Sebastian Crowley in the sixth form; who I *know* Keesh fancies too, it's just she's not admittin it.

'Sorry, Keesh,' I say. 'Your mum not so hot, then?'

And Keesh just looks at me. An I'm thinkin, *This is* not *good*; I'm thinkin the Big C or something. Yeah, I know there are drugs out there that can zap the crap outta those C-cells. But what if you're in the wrong postcode? What if they palm you off with sugar pills, cos the blitzing drugs are too expensive for *your* particular skint GP? What if the entire NHS is friggin bankrupt? Curtains, that's what.

'What's up with her?' I say. 'Nothing serious, I hope?' Thinking, it must be pretty serious for Keesh to look like this. Because, despite her sensitive nature, Keesh is no pushover.

'Depends what you call serious,' Keesh says, a hand going up to her cheek.

She's started wearin these stick-on nails; they've got swirly black targets on them. Vicious-looking things for Keesh. Demonic – but in a nice way. And I'm standing there, arms full of maths books, wondering what effing use maths is to me. Since, pretty soon, we'll all have some dinky bit of BlackBerry 'n' Apple technology tucked under our skin, a bit like me grandad's pacemaker, that'll calculate every friggin thing in the known universe. And I'm so in my own space that I don't take it in. It's like I wanna blank it.

'He bloody whacked her, again, didn't he?' Keesh is saying. 'Knocked her down this time.'

It's the 'again' and the 'this time' that bother me, an I dump me maths books on the bench and look up at Keesh, an Keesh is looking at me like *she's* ashamed, like it's her fault she's got a piece of shit for a dad.

'Mum's got this bruise,' Keesh's hand going up to her face, 'just here.' Her fingers running down her cheek, her other hand going up to clasp it, like she was having to protect her own face from her dad's blows. And all I can think is how lucky Mum and me are *not* having some man about the place spoiling things for us. Cos, most of all, that's what I remember: things being spoiled; meals goin cold because of their quarrelling, because he was late, or because there was a sad lump in my throat that wouldn't come up, wouldn't go down; weekends when the atmosphere in the house was spoiled so much I'd actually looked forward to Monday mornings. Not to mention that spoiled holiday. The one that was gonna make everything right again. The one that never happened. All spoiled by him. Several years of my life spoiled by him.

I missed him at first. But pretty soon I got to like how peaceful the house was without him. Except, at the beginning, when Mum would sob herself to sleep. I'd cover me ears with the pillow, pretend not to hear. Tell myself she'd get over it soon enough. And she sort of has.

And there's Keesh, standin' in front of me in the cloakroom, tears running down her cheeks.

'Oh, *Keesh*!' I say, wrapping my arms round her.

Thursday evening an it's cottage pie with green beans. Sorry – *shepherd's* pie, cos Mum always makes hers with minced *lamb*.

I'm upstairs doing me homework when Mum comes in. She said she'd be a bit late. Silly cow reckons she shouldn't leave me on my own *at all*. 'I'm gonna be *fourteen* in four months!' I remind her. 'Pull yourself together, woman. Grandad was workin at *fifteen*!'

'As an apprentice, Za,' she goes.

'Yeah,' I go. 'Workin!'

By the time I come down (only two minutes after I hear her come in), the table's laid, the pie's in the oven, the beans waitin to go on, and I can't see how *any* woman could compete with Mum in the home management stakes. How any man worth his salt – worth anything – would *want* another woman.

'Like the hair,' I say. 'So, what's it in aid of?'

She shrugs.

She's had a few more highlights put in, and it's all feathery round her face. A tad too fluffy for my tastes. A bit like that new weather girl on telly: the one who wears *really* naff jewellery. I preferred Mum's hair when it was all the same length, so she could pull it back in a ponytail. Practical. No nonsense. But I don't say that, do I? I just tell her she looks pretty. An she sort of blushes. Which is odd. And it gets me thinkin there's something here she's not telling me. Well, it had to happen sometime, didn't it? After all, it's been two and a half years. And she's not gettin any younger.

'Keesh wasn't at school today, Mum.'

'Oh yeah? Did she call in sick?'

'Miss Abdullah hadn't heard anything.'

And this feelin is risin in me guts, like it's reaching up to throttle me.

Twenty minutes later we're sat at the kitchen table, the both of us a bit out of it.

'Eat up, Za!' Mum goes. 'There's that bit of rhubarb crumble left from last night. Remember?'

But tonight my healthy appetite has forsaken me. And with a BMI of 21.8 I reckon I'd better watch it. Though Mum still expects me to scoff like I'm some sad waif straight outta Oliver; one havin to eat for two: me *and* her.

'It wouldn't *be* left over,' I tell her, 'if you'd managed to eat your share!' Feelin that lump in my throat again, that scared feelin, and I *know* something's up. Keesh and me are like the sisters we never had, y'see. Like that, but *more* like that, cos I don't hate *anything* about Keesh.

Mum sighs. 'Yeah,' she goes, 'you're right, Za. I'm gonna pull myself together, like you say.' And she picks up her fork and spikes a bean. 'Don't worry. I bet Keesha'll be there tomorrow.'

But I wouldn't put good money on it. An I don't tell Mum that I've rung Keesh's mobile twenty times since I got home, texted her four times, and called their landline five. *He* answered that last time. Bellowed, '*No one's fuckin' here!*' and slammed the phone down. Sounded mad as hell. And now I've got this picture in my mind of him comin in from the backyard to pick up the phone, a shovel in his hand. But then, they've only got paving slabs out there, that tatty old shed and his bloody bike. Which could be worse, come to think of it. Cos don't bodies often get buried under paving slabs? Perhaps I should've told Miss Abdullah what Keesh told me?

'Mum…? Think I'll speak to Miss Abdullah about Suze. What d'ya reckon?'

But Mum's not listening. She's gazing outta the window, lookin all dewy-eyed, while actually *eating* her shepherd's pie. And she's gotta be seeing more than that godawful fence our new neighbour's just put up (it's got prissy trellis arches all along the top, and they've gone an painted it *purple*! So, now we've got their messy drips running down our side), cos there's a weird smile creeping across her face.

'Mum?'

'Keesha'll be back soon, sweetheart,' she says in a dreamy, outta-this-world sorta way, staring out.

I've not seen much of Keesha's dad. He's the sort of man women don't see a lot of. Always workin. And if not, most likely, he's out front cleaning his bloody car. Or out back, tinkering with that old bike he bought, just so as he had something else to tinker with, some excuse for *not* being in the house doing somethin useful. He's no new man, tha's for sure. A right blast from the flippin past – and not in a nice way.

Keesh is amazin, considering she's the spawn-child of a doormat and a rod of iron with a brick for a brain.

'I'm gonna speak to Miss Abdullah tomorrer, for definite, Mum,' I say.

I shouldn't hide it, too, should I? That's what these *Girls and Violence* classes are s'posed to do: teach us to come out and face stuff. It's like the Big C used to be before *it* came out. Now it's just cancer. There's worse things. Like being hacked to bits with a machete, or pummelled to death by some sad twat who, twenty years before, got down on one knee and said, 'Suze, darlin, I love yer. Will you marry me?', looking up, wet-nosed, like some adoring puppy dog, like it was bloody true. Yeah, we women've *gotta* speak up.

'Think I'll do that, Mum. Tell Miss Abdullah. *Yeah?*'

'Hmm,' Mum mumbles, her mouth full of mash 'n' mince.

And since I don't wanna discourage her from eatin it, I say, 'Oh, nothing', scooping up another forkful of mash myself, thinkin, *Something tells me there's a bloody man at*

the root of that new hairdo. Make the most of the peace in this
house, girl, cos it ain't gonna last.

It's three weeks since Keesh went home to cottage pie and
peas for her tea. It *is* cottage pie in Keesh's house. Suze
mostly buys Aldo's economy range; loadsa ready meals:
lasagne, pizzas, stuff like that. Vegetables come in tins or
freezer bags at Number 29. If Keesh wasn't such a bright
spark she'd be the sort of kid who thinks chips grow on
trees and sweetcorn's something the Green Giant chucks
down from heaven when he's in a good mood. It's instant
everything over there – including anger.

Aldo's cottage pie's *allegedly* made with ground beef.
But I reckon there's more beef in those black 'n' white cows
grazing in the green field beside the pink thatched cottage
on the cardboard packaging than ever makes it into that
plastic container.

Last week, when I told Mum what Keesh'd told me,
Mum goes so far as to suggest, 'All that convenience food
might've had something to do with it. Well,' she goes, 'it
can't do much for a man's temper, can it?'

I don't believe what I'm hearing. '*M-um!*' I say. 'Jesus
flippin Christ! What *are* you saying? If Keesh's dad'd been
living in this house he would've been as sweet as one of your
apple and mince pies? If Suze'd had a few cooking lessons
from you, everything'd be hunky-dory?'

Looking a tad ashamed, Mum says she was saying no
such thing, but *everyone knows* kids concentrate better if
they eat better, so why shouldn't it hold true for a grown
man?

She might have a point. Since, seems t'me, 'grown man' is just one whopper of a euphemism for a pain-in-the-rectum boy.

She'd put it on the table, had Suze: the plate of cottage pie and peas she'd given a coupla minutes in the microwave. He'd just come in, Keesh said. She'd heard the front door slam. Keesh was standin at the sink, washing up, when he stuck his dirty hands under the tap. 'Hello, Dad,' Keesh probably said.

'Hello, luv,' he might've said, all sweet and gentle, like – like *my* dad used to do, before he became a bad-tempered pain in the arse. I can't say *exactly* what Keesh said, cos she still isn't pickin up or texting me. All I know is, her dad was sat down for a second or two – long enough to eat a forkful of the slimy gunk masquerading as food, then – *Wham! Bang! Crash! Wallop!* – he's up, the chair's over, the plate's smashed against the wall, and the mush of minced offal is sliding down it. All because it was '*bloody lukewarm!*'

And, do you know when Suze gets that crack across the cheek, like she's a bit of cheap market crockery, like she's no better than an Aldo's bottom-of-the-range cottage pie? When she apologises to the shit-arse, that's when. When she says, 'Sorry, darling, it won't happen again' (but probably without the 'darling') to that beefy, thick as shit brick-house with mad bull's brains, who'd got home forty-five minutes later than he said he would. *Too right you won't do it again*, he thinks. *Thwack!* And she's down. And Suze is halfway to the floor already. Half his size, for Christ's sake.

We mustn't be doormats, y'see. We gotta respect ourselves. Cos, let's face it, men ain't up t'doing it. They use the R-word like it's goin outta fashion, strutting about with their knives an' guns an' macho bling, like they flippin own the place, or hang about with their hoody mates, tubes of booze in their hands. But they are *the* biggest bunch of lowlifes on the planet. They've got more respect for a hunk of road-rage metal, that's *way* off the scale when it comes to green energy, than they have for us girls. Most of em look at us and think, *Totty. Slag. Easy lay.* I know. I've seen em do it. But they haven't done it to me. *No way!* And from now on I'm making sure *I* don't look like anything *they* might wanna look at.

Maybe even Sebastian Crowley's like that? Maybe all that girly hair, that tranny, AC/DC look, is just a thin disguise to hide the fact that he's a thick-as-shit aggressive twat. Think I'm done with men before I've even started. What's the use? They all turn bad in the end. Look at my dad.

Friday, when I get home, Mum's chopping up a load of meat, the kitchen stinks of garlic, and she's already opened a bottle of red.

'Burf… *Bore-gig-non*?' she goes.

'What?'

'Thought I'd give it a go. Did I say it right, Za?'

'How should I know? I do Spanish, dun' I?!'

'Oh yeah,' Mum goes, in a ditzy sort of way.

'So what about that fish pie?' I say. It's sitting on the worktop, where she put it to defrost this morning.

'We're having it! This is something special for tomorrow night.'

'What's so special about tomorrer night? Apart from the *Dancing on Ice* final.'

'*We* are having someone round for supper, that's what.'

'*Supper?!*' I say. '*Must* be special. Who is it? Prince flippin Charles?'

She smiles and shakes her head.

'So can I leave the prince to you, then, sneak upstairs an watch the final in peace?'

I don't ask about this fella. Don't warn her if she brings anyone home who looks *remotely* like Simon Cowell or Andrew Lloyd Webber I'm outta here. Fact is, I don't wanna know – not now everything's got so peaceful. Can't help thinkin what we'd be givin up. What *she'd* be givin up. Mum'll have to think about that before she chucks in the towel for a second round. What if he's another one who comes on all sweetness and light, wouldn't hurt a fly, then, before you know it, he's weighing into her with a knockout blow? I don't want it endin in tears again. I've had enough of all that.

'I'll get my homework out of the way before *supper* then, shall I?' I say.

She's too absorbed in chucking her chuck steak 'n' garlic into the pan to take much notice of me.

Pausing at the door, I say, 'Did you try Suze at work for me?'

'Oh yeah. She wasn't there. Called in sick, apparently.'

So, I'm thinkin, *how come Suze's not pickin up at home then?*

'Hello, Zara,' he goes.

Saturday night and the 'supper table' has been laid in the dining room. Which, since now it's not so much a dining room, more a den for Mum and me, means the both of us have spent half the day tidying it up.

When I come downstairs her *date's* standing in the kitchen, a bottle of wine in his hand.

Forced by Mum to 'make an effort', I've put on clean jeans and her favourite T-shirt. 'Do you *have* to scrape your hair back like that?' she says that afternoon, taking my clippers out and fluffing up me hair with her fingers. 'For tonight, Za?'

'What's the big deal about tonight?' I say. '*You're* the one wanting to sleep with this bloke. If I do any of that sex stuff,' I tell her, 'and it is a *big* if, it's most likely gonna be with a woman.'

'Oh, Za!' she groans, turning to faff over her chocolate puds. 'Do *not* put that one on me right now. *Heavens!* Is that the time?'

Her Prince Charming's got this poncey silk jacket on, and he's wearing a spivvy purple tie, with a pattern on it that makes me feel a bit trippy when I look at it. He looks like a friggin ITV newsreader.

Mum takes the bottle of wine from him. 'We'll be eating at 7.30,' she tells him, 'if that's all right with you?'

Why ask him? I think. *I'm the one used to eating at* six-thirty. *Don't I have a say in this?*

'So!' he goes, looking straight at me. 'How's things?'

What things *are we talkin about, exactly?* I wonder. Things *have settled down nicely, thanks.* Things *are almost OK.* Were *OK until you turned up to spoil them again.* But I don't say that, do I? I just say, '*Things* are fine, thank you very much. So, how's the girlfriend? Couldn't she join us tonight? Or is it *her* turn to two-time you?'

'Zara!' Mum goes. 'I thought you'd be *pleased.*' Her wide eyes staring at me, angry, but lookin kinda lovely, in a girly sorta way, that *really* doesn't suit her, with too much glosser on her too-pink lips and lashings of mascara; and she's still way too skinny for that scoop-necked top. But lookin sorta vulnerable. 'Your dad's here just as much for you as he is for me.' (She has *gotta* be kiddin me!) 'So don't go spoiling things, Za. Let's all just have a nice evening together, shall we?'

That's rich, I think. Cos, *if my memory serves me well, it was someone of the opposite gender, someone who's standing way too close to me at this minute, who did the spoilin around here. Someone who's magicked himself into Prince flippin Charming.*

'You're looking quite grown-up, Za,' Charm-Pants says, batting his dark eyelashes and giving me a sheepish look.

It reminds me, that look, that, although he *behaved* like a macho, selfish prat, he's always been a wimp at heart. Reminds me of one of those many times when he was late home. Reminds me of what he said: 'Sorry, luv,' his lying eyes looking down at his plate, eyelashes flick-flicking, 'missed the 5.52 by a whisker.'

Whisker my eye. Pussy most likely.

Reminds me of something Mum said not long after he walked out on us. 'Y'know, Za,' she said, 'most men don't know what it is they want, until they see it in another woman.' This little gem of wisdom coming back to me as he's looking at me, smilin, waiting for me to smile back. And I bite my lip and don't say what I wanna say, which is, *Wish I could say you'd grown up, Dad.*

'I think it's warm enough to have a few nibbles outside,' Mum goes. 'What d'ya reckon, you two?'

We two troop out to where I've already hauled out the chairs and table, and Mum has already put olives and nuts and those awful pretzel things that taste like cardboard out in little bowls, and we sit there like three weirdos in a Pinter play. But not the one we're doin in Eng Lit, cos there's just one woman in that one, and a loada sexist pigs; aka men.

'That fence,' the spoiler goes, long pause, starin out, 'isn't up to much, is it?'

Pause again. *Actually, Dad*, I'm thinkin, *it's up against four soddin concrete posts!* But since I'm s'posed to be *making an effort* I just shake my head and say nothing, and we three pause some more.

'Probably means this side'll have to be painted purple, too,' he says, already acting like he owns the place. Then I remember, he still does.

I thought having me outta the way for the night might appeal to that perverted side of Mum that still fancies a man who can pour a heap of shit over her, yet come back smellin of roses himself. But, at first, she won't have it.

'Come on, Mum. It's *gotta* be OK. It's eons since I've seen Keesh.'

'It's quite a way, Za.'

'It's not! It's twenty flippin minutes on the train!'

'But will it be *safe*?'

'Mum! It's a *refuge* for Chrissakes! The clue's in the name. It's full of nothin but women, *and* it's bang opposite a police station. So what's to be afraid of? Probably safer than spendin the night here with you an him.'

'*Not* funny, Za. Your dad may not be *the* most perfect man in the world, but he's not got an ounce of violence in him. That's what I loved about him… what I…' she goes all dewy-eyed again and I realise I'm fighting a losing battle here; I'm gonna have a dad again whether I want one or not, '…*still* love about him. He'll be sorry to have missed you. Shall I see if he can come round midweek sometime?'

'Whatever.'

Keesh and Suze have been in the refuge for five weeks now. It's all wrong. Her shitty dad still in the house an the two of them shacked up there.

Keesh sounded a bit choked when I told her my dad had showed up. I was just having a bit of a moan, like you do, pointing out what selfish twats men are. Should've thought before I opened me big mouth. But before I can say, *Sorry, Keesh, I'm being an arse*, Keesh is saying, 'I'm pleased for you, Za. He must really love your mum and you. Bet you'll be pleased, too, soon enough.'

That's Keesh for you. Holed up in a refuge, havin to start over at some crap school, a shit-arse for a dad, an yet she's still wanting the best for others, the best for me. I think I'll always love Keesh better than some dipstick man. Keesh is the best.

'What about *Wednesday* evening, Za?'

I'm in my room, battling with me maths homework, when Mum pops her head round the door.

'For what?' I say, not looking up.

'*Zara!* You *know* for what. For your dad to come round for tea, that's what.'

'Oh, so it's back to *tea* now, is it?' I say, smilin. And Mum stretches out an arm and pretends to whack me round the head. 'Can Keesh come for a sleepover one weekend soon? Like, the one after next?'

'Sure she can.'

I gotta find my own refuge now. The glory days of sisterhood in this house'll soon be a thing of the past. Mum may be wanting to plump up those old mammaries to please her man, but that ain't me, babe. I'm thinkin of getting one or two T-shirts printed for the NFF: my New Feminist Front. We're a non-violent backlash group, rising up against the bling-and-streetwalkers brigade, who, pretty soon, when science can produce babies *entirely* in test tubes, will *completely* bypass the whole sexist system. Bypass sex itself! I'm gonna put some of my ideas to Keesh when I see her tomorrer. One T'll say *I'M FLAT-CHESTED 'N' I'M PROUD*, an another, simply, *FUCK MEN!* Cos, let's face it, once the test-tube technology is up 'n' running, it'll be a slogan full of post-sex irony.

'Oh, Za,' Mum says, poppin her head around the door again, 'don't forget to give my love to Suze and Keesh tomorrow, will you?'

She's got some weird green mask smeared all over her face. It clashes somethin rotten with the purple towel wrapped round her head.

'Cos I won't,' I say, looking up, smiling.

And Mum forgets not to smile.

'You're crackin up,' I tell her, as green dust drifts down to settle on the carpet.

The Summer
of the Trueloves

P assed by the house yesterday. It's not far from where I live now. Could've driven there in ten minutes, walked it in half an hour – had I had the urge. Kept clear all this time. The four of us had started going there for one reason, one reason alone, and then stopped for the very same. Life had suddenly got a bit too serious. At least it had for me, the least of them.

I was the youngest of the famous five of '67: sweet sixteen that September. Too young and, even if I hadn't been, probably too stupid to join Roge and Billy in the sixth form. So I never got to see much of them after that some-like-it-hot summer. And without Number 49's back garden, we were as good as strangers again. Should I raise a tentative hand across the playground, Roge might respond by lifting a bulging file in the air, as if to say, *Look, mate, I'm too overburdened by the weight of this homework – not to mention the weight of what's gone before – to respond to your immature overtures.* Or Billy, the cheerful one – still not keeping pace with the times, still thinking he was hip – flicking a comb through his slicked-back hair as he brushed past me – might give me a quick, unsmiling thumbs-up, not stopping, walking on by. Walking on like he wanted to walk back a year and be sweet sixteen himself all over again, run through 1967 all over again – be a kid again.

As for the other two? Well, Jimmy and Rod had just completed a short course in growing up, hadn't they? Had been forced to tune into that, and drop out.

It was one of those summers. The sort that feels heavy with promise. Something was going to happen. And if it wasn't going to happen, then you were going to make it happen. You needed it to happen. Wanted the excitement of... well, you didn't know quite what, but, whatever it was, you knew it was coming, felt it in the muggy July heat. At least your body felt it. Your mind? Christ knows what that wanted. Because you sure as hell didn't.

Even Roge and Jimmy, the clever ones, were a little less clever that summer, geared up as they were to show off their 'manly' sun-soaked physiques, what intellect they had scrunched down, scrotum-sized, into their body-hugging bathing shorts, all high-minded thoughts now testosterone-fuelled and heading in one direction.

Forty-nine Craven Crescent, a mock-Tudor Edwardian semi, looks a tad better maintained than it was back then. Two tall terracotta pots ablaze with red geraniums have replaced those funereal concrete urns that had bugger all in them, aside from a few self-seeded weeds and the milkman's dog-ends; a neatly clipped evergreen fills the space the wild-and-woolly butterfly bush used to take up, lolling every which way into the street; and there's a fancy wrought-iron gate instead of the barely-hanging-together rotting bits of wood Rod's dad, not being much of a DIY man, never had the energy, or inclination, to fix up.

Never quite discovered where Rod's father's inclinations lay, our paths not crossing much in those few short weeks of the summer holidays. Though he seemed a decent enough sort of fella. You knew that much. Knew it when you looked at him. Then looked at her, and thought, *Christl! She could have done a helluva lot better than that.* Envying him his position, while, at the same time, a little voice deep inside you whispered, *But perhaps he* deserves *better.* Long-suffering, some might have said. One of the luckiest buggers alive, the four of us. Maybe, dare I say it, even the five of us?

For, in the conventional manner of the time (we're talking provinces here, not Swinging London), Ralph Truelove was married to a woman who, for some unfathomable reason, had agreed to become Mrs Truelove. And perhaps for Ralph it had been true love. Still was. Maybe it was for her too? Love moves, they say, in a mysterious way. But it didn't look much like it to me. Not that we saw the two of them together that much to judge. We'd scarper soon after he got home from work, and he, understandably, didn't plead with us to hang around. But in the rare moments we *did* see them together, I don't recall a single second of intimacy between husband and wife. Though, come to think of it, I don't recall seeing my own mum and dad being that lovey-dovey either.

But then Rod's mum was no ordinary mother. Rod's mum was a cut above. Rod's mum wasn't really a mum at all. Billy, Roge, Jimmy and me knew that much. As, I suppose, did Rod.

The four of us had been drawn to Number 49 like drone bees to the honey pot, knowing Mrs Truelove to be the queen, the one in control, the one having it her way. Even I, the stupid one, could see that.

It was late July; a few days before school broke up. We were skiving, as, of course, was Rod, but she didn't question why we were strewn about her back garden at 2.30 on a Thursday afternoon.

'Afternoon, Mrs Truelove!' Roge said, in that polite Roge way of his, jumping up when she appeared.

She'd been upstairs washing her hair. We'd heard the water running. Seen the shape of her through the frosted glass: her arms moving; what looked like a bare back bent over the washbasin.

A large turquoise towel, wrapped around her like a stole, covered her right shoulder and much of her torso, while managing to reveal her tanned left shoulder and upper arm; drops of water, trickling down from her thick, dark hair, sparkled on her skin.

'Come on now, boys!' she said. 'Call me Judy, for heaven's sake! After all, you're not exactly kids any more, are you?'

She was wearing the same white shorts she'd worn on sports day, four weeks before. And, for a moment, the way the towel hung about her, the way no shoulder straps, no halter neck was visible, we could imagine she might be wearing nothing *but* those white shorts.

Rod, giving his mother a scowling sideways glance, strode past her into the house. 'Kettle's boiling!' he shouted back at her. Ignoring him, saying nothing, she just stood there, enjoying the moment she'd set up, savouring us savouring her. That's how it worked, you see. And we were up for it to that extent.

'Not sure I could manage that, Mrs Truelove,' I said. 'Sounds a bit disrespectful to me.'

'Well,' Billy said, 'I guess if I can say it in a *respectful* way, I'll give it a go every once in a while.'

'Hey, fellas!' And, slipping the towel from her shoulders to reveal the purple boob tube beneath, she wrapped it, turban-like, about her head. 'I am no maharajah to be worshipped. I'm an *ordinary* woman. And come on now, it's 1967! I want equality, not *respectability*.'

'Right on, Judy!' Jimmy said, rising from the grass.

Removing the towel, she bent forward to rub her hair with it.

By now Jimmy had joined her on the patio. The towel in one hand, she ran the fingers of the other through her damp hair before turning to look up at him. And Jimmy, the tallest and gangliest of us, giving her one of his piercing blue-eyed stares – the sort I'd only ever seen him give to his girlfriend; his soon-to-be-*ex*-girlfriend – a hand grasping one end of the towel, said, 'Why don't I hang this up to dry for you, *Judy*?' She not letting go of the other end, but holding on to it for a second or three that seemed like forever, holding on to it and pulling on it, to pull Jimmy a little closer to her. And although the distance between them was a yard or more, when she looked up at him, her dark tousled hair every which way over her forehead, brushing her eyes, it was electric! And I wanted to be Jimmy more than anything in the world. To be as tall as Jimmy, to have the guts of

Jimmy, the intelligence of Jimmy, while, at the same time, hating Jimmy for being the one who was standing there.

Then, fixing him with such a look, she said, 'You, Jimmy, are just the sweetest boy', before letting go of the towel.

'*Fella* will suit me fine, Judy. Or, better still, why not just stick to Jimmy?'

'Will do… *Jimmy*!' Holding his stare, before, turning on her bare heels, she walked back inside.

'Roderick!' we heard her shout, all sex washed from her voice. 'Where the hell's that damn tea? There's a packet of ginger nuts in the tin, if you want them', as we three turned to look back at Jimmy, nose pressed to the towel he'd just pegged out on the line. Triumphant. Lost.

'What's she like, his mother?' my mother asked me.

It was the morning after my first visit to Number 49: December '66. I'd gone there mainly because Rod, having come to my house so often, felt obliged to invite me back.

My mother rather liked Rod. Rod was, on the face of it, the innocuous, trustworthy sort of boy a motherly woman like my mother would go for. There was something in Roderick Truelove that made the maternal types want to brood over him, in a way his own mother probably never had.

'Wears a bit too much slap,' I said.

On first seeing Judy Truelove, in the kitchen of Number 49, I hadn't thought much of her – except, perhaps, that she looked oddly out of place in a kitchen. But an hour later, dressed up, ready to go out, and smelling like heaven, watching her drift across the sitting room, a couple of mugs of instant, a chunk of bland cheese and a packet of TUC biscuits on a tray... well, it was quite a different matter. From then on I couldn't stop thinking about her.

She was wearing a red V-neck sweater tucked into a slim-fitting tartan skirt, a shiny black patent belt pulled tight round her waist. Her short black hair – thick and wavy, brushed back from her high forehead – curved down to hug the back of a rather attractive neck. It mesmerised me, that neck of hers. Rod must have seen my eyes cast in that direction because, addressing his mother in what I later realised was an unusually bossy tone, he said, 'Thanks, Mum. Go on now! Get off and enjoy yourself!' And suddenly she was gone, leaving me to wonder if Elizabeth Taylor was the most beautiful woman in the world, since Rod's mother had the looks of Liz, with the added benefit of a body that was both curvaceous in all the right places and slim in all the right places. What the hell must Mrs Truelove be?

'Lips the colour of a bloody postbox!' I told my mother.

'Without the bloodiness, I hope,' my mother replied.

'And kinda old-fashioned. Looks like she stepped straight outta the 1950s.'

'Is that right? *That* old-fashioned?'

I looked up at my mother's Plain Jane face, at her straight-as-a-die mousy hair, at her small, thin-lipped mouth that might see a smear of lipstick come her birthday or a rare night out, and felt my heart leap at the very thought of Rod's sexy mother, envying my schoolmate, while pitying the position having a mother like Judy Truelove put him in.

'Did she give you a nice tea?' my mother asked, flipping the bacon rashers over.

'It was OK,' I answered, watching the egg slipping from shell to saucer, 'though I'd say she's not much of a cook. Not a patch on you, Ma.'

'One egg, was it?'

'Two, please. I'm bloody starving.'

'Starving'll do fine, thank you very much.'

Sliding the egg into the pan and reaching for another, my mother said, 'No wonder that poor lad looks so pale. You'll have to invite him round here more often.'

I said I would, while knowing I no longer wanted Rod to come to my house; I wanted to go to Rod's house any chance I got. I would live on TUC biscuits, mousetrap cheese and substandard coffee for weeks on end, for months, if needs be, if only I could feast my eyes on Judy Truelove, could dream all the impossible dreams imaginable. But, as things turned out, over the next few months my mother got her way. However many hints I dropped, Rod refused to pick up on them. And since my house was en route to his, Rod would often suggest we do our homework together at mine – an offer I wasn't in a position to refuse. And even if Rod didn't suggest it, my mother, keen to feed him up, would be on the lookout. 'Stay for tea, Roderick?' she might suggest, suddenly appearing at an upstairs window, or popping up from behind a shrub, shears in hand.

Rod knew what he was doing.

Having seen me as an innocuous, sexless type, just like him, he'd copped me looking at his mother and thought better of it. Not that I ever said anything to him, of course. Well, it's not the sort of thing you confide in a classmate about, is it? And, anyway, at that age, it's all overblown thoughts. You fantasise day in, day out. Spend half your life in cloud cuckoo land. As for Rod? Whatever he thought of the woman who was, so improbably, his mother, he had no intention of discussing his thoughts with me – with any of the four of us. Judy Truelove was out of bounds for discussion. Out of bounds full stop. And as a consequence, I managed only three brief visits to Number 49 before that momentous sports day.

I'd come late to Ravenswood Boys' School. Austin, the car company my dad worked for, had recently opened a depot nearby. My father was told, if he wanted promotion, he'd have to move there. So we upped sticks. Dad gets himself a good managerial position, and I get to lose the two good friends I had. Get them replaced by Rod Truelove. Fair exchange? I don't think so.

'Roderick Truelove will show you the ropes,' Mr Davidson, my new form teacher, informed me. 'Won't you, Roderick?'

'Certainly, sir!' Roderick Truelove said, standing to attention.

'OK then,' Mr Davidson said, standing to attention himself, shiny black shoes aligned below crisp turn-ups, 'I will leave you in Roderick's capable hands. Mmm… Do I smell cottage pie? Well, bon appétit, you two!'

One no-hoper linked to another, I reckon was how Mr Davidson saw it. Or, more charitably maybe, one lost boy helping another.

Like me, Rod had changed schools mid-term – changed counties in his case – to start over at Ravenswood Boys' a term before me.

'Your dad's work, too, was it?' I asked him.

'Something like that,' he answered, characteristically giving nothing away.

This could be hard going, I thought.

And so it turned out. No wonder Rod Truelove hadn't struck up any meaningful friendships. I myself was not overly impressed by this dubious new 'friend' Mr Davidson had lumbered me with, wishing I'd been left to strike up my own friendships, rather than be tied to this sallow, uninspiring youth, with his weak chin and faraway, vacant look. Not that Rod was stupid. Far from it. He could have given Roge a run for his money, had he wanted to. He just never seemed to want anything very much. There appeared in Rod Truelove no desire to affect anyone in any way. No wish to impress or to shock, nor even to move those close to him; or should that be those near to him, since I'm not sure Rod Truelove was close to anyone in particular? Not even his mother, in spite of what happened. And although he'd taken up the baton of responsibility Mr Davidson had given him with some enthusiasm, I could not, in all honesty, have described Rod Truelove as my friend.

But he and I rubbed along through that Easter term and into the summer one. We had some weird need of each other.

Then, late that June, came sports day. Came Mrs Truelove. And soon after that came Roge and Billy, and then Jimmy, latching on to me so they might latch on to Rod, one or other or all of them trailing us home from school, ragging Rod about the 'great garden' they'd heard all about from me.

Ragging with a twinkle. As a bit of a wind-up. Tongue in cheek. But seriously muscling in all the same.

And perhaps some of it was about that garden? Was about the way it felt to be in a house like that, compared to the ordered, predictable households we were used to – at least the households Billy, Roge and me were used to. We three with the OK lives. With dads who worked five, six days a week; who cut their lawns once a week; who washed their cars every other weekend, and, in Roge's case, even went to church every Sunday. We lucky sods with mums who cooked breakfast for us on schooldays – and who, every once in a while, even had Sunday breakfast cooked for us by our dads. We spoilt ones with full-time mothers, or mothers who just worked part-time (as well as working flat out to keep the dishes we ate off Fairy-sparkling, the school shirts we wore Persil-white), who found the disorganised chaos of the Truelove household quite exciting.

Jimmy, on the other hand, was a different kettle of fish. The brightest of the bunch by a long chalk, I reckon he'd grown tired of being the responsible one; the only one with a brain in his household. The one having to use it for the whole damn family: for his worn-out mum, his no-hoper dad, his two dopey brothers and three off-the-wall sisters. No wonder Jimmy wanted to stay away from that overcrowded house. No wonder he liked lazing about at Number 49. That back garden was a blessed escape for Jimmy.

Within a couple of weeks the alpha team had worn Rod down, and they and me – on the other end of the manhood spectrum – were allowed to enter the Garden of Eden, as

Jimmy had dubbed it. All of us revelling in the fact that the disorderly house we walked through to reach it seldom smelled of cold cabbage, *never* of warm, freshly baked cake, but almost always of Judy Truelove's perfume: a scent that took us far beyond the juvenile pleasures of a humungous slab of Dundee; one that sent us on a trail the wiliest of foxes might think twice about taking.

We liked the way the back garden at Number 49 was as untamed as the woman who sunbathed in its semi-wildness. We gloried in the fact that Judy Truelove cared not one jot about pruning roses, deadheading petunias, or cutting dahlias for some church display. And we rather admired Ralph Truelove's similar disinterest in horticulture: the fact that he mowed the lawn (more meadow than bowling green) only when absolutely necessary, leaving a patch just large enough for all of us to sprawl on. Or, once or twice towards the end (when Jimmy, with Judy Truelove's consent, took over the mowing task), where Mrs Truelove herself might erect her sunlounger or spread her soft yellow blanket on the sweet-smelling, newly cut grass, we 'drones' buzzing about her, before settling down to listen to her radio, pretending to read. Rod, on these occasions, would often distance himself from his mother, returning to the patio she'd just vacated to feign interest in his book, while scowling back at us from behind his sunglasses.

A couple of old tyres, strung up by the previous inhabitants, still hung from an old mulberry tree at the far end of the garden, neither Ralph, Rod nor Judy bothering to take them down. I doubt that Rod ever swung in them, or would have, had he lived there from the outset. I found it hard to imagine Rod as a rough-and-tumble boy at any age. And his mother was not the type to pull out a photograph album and gaze adoringly at her rumbustious toddler, her graze-kneed, tree-climbing little boy. On the contrary, Rod appeared only of passing interest to his mother. We – or, more accurately, Roge, Billy and the unforgettable Jimmy – were her main attractions.

I'd sometimes look up at those battered old tyres, and imagine her golden legs swinging back and forth above my head, picture her rounded bare buttocks perched on that worn-out rubber.

An out-of-control hedge had reached unneighbourly heights on Number 47's side: a Russian vine careering through much of it, an old red rambler battling it out for survival. While, on the western side, since Number 49 bordered on Church Road, beyond an ancient apple tree, a tall beech hedge kept nosy passers-by below seven foot from peeking in, as the tower of Saint Michael and Mary the Immaculate looked down on us.

I can see her now, that sports day, standing there as bold as brass in those white shorts, showing *way* too much of her smooth, tanned thighs. See that red top, looking halfway decent at the front – revers, white buttons running down; the sexiest waistcoat in the world – then dipping at the back to be barely more than a band of cotton the colour of her lipstick, the expanse of her brown back above, a strip below looking even more golden above the waistband of those white shorts. Heaven!

'I'm afraid, Mr Davidson,' she said, one golden arm hooked around Rod's shoulder, 'we are *not* the sportiest of families.' The pinkness of her son's embarrassment clashing violently with her top, as Rod attempted to escape his mother's embrace. Then, turning to him, 'Couldn't you manage the long jump, sweetie? You used to be all right at that, at least.'

Billy, who'd just come second in the sprint, was the first to see her, the first to find some reason to, nonchalantly, skulk over to us. Then came Roge, because Billy had. And finally Jimmy, who, looking back, had looked at her differently right from the start.

What exactly happened that day? I'll never know. Though I've a pretty good idea.

It all went on in the long grass beneath the mulberry tree.

Billy and Roge were away on holiday at the time. Billy and Roge were the sort who had regular holidays: a week, sometimes two, with their folks. Billy and Roge were the sort who, even at their age, *liked* going on holiday with their folks.

Anyway, by then, the game was up. It only worked if we could all play it at the same level. Not that we'd ever *been* on the same level. There was a caste system. I knew that. Knew I'd always been the untouchable one. And, by then, Billy had got himself a girl he was sweet on, and Roge, bored after a few weeks of hedonism, was getting more and more serious, not wanting to waste his life 'being a layabout'.

And so, those last eleven days – the beginning of the end – it was just Rod and Jimmy and me.

Rod and me had been down town that morning. Had hung about the Plaza. Had mostly hung about Rocky's

Records, in vinyl heaven, listening to a load of stuff we couldn't afford to buy.

But by lunchtime the sun was seeing off the grey clouds and I fancied a layabout afternoon on the grass before Rod's dad got home. Fancied seeing Judy Truelove's body lying out there. Fancied doing a bit of reading, too. I'd got into *The Catcher in the Rye* and, Judy Truelove notwithstanding, was looking forward to being consumed by something powerful enough to block out my fantasies.

I'd stopped for a piss in the downstairs loo. Rod had walked through to the garden. Stopped there longer than needs be for a quick leak.

I'm unzipping my fly when I see this women's mag on the floor; read, in shocking pink letters on the cover, *The Female Orgasm Exposed!* Think, *Well, best bone up on this.*

I'd flushed, and was zipping up when I heard it: a strange noise. A yell? A moan? God knows. The cistern was making such a din, I couldn't tell. Nor could I tell where the noise had come from. The TV? But what would be on at that time of day? It wasn't the sort of sound you'd hear on *Trumpton.* The radio, maybe? Or those invisible neighbours behind the hedge?

When I walked out onto the patio she was standing there, her big eyes staring, bigger and wilder than ever.

She was wearing the same sexy top she'd worn on sports day. Or half-wearing it: the white buttons were all undone, one of her breasts totally exposed, the other half-peeking out. I could see both of her dark nipples. A trickle of red, bright as ketchup, running down between her beautiful breasts, was smeared over those white sports day shorts.

The unzipped shorts were slipping slowly from her hips. She wore no pants. I glimpsed the dark glory of her pubic hair. Her eyes had this crazed look in them, and although as yet she'd made no sound, tears were beginning to stream down her cheeks. Then suddenly she was in my arms, her dark hair pressed against my cheek. Only then, looking over her bare, sweet-smelling shoulder, did I see Rod emerging from the long grass, pale as death, a blood-stained knife in his hand.

I forced her to sit down on the sunlounger, where, curling up like a baby, she began to cry like one, and ran across the grass to Rod. He'd dropped the knife by now.

Following the trail of downtrodden grass I found Jimmy stretched out on Judy Truelove's yellow blanket, hands gripping his abdomen, blood seeping through his fingers. 'Jesus, Rod!' I cried. 'What the *hell* are you doing? *Call a bloody ambulance! Jesus!* It's OK, Jimmy,' looking down at poor frightened Jimmy, 'it'll be OK.'

But when I turned round Rod was still standing there, still staring down the garden at his mother, indecently crumpled on the lounger.

I pushed past him, hurrying back into the house.

When I came out he was crouching beside her. He'd wiped the blood from her breasts with his shirt and done up her clothes.

'For fuck's sake, man! *She's* OK! What about poor Jimmy?'

Rod gazed blankly back at me like he didn't quite know what I was talking about. And maybe, by then, he didn't? Maybe that was the truth of it? Maybe both of them acted instinctively, both in their weird and wonderful ways not knowing quite what they were doing, both not caring a jot about anyone but themselves.

Jimmy was charged under the Sexual Offences Act of 1956: indecent assault on a woman. Got three years. Borstal. Way out at Winterfields. Siberia, some people called it.

How it all panned out I'll never know. Though I've a pretty good idea.

Anyway, the three of them went off in the ambulance. Questions were asked. Lies were told. But at least, I thought, she cared enough for Jimmy not to go as far as to say he'd raped her. Cared enough not to allow Rod to incriminate Jimmy any further. Which, remembering Rod's pale face livid with rage, I suspect he would've done.

The most innocuous boy in the school swore he'd come upon Jimmy forcing himself on his mother. Swore he'd heard his mother's screams from the kitchen. Swore he'd grabbed the knife for self-defence before running out there. Well, that was his story.

A detective came by for mine the next day. But since I hadn't actually seen what went on, what could I say? I told him what I *had* seen. Just that. Nothing more. And, in that way, I let them do it, didn't I? I let them ruin Jimmy's life.

The *For Sale* sign went up five months later. Five months after that they were gone. Rod had already dropped out of school, of course. Hadn't returned that autumn. What with Jimmy's court case coming up, he wouldn't have been *the* most popular boy in the school. Whether he started over, mid-term, in some other boys' school in some other county, I couldn't say. Perhaps it was a regular occurrence? With grown men before. With growing boys now that the boys were big enough. Were up for it, so to speak. Though I hope the games she'd played hadn't been quite as bloody, quite as cruel, as this one turned out to be.

A week ago, it was: last Friday evening. The phone goes. I pick it up. Hear this smooth-sounding guy on the other end of the line saying my name in a questioning tone. Well-spoken, sensitive sort of voice, so I don't immediately hang up, because this fella's obviously too mature, too intelligent to end up working in a call centre. Too right he is. The fella turns out to be Roge.

Roge'd come back this way to tie up the sale of his mum's house. We arrange to meet next morning in the swankiest coffee shop in the Plaza. One I'd not set foot in before. Roge's choice. I would've suggested Starbucks.

It's like a blind date: Roge telling me what he'll be wearing – grey jacket, black collarless shirt, black jeans – before reminding me his hair is no longer black. Me giving him my description. Roge comes out on top, wouldn't you know.

We sit in soft leather armchairs on either side of a smoked-glass coffee table, sipping coffee from cups way too small for my taste. Roge is looking as smooth and relaxed as you please; while, thanks to the low-slung leather armchair, I feel paunchy and awkward in comparison, and wonder if I've a moustache of froth on my upper lip Roge's not telling me about.

He's big in the dreaming spires of academe, is Roge: Oxford.

I take even smaller sips of coffee I can barely taste, trying to make it last, and think, *Same school, same chances then; different worlds now.* Different bloody brains, that's why. Roge's grey matter was always as sharp as the cut of that grey jacket of his.

Turns out Roge recently crossed paths with Rod – well, *almost* crossed paths. I reckon Roge got in touch with me for that reason alone. It was more about him having seen the Trueloves, about him wondering if *I'd* seen the Trueloves, than it was about him wanting to see me. I mean, he must have been back this way, visiting his mum, loads of times before now, before he finished converting part of his Georgian pad into a granny flat for her. Oxfordshire, of course. A couple of acres attached, apparently. Typical good-guy Roge stuff, though: doing right by his mum. She'd spent the last six months in the Parkside Care Home, and he wasn't having her staying there.

It was there Roge saw him. Saw a tall, sallow-faced man progressing across the lawn, a bent-backed, white-haired woman gripping his arm.

'And I somehow knew,' Roge said. 'I don't know why.'

Her hair, he said, was pure white, that golden-brown skin now almost as white as her hair. Bleached out. Like she'd not seen the sun for decades. Whereas Rod's floppy mouse-brown hair was bottle-black. 'As if,' Roge said, 'he wanted to look like she used to look'; adding, 'not that there was ever much hope of that.'

The two of them, he said, gave off a strange aura.

'Well,' I said, 'they were a strange pair, let's face it.'

My memories aroused, I wanted to know more. Had the Trueloves divorced? Had Rod married? Divorced? Or had he spent his entire life with his mother?

'Sorry,' Roge said, 'can't help you on that. You see, I chickened out. Didn't actually speak to them. Something in me said, *Uh-uh. Walk on by. Don't go back there.*'

That's the rational bit of Roge, you see. The bit that wasn't quite as bright as Jimmy, but, in the end, the bit that made him the brightest of the bunch.

'Wondered, since they were so close to home, if *you* might have been in touch?' Roge asked, leaning forward to take another sip of his coffee, adding, 'Or, come to that, heard from Jimmy or Billy, over the years?'

'Nope! Not a thing,' I said. 'You?'

Smiling, a ring of confidence encircling him like a halo, Roge said, 'Billy, that's all. Way back. A postcard from San Francisco. The early '70s.'

'Went for the drugs, did he?'

'More likely for the free love.'

'But,' I said, 'there's always a price to pay for that, eh?'

'Got a Christmas card from him for a few years. All I can tell you is that in the late '70s he was working somewhere in Silicon Valley. Whether drug-free or woman-free, I couldn't tell you.'

But I couldn't care less about Billy. He could be up to his eyes in all the chemical ways to get out of his head he could lay his hands on, could've laid as many Hollywood starlets as any man could handle, for all I cared. Looking over to the still-chiselled chin of my old school 'chum', a year older than me back then, yet looking ten years younger than me now, I said, 'And Judy Truelove? Did she... did Judy look...' – I didn't want to say it, didn't want to think of her in that way – 'did she look OK, do you reckon? Mentally OK, I mean?'

'Think so. Yup! Those big dark eyes were smaller, duller, as you might expect, but bright enough, I'd say. The two of them were chatting away together. Looked very chummy, in fact. Looked a damn sight happier in each other's company than they ever did back then.'

'God, she was beautiful, wasn't she? Like some Hollywood film star.'

'She was *dangerous* like some Hollywood film star,' Roge said, 'I know that much. She was a summer diversion that got out of hand.'

'A diversion for you, maybe, Roge, but not for Jimmy. Jimmy fell for her, hook, line and sinker. Jimmy really loved her.'

'You think so?' Roge said, looking up from his empty cup, while I wondered if it would be unsophisticated to order a second cappuccino. Then, seeing the look in my eyes, he said, 'Who knows? Maybe you're right? Maybe he was in love with her at the time?'

I'd always hoped Jimmy had loved her. It made it less painful, somehow. I mean, to have your life ruined just for lust, for sex alone...

I dropped by Number 49 a couple of times that autumn term, my speech on how much I missed my old school 'friend' well rehearsed. The first time, she answered the door. 'Rod's out!' she said coldly, not even acknowledging who I was. 'I'll tell him you called.'

I'm the boy whose shoulder you cried on, I wanted to say.

The scent of your skin is in my nostrils, even now. But by then she'd gone, leaving me standing on the doorstep. I mean, she'd never turned on the charm for me, had she?

The second time Rod came to the door. My toe on the threshold, I smiled, thinking he might at least ask me in, when the smell of her perfume and the swish of her skirt made me look up. And there she was, coming downstairs, a towel wrapped around her lovely head.

'Roderick and I have things to do together this afternoon, I'm afraid,' she told me in a clipped, unfriendly tone, by now in the hall, her well-manicured hands gripping her son's bony shoulders.

Rod, saying nothing, smiled back at me, a strange, triumphant, self-satisfied smile, before 'Goodbye then!' he said, shutting the door in my face.

A dismissive wave of her hand, her red-lacquered fingernails glinting in the sunlight, my last sight of her.

By this time, Roge has filled me in on the up-and-coming careers of his two beautiful kids, a boy and a girl; has whipped out a photo of his beautiful wife: dark hair, big eyes, Audrey Hepburn's slightly less attractive older sister. 'Always carry one of her!' he tells me. 'Have from the outset. It's a habit I'm afraid to break.'

While I confess to having no such photo to show him, and, since my children's achievements do not compare, say very little about them.

'Well,' Roge tosses a healthy tip into the saucer, 'I'd better make a move!' His well-manicured thumb and forefinger pull a card from his slim black wallet. 'If you're ever up our way?' he says, handing it to me.

The tips of his polished nails are as white as the card I slip into my breast pocket.

'Sure thing,' I say. 'Let's keep in touch!'

And we rise from our squeaky leather armchairs, confident we will never see each other again.

As for me? I went steady with the first girl I fancied. The first who appeared to fancy me back. The first who gave me a second look.

I met Kathleen in the September of 1969. She had regular, plainish features and straight, mousy-brown hair, a bit like my mother's. Was a bit shy. A little afraid to look me straight in the eye on our first few dates, blushed at any vaguely intimate thing I said to her for the first six months, and jumped at the chance to marry me six months later. We were engaged for two years, and married when I was twenty-one. We rented a small flat for three years, then bought a two-up two-down two streets from my folks' place.

We've had three kids since then, have two grandchildren now, and we've moved one more time. Wanted a bigger garden, you see: for our kids back then, and for the grandchildren now.

I clean the car every other Sunday. Mow the lawn most weekends, in mowing season – which, these days, seems to be nearly all the year round. I keep the edges clipped, the hedges trimmed. I don't like it too wild. Like to keep things in reasonable shape. Keep things neat and tidy – as does Kath. We're compatible in that way. And as long as I don't take life too seriously, as long as I don't analyse it to death, all things considered, I've no regrets – not really. You make what you can of life, don't you. What you're capable of making. We jog along, Kath and I. Passion? Lust? It's for the young. You grow out of it, I suppose. It becomes a distant memory. Something beyond your grasp.

Let Her Go

Your head is just breaking the water when I hear that tedious new ringtone of yours – mercifully muffled by your beach towel. 'Do you have to bring your phone to the beach?' I'd moaned earlier. 'We are *supposed* to be on holiday.'

'You know what it's like,' you'd said; 'someone might need a quick comment, a quotable line. I can never be *totally* out of touch.'

What liars we are.

I let that awful, tinkly, tinny tune go through several more ring cycles – less painful, less drawn out than Wagner at least – watch your sea-slicked seal head rise up, watch you turn to look back to the vast expanse of ocean, unwilling to leave this element that is so much your own. Torso fully exposed now, you wade a few steps, stop once more, turn once more, hands on hips, back to me, looking back. Reluctant to face the deserted beach, no doubt. Your 'flipper' feet unwilling to make contact with the desiccated land, unwilling to rejoin the landlubber lying here waiting for you. Although, looking back myself, haven't *I* always been the fish out of water?

The caller persistent, I decide to do the unthinkable. Rules, they say, are made to be broken. Though you and I have always prided ourselves on our mindfulness of rules, the concern we have for each other, the boundaries we respect. We have, you could say, made it a rule: a stick with which to measure our (so-called) easy-going, independent spirits; one we need not beat ourselves up with, since we *do* stick to the rules. No wishy-washy one-for-all-all-for-one sentimentality for us. Oh no. We respect each other's privacy, each other's bank accounts, each other's digital interactions. We two of the original me/myself/I generation honour each other's individuality. *We are good at holding on while letting go.* It was you who coined that arsehole oxymoron of a phrase. Except, I seem to remember, you said, '*You* are good at holding on while letting go.' It was back in the days when I was fool enough to take this as some kind of compliment.

I am unmuffling your smothered phone from its multicoloured cocoon when it comes to me: who would bother to call, rather than text you? No one calls you now – except me. And you and I both know *I* don't count. All manner of correspondence done, arrangements made with all and sundry, without a single word said by you, heard by me. Who, I ask myself, would be this persistent? Who would feel a need for such urgency? And suddenly, in spite of having no warning signs, no reason to expect it, I know who is making the call, know why she is making it.

Meanwhile you are, quite literally, dragging your feet across the sand. Dry land already tiring, already tiresome to you. So much effort a body must make just to stay afloat on boring old dry land.

'Yes, Izzy,' Louise is saying, 'she's gone. Too late to do anything. Can I speak to him? Is he there?'

'He's here now,' I say. 'Louise!' I tell you, as droplets of seawater drip from your hair to dot my oily thighs. Lingering there, they remind me of those little golden domes of plastic that keep dropping off the insides of our kitchen-unit doors. And I notice several extraneous pubic hairs have escaped my home waxing treatment. Notice pink pinprick spots left *by* my home waxing treatment. While you demand details from Louise: time, place, time before the ambulance arrived; ask what more might have been done, say what should have been done, who could, *should* be blamed, sued, shouted at. You appear to almost blame Louise for not being there earlier; she who is there every Saturday afternoon. You exercise your phenomenal powers of outrage, while showing not one smidgen of sorrow.

He's in shock, I tell myself.

'Bye then, sweetheart,' you say. 'Chin up!'

And, dropping the phone, you reach for the towel and energetically rub your hair with it. Before, sitting down, garish towel around your neck, you stare out to sea, where, I imagine, you would rather be.

I stare at your profile: the one to which some of that rugged youthfulness still clings. Has, according to you, recently returned. And, though loath to admit it, I have to admit it: you *do* look younger. 'You see!' you've said. 'You were right, love. It *is* never too late. Fifty doesn't have to mean you're over the hill. A bit of abstinence can really have an effect. I should have listened to you years ago.' Why didn't you, then? Why wait? Why wait until now? As if I didn't know.

I suppose at this point a wife should hug her husband, should comfort him in his distress. But then at this point a husband should *look* distressed. Should even manage to say to his best beloved, *Are you OK, love? Bit of a shock, eh?*

'I should've had a few more words with poor Louise,' I say to fill the silence. 'Back there. Coping on her own.'

'Oh, you know my sister. She's a coper par excellence. Always has been. Nothing much fazes Louise.'

Not even death? I think. Surely death has a way of fazing us all. Is that not its main purpose in life: to scare us into living, after the grief has passed?

'We'd better get back to the hotel!' I say, standing up.

You remain lying there. Lying quite still, as still as death, your eyes looking up at me. You look, dare I say it, somewhat bemused. *Pack up?* your expression seems to say. *Why? We've only one day left.*

'The funeral won't be for ten days or more,' you say, unmoved, not moving.

'But seeing her?' I say. 'And Louise? The preparations? We can't carry on as if nothing has happened.'

'One day,' you say. '*One day*. Don't worry, I'll do my bit when I get back.'

And you proceed to stretch out your newly slimmed-down torso, flex your freshly toned arms, hook your well-manicured hands, with their beautifully buffed fingernails, beneath your head, and, sunglasses in place, stare up at the blue sky for all the world as if you are on holiday.

How will this pan out? I ask myself. Now that the woman you loved the most, hated the most, is no more, who will be next in line for your troubled heart?

'My mother hates me!'

You said this. You told me this. Told me this within two hours of our first meeting.

We were in The Roma. It was late. Very late. Back then Carlo lived above the shop. Kept open until the last punter left, whatever the time. Carlo was never in a hurry to boot his customers out. And that evening, young and believing ourselves to be falling in love, we two were in no hurry to go anywhere.

'Surely not,' I responded. 'It's counterintuitive. Almost all mothers adore their children. Almost all mothers mollycoddle their sons.'

'Almost all,' you said, 'but not mine. Mine mollycoddles my sister. Hates me. You'll see!'

Overcome by the prospect of a future with someone who wished to see his future with *me*, overwhelmed by the fact that for the first time in my life I was with a man whose intentions, even at this early stage in the game of love, appeared to be entirely honourable, this all-embracing pleasure managed to override my initial desire to expose the soft underbelly of your hard words.

We had sex in the small hours in my bijou garret bedsit in that Dickensian yard just off Goodge Street. It's a brutalist hulk of concrete now: a car park. 'Very *La Bohème*,' you said as I drew back the curtain to expose my kitchenette. 'Where's the bog?'

'Next landing,' I told you. You were not impressed. This was really roughing it for you.

I have never been able to clearly recall the sex we had that night. I don't believe either one of us was, as they say, blown away. And yet I do remember feeling... comfortable. Yes! Comfortable. That was it. Feeling comfortably at ease with you, and with myself. Which was new to me – in that position, at least. Insecure as I was in respect to my face, my body, my entire persona, previous sexual encounters, though more memorable in terms of the quality of the sex, had, for me, been obstacle courses of embarrassment. Courses where I had felt myself a failure: a spotlighted, stage-struck performer, fearful her make-up might melt in the glaring heat of her fiery desire. Felt, orgasm or no orgasm, on the outside looking in.

Until then, I'd got into the habit of draping gauzy scarves over lampshades in order to attain that flattering rosy glow, while fearing the cool, clear light of day come the morning. But with you, joy of joys, none of this applied. You may remember – though I suspect you were asleep by then – that after the long-forgotten act, I went upstairs to my, quote, 'scuzzy bathroom', where I cleansed my face of blusher and mascara and brushed my teeth, for all the world as if the bed below me was empty (as it had been every night of that year and much of the year before), a voice inside my head saying, *There is a freedom in this; there is commitment* and *freedom*. And, returning to you, I lay my greasy, freshly moisturised cheek against your warm back. You, oblivious of my absence, my presence.

It worries me now. Has worried me since. How little we needed to impress one another, to be special for one another. For amongst all our rules, our obsessive need to 'protect' our identities, the rule of give and take has not played a big enough part – in my opinion. I wish I *had* wanted to look beautiful for you in the morning; I was passingly attractive back then – am still. I wish you had chosen to take a similar pride in yourself. Had not waited twenty-five years to get yourself in shape for someone else.

The truth must have hit you, eventually. Hence the makeover. Although I think your mother sensed the mismatch from the start. I detected discomfiture in her face on first seeing us standing side by side. You said it was because she was a 'jealous old bitch' who couldn't bear to see you happy. Which may have been true. I bought that line at the time. But why, if she was a jealous old bitch, did we spend so many weekends in her company? You surly, snapping at her half the time; I so unused to the protocol of what to me was, near as damn it, upper-class society. I felt I was tiptoeing through a minefield of etiquette, felt so on edge as to be practically struck dumb. Felt like a child from another era who only spoke when she was spoken to. No wonder your mother disapproved of your choice of spouse. For, at the start, there was little evidence her future daughter-in-law had any neurons up there in good working order.

Do you recall that first weekend Louise came down too? What a relief! I could begin to be myself.

My first thought was how *un*mollycoddled Louise was. My second, how much your mother – despite being only in her late fifties at the time – demanded of Louise. As well as how much poor Louise was prepared to give, and how little thanks she got for her labours, you, lying back, the only man in this harem household.

'He left us!' you told me, your admission coming as a result of my persistent questions.

By then I had known you for several months. You were fourteen when your father left, you told me. Told me you would never forgive him for it.

'Why did he leave?' I asked you.

'Probably because he'd had enough of the bitch he married,' you said.

'But you stayed in touch, surely?'

'Why would I? He pissed off. He made his choice. I forgot him.'

I asked if there had been another woman. One who might have been a better mother to you than your mother. I told you, at fourteen, you could've chosen to live with your father.

You shrugged, smiled that strangely oblique smile of yours. 'There *was* no other woman,' you said. 'My mother's enough to put a man off women for life.'

How true.

I once asked Louise about her father. She would have been eleven when he left. Not a good age for a girl to be abandoned by the first man she has known, the first she has loved. Louise showed me a few faded photographs of him, secretly, one Sunday afternoon. Showed me as a prepubescent girl might, pulling them protectively from her bag, looking furtively over her shoulder, as if fearing she might be found out. He was dark like you, olive-skinned, beaming; Louise a golden-haired, sunny bundle in his arms. *How time has diminished her*, I thought at the time. Have thought since. Where does it all go? All that optimism. All that hope.

'Where are they?' I asked you. 'Where the *fuck* are my pills?'

'They're preventing all those itsy-bitsy bits of microbial life from reproducing, I expect,' you answered. 'I flushed them down the bog!'

And I let it happen, didn't I? I let you decide my future. Let you tie me to you. Tie me down. I let a child be born because it was what *you* said you wanted. Where were our boundaries then, pray tell? I let a few soft-centred words, your rough lips on my neck, your insistence wipe out my inner fears, my regrets, *my* wishes. Yes. I had wishes. Hopes. Desires. I even had desires that went beyond you. For a while, that did not include you. Shame I did not voice them. Shame I did not act on them. Shame our son was born. Yes. In a way, it was a shame. Poor Josh. If he knew… But he can't know, can he? Which is why I've spoilt him rotten. Which, as you know, doesn't help. Another cover-up. Protection come too late. We've both needed that, haven't we? Both of us, as they say, have kept ourselves to ourselves. Kept the fucked-up bit of ourselves holed up inside.

Will you cry at her funeral? Will you show some genuine feeling at last?

You must know she's been calling you. Texting you. Why can you not at least talk to her? Tell her what's happened?

Tell her how you *feel*? You must have done a lot of 'opening up' to her before now: before your mother's death got in the way of your affair. Anyway, I've saved you the trouble. I've told her for you. Told the woman who only a month ago was your new best friend. I assume she's the A-M-I-E sort of Amy, since she sounds pretty young to me. Sounds pretty, too. Don't know if a pretty voice indicates a pretty face, but my guess is this Amie, your *amie*, is pretty. You'd go for pretty, wouldn't you, if pretty would go for you?

No! Don't get me wrong. I have *not* been snooping. You and I have rules. Hell! Why let everything fall apart? I'm holding myself together. In fact, better than that, I'm working on rebuilding myself. You should try it. You *need* to try it. You're a fucking mess! Despite all that 'getting in shape', the diet, the fake tan, the new haircut, new ringtone – a favourite of Amie's, I suspect. Despite all this, you are one *fucking mess*! One heap of *shit*!

She called on the landline, did Amie. Called more than once. Called several times. We've become quite close, she and I. It's rather nice, the old landline springing to life now there's a death in the family. Poor Amie was *completely* in the dark, of course – until I enlightened her. You've let her down *big time*: Amie's words, not mine. Though, sweet, unknowing thing that she is, she softened when I told her you had 'lost' your mother. I deliberately used that childish euphemism, overused by church, state and owners of furry animals, which, as you know, offends my atheistic sensibilities. I only use it now because it seems altogether apposite. Since I have the sense you are still looking for her, looking to find a way back to her. Looking, as the Americans say, to find *closure*. Too late for that, buddy. Instead you've closed down. Closed up. Shut up. Put the shutters up on Amie, on poor Louise, and on me. But what's new in that respect? Now you commune only with the dead.

Our marriage was a strained affair. Oops! Freudian slip. Meant to say our marriage *ceremony* was a strained affair. Guess I was right the first time. You looked ill at ease in your tailcoat. I felt trapped in that flouncy crinolette concoction that was as winter-white and stiff as the royal icing piped around our five-tier wedding cake. Felt like a giant cake decoration myself in all that crumpled silk, that stiff netting, the dress moving independently of my body. Where was my body? I was certainly out of my mind. Halfway up the aisle I wondered if, by magic, I could slip out of that dress, could run in my (supposedly) sexy underwear and stockings to hide behind a gravestone, to escape into a wheat field. Could let the dress continue up the aisle of its own free will. Let *it* say, 'I will.' Let it marry you: the man who was about to become my husk of a husband.

We've never spoken of our Big Day, have we? *We're not the type*, you'd say. *Why did we do it?* I'd say.

My parents, who could barely afford their contribution to this madness, looked awkward, mingling uncomfortably amongst the groom's guests; looked even more uncomfortable than was I.

I still have a clear picture of you putting the ring on my finger. Sliding it on as if you were playing that children's game – the one where a buzzer goes off if the guided ring touches the wire – your face cool, detached. Frightened.

Afterwards, cake frills and fripperies removed, the tiers dismantled, waiting to be sliced and shipped in silver-belled boxes to distant relatives unwilling or unable to attend this alleged joining of one man to one woman, married to you, not hiding in a wheat field, dressed in our comfortable if formal going-away clothes, we made our fond farewells.

My parents wished us 'all the best', my mother, hugging each of us with egalitarian vigour, kissing her new son-in-law with as much warmth as she'd kissed me; my father, triumphant at her side, a job-well-done expression on his face.

Then came your turn. Your *side's* turn.

If I asked you now, you would probably say you don't remember. But I would know you were lying.

She stood in the shadows. Did not step forward as my parents had done. In fact, having previously been in the foreground, she appeared to melt into the background, so that you were forced to search her out. Leaving me standing there in my neat dogstooth suit, my inner puppy, wishing it had the strength to growl and snap, whimpering silently inside.

'He's probably gone for a quick leak,' my father said, managing a cheerful smile, just as you reappeared, after what felt like forever, your hand in hers.

She walked toward me, took my hand – just the one: the one *without* the band of gold on it – took it awkwardly, as she leant forward to kiss me on the cheek. No warm embrace for me, from the inaptly named Cordelia, now that my place in the family had been legitimised. Then, letting my hand slip from hers (as you might a piece of wet fish you rather wished you hadn't touched), and turning to you (you standing by *her* side, not mine), she wrapped both her arms around you. While I, embarrassed, suddenly aware, watched your lips brush her forehead, your nose nuzzle her hair, as tears streamed down her delicately rouged, fine-boned cheeks. Stood there waiting for it to end. *Let her go!* I willed you as each second ticked by. *Let her go! I'm here now. I am all you need.*

Liars in love. Liars both.

You dive too deep. Always did.

On that first holiday, that first summer after our honeymoon, on the Spanish coast. Remember? South of Cadaqués. You took to diving off the rocks each day. To escape me? To scare me? Anyway, you left me watching from the safety of the beach. Left me unable to relax. Terrified. Thinking, *If there are rocks above, there are rocks below.* My heart thumping somewhere between my ribcage and my mouth. Yet still you dived, day after day. Still you walked away from me, day after day, bent on climbing higher and higher, diving deeper and deeper, staying down longer and longer, my scaredy-cat voice receding in your watery ears. You go to extremes, don't you? Always have: you, the quiet, keeping-mum boy. So why not go there? Go back to the beating heart where your life began, your diver's body, lithe as a baby seal, embracing your first watery home.

One Slip

A balmy summer's day and he had come to walk in the park. A different park now, a different town, a different part of the country. He was coming to terms with aloneness. Tried not to remember the man he once was.

He had moved to the town in late spring, riding on a surge of equinoctial optimism. Well, what else could he do? Though an alternative had wormed its way into his world-weary winter brain.

Contracts were exchanged on a bright April day. At the solicitor's office, smart in his grey suit, he had almost felt human. 'Chain-free!' his solicitor had said, all smiles. 'So not too long before you can move in, Patrick.' Said to cheer him, he supposed. Except, devoid of chains as he was, it had done quite the opposite. And, wouldn't you know it, on the very day he moved, the weather had taken a turn for the worse: showers or spells of rain or heavy downpours, day after day, week after week, a spell of disenchantment cast across the entire country – and across the face staring back at him in the mirror, looking as gloomy and grey as his hair. Where had all that youthful black gone?

It was the jet stream again, he supposed. Although the meteorological men and women had ceased to mention it.

Ashamed to, no doubt. Probably all jetting off to far-flung holiday destinations themselves at the drop of a sunhat, power-showering twice a day, without a thought. Everyone's fault. Yet no one owning up. No one willing to change their bad habits; to deprive themselves of anything.

Then, July nearing its end, had come sunshine. Days of it, with not a cloud in the sky – but plenty of vapour trails criss-crossing every which way. 'At last the jet stream has moved!' the smiley young weatherman in the silky suit had cheerfully announced. Although he had appeared equally cheerful when forecasting torrential downpours, even floods. Summer had finally arrived and Patrick had begun to use his 'charming garden'. Estate-agent speak, not his own. Where its charm lay, he could not say. It was tiny. Not much bigger than the kitchen table he used to eat at. Though no longer *his* kitchen table. No. No farmhouse kitchen any more. His was a galley kitchen. Though he was no slave to it. Rather wished he could be. *Patrick's a far better cook than me*. Forget those words. Forget her voice. Forget!

He had sat outside in his charming garden these past few nights. It was too hot to do anything else. Had taken a plate of limp salad to sit at the small pedestal table bought, cut-price, with his employee's discount.

Never much of a DIY man, it was strange to be working in such a place. Still, there were several other employees of a similar age, which helped. Though he had yet to find common ground with any of them. 'A teacher?' they'd say. 'My! And a *head* teacher, too!' He had not gone into details. Had avoided explanations. Curious, they would quiz him in his lunch break, he dodging their questions. They soon got the message. And, although polite enough, a few still friendly despite his standoffishness, they had let it be. He could not, somehow. Could not externalise it. Could not make it real. Not yet. Maybe not ever?

It was all right working at the store. It was bearable. The place was so large you could move about it and not feel yourself caged in like some ageing, broken animal.

Looking out from his rain-spattered kitchen window, he had grown quite fond of his bijou garden. At least he had before the heat had forced him into it. Now, after sitting out there, four nights in a row, sipping lager and attempting to read his newspaper, he was already tiring of its claustrophobic charm. If only he could concentrate. If only he could read a novel in the way he used to. If only he could escape his own interior landscape: the bumpy terrain of self-loathing and self-pity he travelled daily. Out there he had felt himself a lone player on the thrusting stage of life, all those windows staring down at him on three sides, silently poking fun at the poor sucker, all alone again. *How are the mighty fallen*, their glazed 'looks' seemed to say.

And so, that afternoon, he had made a promise to himself: had vowed to go to the park that evening, vowed to mingle with the non-working world. And, returning to the flat (it could never be home), without putting on the light and, as a consequence, that ghastly extractor fan that made you feel you were living in a hotel, he had splashed his face and neck with cooling water, pulled on his old stripy T-shirt, slipped into a pair of cool cotton chinos, and come here. Had thrown himself into it. Well, he had to start somewhere.

He had not allowed himself to enter the park until now. To enter any public park where he might see children playing, having fun.

Confronted by the children's play area within seconds of walking in the gate, his heart racing, he steeled himself as he passed by, daring one quick look. There were a few older children on the swings, two young lovebirds on the whirligig, but no little ones, no toddlers. A bit late for them, perhaps.

Ahead of him, the path extending to a paved area on one side, he saw a small café. Barely that: a stall, its deckchair-striped awning attached to a van. A skinny young man was folding up the tables and chairs and loading them into it. In line with him, Patrick said, 'I guess you're closed up now, eh?'

'Guess I am,' the young man said. He wore a baggy WOMAD vest. A gruesome tattoo, coiling the length of his left arm, encircled his neck. 'But if it's just a can and/or a packet of something, then I'm cool with that, mate. Open for biz tomorrer,' he informed Patrick as he gave him his change, 'at eleven! Should you happen by.'

And walking on, the can of lemonade and bag of smoky bacon crisps in his hand, Patrick realised he was smiling. *I should do this daily*, he told himself. *Rain or shine. Should run like I used to.* Would that still be possible? To run? To actually enjoy running? Except, back then, his running had been an act of self-preservation, a form of affirmative action, a necessary part of his staying alive. Did that matter any more? He could not answer that question one way or the other. Which might be seen as an improvement, he supposed: his having an indifference to life, rather than a complete disinterest in it.

There were quite a few people littering the grass, already bleached of its rain-drenched greenness: a few solitary sun worshippers desiccating as much of their youthful skin as they could without being totally naked; two dog walkers, their hounds haring towards each other through the picnickers; a couple of runners, both women, both plugged into whatever musical accompaniment must run with them. Humankind in all shapes and sizes – a bit too many oversized. A smattering of colours. Not quite the multiracial mix he had been used to, but at least there was a bit of a mix. He missed the kids at Greville High. Not that they would have missed him. The sixth form would have graduated by now; were already starting out on their adult lives. So much to look forward to. How he missed… *No. Don't go there.*

Approaching the duck pond, he saw a vacant bench. A perfect place to sit, sip his drink, crunch a few crisps. Lose time.

The small child was playing on the grass close to the pond. She looked no more than three. Had she been abandoned? She was too small to be left alone near the water's edge. He would sit and watch over her. Ensure her safety.

Her hair was a soft baby blonde, her cheeks as pink as a cherub's. From her little dress – a pale, girly, frilly thing – two feathery white wings sprouted. A sparkly starred wand in her hand, she was waving it in the direction of the ducks – which were not instantly transformed into swans. He could not take his eyes off her. How beautiful she was. 'Beautiful,' he heard himself say out loud, biting back a tear. Should he go over to her? Should he ask where her mother was?

'My angel!' a voice beside him said. '*Not!*'

Absorbed in his own world, Patrick had not heard the woman sit down at the other end of the bench. Tall, he imagined; her long, thin, bare legs splayed out in front of her, flip-flops on her bony feet. The flip-flops worried him. Unsafe footwear at the best of times, surely they were unwise footwear for a mother of a small child? How could she run after her daughter, should she need to? How could she guard her child from danger in those silly things? They were only of use on a sandy beach, if that. He felt like telling her so. Her thick, dark hair was quite unlike the child's.

Her sharp features briefly turned to him, she said, 'They were fresh out of little devil costumes! Which might have been more appropriate.'

'Surely not,' he said. 'She looks adorable.'

'Appearances can be deceptive, y'know.'

He did know. He himself had been trying to keep up appearances. But it was hard.

'She must give you such joy,' he said, fearing she might see the tears threatening to spill from his eyes. Fortunately her eyes were on the child – as were his – and he managed to pull himself back from the brink.

The child was waving back at her mother, while looking apprehensively at the man her mother was talking to. Small children were such possessive creatures. That was what was so wonderful about them: being loved by them in that greedy, grabbing way. The child's gaze, meanwhile, had returned to the ducks. *Loving*, Patrick thought, an index finger wiping away the last trace of weakness, *and so very, very trusting. I* can *do this. I can still have some sort of life.*

'They had this little party, y'see, down at the playgroup this afternoon. Anniversary. One o'clock club's been there ten years now.'

'So you've other children?'

'Uh-uh. Just this one. I was a late starter,' her long-fingered hands fanning out on either side of her fine-boned face, 'as you see!'

He wanted to say something complimentary, but, never having been much of a smooth talker (Fran had often said flattery was not his strong point, no doubt wishing it was), nothing came instantly to mind. *Forty, perhaps?* he thought. *Forty-two at most?*

'My little angel, here, was the product of a rather devilish adulterous fling. I was forty-four. Past it, I figured. Didn't expect… well… didn't think, did I?' Gesticulating in the child's direction. '*Et voila!*'

How open she was. How relaxed. How honest.

'Lilly was so excited about being an angel for the afternoon. God knows how I'm gonna get those wings off her to get her into the bath.'

'Maybe you could ask him? Get some advice.'

She turned to him, a puzzled expression on her face, then, a smile of recognition rippling over it (*Ah! So she does have wrinkles!*), 'Oh!' Her thumb gesticulating heavenward. 'You mean him up there. Don't think I'd be in God's good girls' directory, do you? Lil! *Lilly!* Think I'd better go get her. You've gotta have your eyes everywhere with a kid, haven't you?'

Another time he might have got up at that moment, might have hurried off as soon as her back was turned. But something in him, something in her, made him stay, his gaze drawn to her skinny frame as she picked up her pale be-winged bundle, her antithesis of a daughter, and returned to sit on the bench.

Patrick held out the opened bag of crisps; the child's small hand dived in.

'I'm sorry. Should've asked. Is she allowed?'

'Every once in a while. Yeah. Why not? I'm fighting a losing battle, I know.'

Then, taking a plastic container from the carrier bag on the bench beside her, lowering the bag to the ground and putting the opened container in its place, she said, 'Here! Have one! Have more than one. Left side's grown-up sarnies: cheese 'n' pickle. Right's kid's grub, i.e. peanut butter 'n' banana.'

'May I?' His hand hovering over the peanut butter and banana.

She smiled. 'Y'know, I would've sworn you'd be a cheese 'n' pickle man.'

'Not the sort of man who takes food from babies' mouths, you mean?'

'*Definitely* not that.'

Was this flirting? Or was it simply friendly interaction? He had lost the ability to judge. Should he be doing this? If he had not stopped to think, stopped and felt guilty for feeling anything, he would have sworn he was feeling happy. Happy? Surely he must never expect that. Not any more.

'You OK with that?'

The sandwich hovering near his mouth, he had yet to take a bite. She was looking a little worried. Maybe she was wondering if this stranger was a nutter after all?

'See! Said you were a cheese 'n' pickle man. Lilly'll eat it if you've changed your mind. Won't you, Lil? Right little trencher kid is Lil.'

Lilly's mother's name was Kate. Kate and Lilly lived in a flat just east of the park.

'No garden, though. Tough in this weather. Tough in any weather now she's growing.'

Patrick admitted to having a garden, just about. Should he admit to living alone? Or would that make her wary of him? Perhaps this was pure friendliness? Perhaps this was what pure friendliness was all about? He had forgotten how to interact normally; was becoming an old fool before his time. He should not have come here, should not have looked at the child. He was fifty-nine years old! If Fran were to call him tomorrow and say, *I've made a mistake, Patrick. I shouldn't have divorced you. It was foolish. I was wrong*, would he not agree with her? Would he not pack his bags, leave his galley kitchen, his inappropriate job, and return to eat supper with his ex-wife at that big kitchen table?

'You have kids?' she asked him.

'One: a boy.'

'Close by, is he?'

Had she already made the assumption he no longer had a wife? Perhaps there was an aura of rejection about him? Perhaps he had the ragged-edged look of a man alone, a man unloved, uncared for?

'No. London… Correction! He *was* in London.'

He was actually talking about himself. Had answered her honestly. This was new. He'd not done this in a long while. He had become used to bluffing – lying, even. It was easier somehow. This was dangerous territory. At any moment he might break down, might blub on that bony shoulder of hers and send her running away. And would that not be for the best? Wouldn't that be best for little Lilly? If they were to become friends – just that, nothing more – would he dare pick Lilly up? Dare toss her in the air? Dare to do all the things a parent, a grandparent, does with a squealing, giggling toddler?

'But,' he went on, 'he's moved to Sydney now.'

'*Australia!* Well, I guess that's your holidays sorted.'

Lilly's hand was in the crisp packet again. He had been holding it, loosely, in his hand, had seen her bum-shuffling along the seat to rummage in it, and left it there. He could feel her small fingers fumbling on the other side of the foil.

He bit hard on his bottom lip. 'Can she?' he finally asked Kate.

'What the hell!' she said. 'Though you wanna watch it, Lil, or you'll be a right little porker.'

Looking up at her mother, a broad grin spreading across her chubby-cheeked face, Lilly's small hands took command of the crisp packet.

'Go ahead! At least if you grease up your angel outfit, I'll have a better chance of getting it off you without a fight.'

He thought he might let it pass, her Australia remark, but found himself returning to it. 'No,' he went on, 'I've not been to Australia… Not as yet. Well, to be honest, I've no plans to… You see,' he paused, and her face showed some concern as he heard himself say, 'you see, my son…' He had not said that word for so long that the sound of it hitting the air almost made him gag. Clearing his throat, he went on, 'My son and me… we're, as they say, estranged.'

'Estranged *et à l'étranger*. That's a double whammy.' She had a nice voice, but not a highly educated one, and her perfect French accent surprised him.

She was a translator, it turned out: French, Spanish and Italian. She admitted to being a quarter Italian herself. Before 'You-Know-Who' was conceived she had worked in Brussels and Strasbourg. 'Still, my high-flying days are over now.' She managed, 'just about', doing freelance translation work from home.

So they were in the same boat: both brought down by circumstances beyond their control. One split-second decision, one little slip, and your whole world is turned upside down. Except Kate appeared happy in her new world. Why would she not be? She had gained a child, had gained Lilly. No loss there.

'One cheese 'n' pickle going begging!' She was holding out the container. It seemed greedy, rude to take it. 'Go on! I'd eat your last sarnie, should you do the same.'

Was she hinting? Suggesting? Would she trust him with little Lilly if she knew?

'I'm not sure you would,' he said. 'You haven't seen my doorsteps.'

'Try me!' she said, turning to put the container back in her bag.

Wishing he could have seen the expression on her face, he bit into the sandwich. Looking down at his watch, he realised more than an hour had gone by. It had flown. He could have sat there for another hour.

'Better get my devil in disguise back home to bed, I suppose. Plus, it's a tad cooler now and I've heard tell angels don't take kindly to wearing cardies. Crushes their wings. *Right!*' She stood up. 'Come on, you!'

Her greasy fingers still clutching the crisp packet, Lilly looked first to her mother and then to Patrick.

'All done, there?' Kate's hand reached out for the empty packet. 'Give me that, then! Time for angels to go beddy-byes.'

Not altogether convinced that it was, Lilly wiped her mouth on the back of one hand, then, scrunching the crisp packet as hard as she could between both of them, she turned to Patrick. 'Tank-oo, man,' she said, pushing the greasy foil into the palm of his left hand.

'Patrick's not a rubbish bin, Lilly.'

'Thank *you*, Lilly,' Patrick said, standing up himself. 'I am delighted to be your rubbish bin.'

The child in her mother's arms, there were a few seconds of embarrassed silence in which Patrick pictured Kate sitting at his cut-price table, imagined little Lilly running about the claustrophobic garden. Concrete slabs, though. Was there no way forward without going back? No happiness without pain? No hope?

'Well,' she said, breaking the embarrassed silence, 'if this weather holds, we'll most likely be here tomorrow...' She paused. 'With or without sandwiches.'

His chance to say something. *Go on!* Say *something*.

'No doubt my daughter'll be in her usual devilish daytime gear. That is, smeared with paint or mud, pasta sauce or peanut butter.'

Too late! He'd missed his chance. Though he could still say it. *Should* say it. Wasn't that what Kate wanted? He could get some tuna, some cucumber, some mayonnaise; he used to rustle up a splendid home-made mayonnaise. But what if this was all a friendly game, a pleasant way to pass an hour? She might have a boyfriend half her age. Might not be in the least bit interested in a grandfather down on his luck. Why would she be?

Standing side by side, she was almost as tall as him; Lilly in her arms, head-height. *Just say it! Say,* Maybe see you tomorrow, then? *Nothing more than that.* Was that so hard?

'Say night-night to Patrick, Lil.'

'Ni-nite,' Lilly said softly, one greasy-fingered hand in the air.

'Night-night, Lilly,' he said, the pad of an index finger touching her soft palm. And then, turning, without looking back, 'See you!'

'If the sun's out, we'll be here!'

And, the tears welling, he walked on in the direction of the playground.

It had happened in an instant. Life had been glorious until that moment. Everything fitting together: wife, son, job, lovely daughter-in-law, and now this beautiful grandchild. It was almost too perfect. He had often thought that. Thought it *too* often, perhaps. Had often considered the unfairness of life: where we are born, the chances we have, don't have, take, don't take. How life can deal out good and bad, willy-nilly.

He had been running, feeling fifty-five going on twenty-five, his granddaughter on his shoulders, his hands holding fast to her ankles, her laughter in his ears, the sun warm on their faces, the sky as blue as blue. Then, suddenly, out of nowhere, heels skidding, hands... What had happened to his hands? Had he let go? It was a muddle to him still, yet, still, it was as clear as that clear, still day: Ellie's shrieks of delight. The cold, dull thud. The silence. All happiness gone in an instant. On his knees... praying. Her bright little face staring up at the heavenly blue, at nothing, an enlarging pool of dark red trickling from behind her pale blonde hair. Why had he not run on the grass? Why had he not run on the bloody grass?! Why had he run at all?

Fran might have been more understanding, might have helped him through those first torturous months with more understanding, had it not been for Daniel. A replica of his father in everything but anger, their son had turned his consuming despair into raw hatred, had turned his young wife against the man who had 'killed' their daughter. Had turned his doting mother against the man she had loved for three decades. Though not loved quite as much as Patrick had thought, it seemed, since, last he'd heard, Fran was planning to join Dan and Jozie in Sydney: Jozie's hometown. There was talk of another child. Perhaps already born. *No. Out of bounds. Don't go there.*

Fumbling in his trouser pocket for a tissue, Patrick wiped his damp cheeks. Through a teary blur he saw the two young lovebirds were still there. On the swings now, one pushing the other. He felt something on his right foot. Looking down, he saw a slimy ice-cream wrapper – dropped by some lazy litter lout, no doubt – had attached itself to the toe of his shoe. Bending to peel it off, he became aware of the scrunched-up crisp packet in his other hand. He pushed the ice-cream wrapper into the overflowing bin, reluctantly released the crisp packet from his grasp, and, turning, strode on towards the gate.

Despite the extreme warmth of the day, a distinctly cooling breeze had developed. Maybe the heatwave was coming to an end? It might be raining by tomorrow. He would check the weather forecast later on, as he always did.

Porkies

After the pig-squealing contest, not long after leaving Trie-sur-Baïse, Huw took a wrong turning. Bethany had an idea they might be heading in the wrong direction, but as her husband had always mistrusted her navigational skills, she had chosen not to get into one of those depressing sexist arguments, Huw's exasperated sigh when making a sudden stomach-churning U-turn the only acknowledgment of his mistake. And, since the atmosphere between them had acquired an unexpected and growing density, she had remained silent, staring out at the flat patchwork of fields, the mountains beyond, with a sudden longing for gently rolling hills, verdant hedgerows, ruminating cattle, the fake squeals and oinks reverberating in her head, a frightened scream gripping her gut. Why had they gone to *La Pourcailhade*? That obscene *boudin noir*. That woman in the mobcap. Those pink-nosed men. She would never eat sausages again.

At last reaching the restaurant, Huw, who had managed a disgruntled groan when a Renault estate 'stole' his parking space, stood impatiently jingling the car keys as Bethany dragged her reluctant body into the humid evening heat, and, in silence, they crossed the square. *How sad*, Bethany thought as they neared the convivial clatter and chatter. *It looks so jolly, so welcoming*, unable to look up at her husband's withheld profile, preferring to imagine his face set fair, as it had been two days ago.

She thought of the haunting cave paintings they had seen then. Pictured a Palaeolithic family, father etching the elegant line of an ibex's horn, mother colouring the back of a muscular aurochs' neck, their children hand-stencilling the rock below – making their mark on history.

Huw was charging manfully on towards a table, oblivious of her presence. Had Palaeolithic man – a man who could produce such stone-on-stone sensitivity – perhaps possessed a greater understanding of his partner's needs than did twenty-first-century *Homo sapiens?* For all his *What a superb Chenin blanc! What amazing truffles! What a treat* ways, what civilised man would take his wife on holiday in order to—?

'*Fuck!*'

Gazing blankly at the menu, while wanting nothing more than a cheese-and-pickle sandwich, Huw's loud expletive, his first clearly enunciated word in almost half an hour, roused Bethany from her reverie.

'All this bloody way and there's no bloody *porc noir!*' Grunting and groaning over an alternative, before ordering duck gizzard salad followed by cassoulet, and filling Bethany's glass with the red wine he himself had ordered, not even asking for her approval, while looking askance at the bottle's label and not straight into her eyes (as any caveman worth his salt would have done), and saying, in that soft, questioning tone, as if he was the kind of man who could etch a sinewy line in hard stone, 'Beth…?' His voice tailing off as the plate of entrails was placed before him and he paused to spike one with his fork. And Bethany wished they *had* bought one of those disgusting blood sausages Huw, having eaten several taster chunks, found so delicious, so she might stuff it in his mouth right now. Might force it down that expanding gut of his. Might shut him up forever. 'Beth' said like that. As if she were one of the *Little Women*: the soft, nurturing one. He would not have spoken to Jo in such a way. But then Jo would not have come on this 'little break', would have told Huw where to stick his 'treat' that was in fact more of a trick.

'Beth,' he'd said, 'we need a bit of time, don't we? Perhaps the kids could spend a few days with their grandparents… You and me, we need…'

A break? she'd thought.

Watching Huw's fork spear another mouthful of gizzard – feeling like throwing up or throttling him, or both – Bethany realised that, had their daughter Tassie not rushed into the kitchen at that moment, Huw, in that soft, sanctimonious, guiltless tone – the tone in which he had begun to address her now – might have gone on to say, 'to talk'. And husband and wife would have talked, then and there, in their newly decorated kitchen, and Bethany would not be sitting in this restaurant now, hungry, yet devoid of appetite, full of love and hate. Huw had got the upper hand, as always; as always, in an underhand way. Yet he could still sit there, calmly chewing on some poor dead duck's stomach. He had no heart.

—···—

Bethany had wondered about the nature of her fiancé's palpitating organ, which, though patently not in any physiological sense connected to the mind, is so intrinsically linked to our emotions, soon after meeting Huw's parents.

The farm her future in-laws owned, owned still, still had animals on it then. Not pristine barn-conversion holiday flats smelling of Forest Glade air freshener, but a small mud-trailing dairy herd, two styes of smelly, inquisitive pigs, and a whole field of chickens. In love with love, Bethany had pictured the progeny of that love running about this place so redolent of childhood.

She had known from the beginning, of course. But was not certain if there had been one beginning or two; such adulterous detail she had not sought to clarify, accepting her husband's excuses, preferring her own pretence; preferring, 'Oh dear. Poor you… Of course I don't mind… Don't worry, I'll keep a plate of it for you', and, 'Yes. Better too much work than too little', to the truth. A truth that might be just a passing fancy, for a while, a different way of seeing. Of seeing someone else. Of not seeing the real Bethany: the woman he took for granted, but loved, and would love again.

Images from the pig-squealing contest kept rearing their ugly heads. Those plastic noses. Those hideous piggy ears. Those bizarre antics, most of them acted out by men. Hogging the limelight. Making pigs of themselves. Why had that useful term 'male chauvinist pig' disappeared from the post-feminist canon? A perverted form of female chauvinism had replaced feminism. One that permitted those who subscribed to it to seek 'liberation' slithering around a pole to please *the guys*. A transatlantic form of sexist equality making us all guys together now. Even here in the Hautes-Pyrénées. '*Au'voir*, you guys,' the young woman who cleaned their room had said that morning. 'Ave a neece day.'

Perhaps they would have had, had they gone to Nice?

'Aren't you having any meat?'

He was looking at her goat's cheese salad, not at her. While, looking into nothingness, Bethany only knew she did not want to look at Huw. For looking into his eyes would both make her want to cry and to kill him. Did he wish to build her up in order to cut her down again? Or was he backing down? He had done so before. Two glasses of wine hadn't given him quite enough bottle. *That's it. Pour yourself another. Don't mind me. I'm just the little wife, the little woman,* little *Beth*.

She knew what he was doing, sitting there chewing on another mouthful of dead duck while juggling the words in his head, shuffling clauses, attempting to soften their impact – make them palatable. Would they spill from his lips this time? Would they drizzle out between mouthfuls of duck gizzard? Huw's appetite always came first. It took on all comers, all emotions.

Perhaps he was hoping she would initiate proceedings, would roll over and admit defeat? Would offer up her own throat to be cut, right here in Le Petit Gourmand? The chef might want to drain her blood. Might serve her up as sausage!

'Some chicken, perhaps? Beth…?'

His voice had acquired that firm yet questioning tone Huw employed when wishing to imply he was in complete control of whatever it was he was doing, in actual fact, he had no wish to do it at all, his gentle enquiry as to where this or that cleaning product, this or that kitchen utensil was, merely a cue for Bethany to sigh and say, *Huw, why don't I do that for you?*

Not this time, Huw. Not this time.

Tassie would love her father no matter what. Tassie had always been Daddy's girl. Huw would still have his daughter's smiles, while she, Bethany, would shoulder Tassie's tears.

But what of Zac? No doubt her son's anger would remain locked inside him, where it would gnaw away at the buoyant boy he had finally become. He might flunk his GCSEs, might escape into drugs, while, like Tassie, smiling for his father come the weekend. Weekends that would dissipate, be squandered, slowly fade away.

'I can't manage… I'm not hungry enough for meat, Huw. I never am, really. You know that.'

He had known that. But that was in the past.

Huw's mood had changed soon after their return from the Gargas Caves, soon after he had checked his text messages.

Unfaithfulness, Bethany supposed, must be an awful lot easier these days.

In the bad old days, before instant one-on-one communication, a MCP's mistress would have had to call the hotel, the concierge announcing, 'A telephone call for Mr Foster!' Or the bellboy, whistling a chirpy little tune as he crossed the lounge, would have presented Mr Foster with a scented letter on a silver tray; Mrs Foster, eyeing the envelope being whisked into her husband's breast pocket, catching a glimpse of the delicate feminine hand, the criss-crossed kiss or the lipstick imprint with which the *other woman* had sealed her missing-you message.

Ah! Those were the days. Life, for all its efficacy, all its openness, had an inbuilt covertness now: 'working' a euphemism, a computerised cover for all manner of illegal, underhand ways of interacting with the virtual world – with worlds *without* virtue.

Surfacing from his thoughts, Huw said, 'We never did quite enough of this, did we?'

So, already *they* were in the past, were history, she, the virtuous one, zapped into another reality.

'Well, children are a lot of work, Huw.'

'But worth it!' he replied.

If he used this moment to tell *her* how worthwhile their family was, when, most likely, some day soon, he would be counting the little 'pinkies' of another child, reading *The Three Little Pigs* all over again, Bethany might make like the Big Bad Wolf and tear out his liver with her teeth. She wanted to be back home with Tassie and Zac, back in that once-upon-a-time land of bedtime stories, wanted this moment to be a decade and a half into the future, with no fears of a Big Bad Wolf blowing their house down. Huw was always home on time then, hurrying back to them, full of love.

His cassoulet had arrived. He could eat cassoulet and think what he was thinking. Think of who he was thinking of.

I'll huff and I'll puff and I'll...

The second time she and Huw visited his parents' farm a large white van had driven into the yard, and Pinky, Perky and Curly, the pigs he had introduced her to five weeks earlier, were unceremoniously herded into it. 'They know, Huw,' she'd said. 'Pigs are intelligent creatures. They'll know what's about to happen to them. Doesn't it upset you?'

Huw said it did not. Huw said it was a dog-eat-dog, man-eat-pig kinda world. 'Get in there, girl!' he'd shouted at the frightened creature, lifting the ramp, sealing their fate.

Their squeals ringing in her ears, Bethany had retreated to the kitchen where Huw's mother, her back to the window, was preparing tea. Putting the kettle on the Aga, she'd said, 'Y'know, even after all these years, I still can't bear to watch em go.'

A few moments later a smiling Huw strode in, tall and handsome and smelling of frightened pig, his eyes bright with love, as Bethany blinked back a tear.

'Tea!' he'd said, sitting down at the table, his gaze drawn to the plate of tender cold cuts his mother had just placed there. And something in the efficient way her lover was able to dispatch the pigs whose birth he himself had witnessed and then greedily sit at the table to eat ham and salad, made Bethany recoil from the cold hand that reached across the table to brush her cheek.

If he did that very thing now, here in this restaurant, would she recoil from his touch? Or would she be relieved that he had cold feet again, and was giving their marriage a reprieve?

He was spooning the remaining contents of the terracotta dish onto his plate. Still he could not begin. No doubt he had sent his lover a message vowing he would.

'Are you *sure* you don't want any of this?' he said.

Bethany shook her head. 'I was a vegetarian until I met you. Remember?'

He nodded, pretending he did.

'I cried that day Pinky, Perky and Curly were sent to the slaughterhouse.'

'*Christ!* You even remember their names!'

'I'm surprised, after that, I allowed you to convert me to carnivorousness.'

Scooping up another mouthful of cassoulet, Huw looked up, looked straight into her eyes and, with half-full mouth managing half a smile, said, 'I'm a good salesman, that's why.'

He would sell Bethany her future, she knew. She could squeal as much as she liked; he would still kill their marriage. There was no stun gun to hand, only wine. Better to drink it, then, to prepare for the carving up.

They would lie to their children, she supposed. They would talk of *joint parenting* – which here, in this country of carnivores, brought to mind bringing up a leg of lamb or nurturing a belly of pork. They would tell Zac and Tassie not to worry. Their parents would remain good friends. That would never change. They would say they still loved each other, and that their love had not gone away but had merely been transmuted – they would not admit to its debasement. They would tell their son and daughter this so many times they would almost believe it themselves. They would treat

Tassie and Zac like children. But Tassie and Zac, knowing themselves to be no longer children, would not believe what they heard, and, their house blown down, would cry into their pillows in the dark – like children.

The waiter was hovering over her. '*Dessert pour madame?*'

'*Non, merci.*'

'*Et monsieur?*'

'*Rien pour monsieur aussi. Merci.*'

An expression of relief and regret on his wine-flushed face, Huw, not looking up at the waiter himself but staring straight into Bethany's eyes, shook his head in agreement. '*L'addition, s'il vous plaît,*' he said.

'*Du café?*' the waiter persisted.

'*Non!*' Bethany said sharply; then, raising her empty wine glass to Huw, '*Rien de rien. Nous avons fini. Absolument fini.*'

Running Away

In my perverse mind it's summertime: that hot summer of 1976. Which, of course, it could not have been since Lukey was born in January. Even so, I persist in seeing it this way: see my mother, in bikini and tie-dyed sarong, drifting from shaded bedroom to sun-scorched balcony, a whiff of coconut suntan lotion wafting through time to perfume this dull autumn afternoon. Bob Marley is playing on the record player, *Running Away* running through my head. Though, again, I am conflating an early memory with a later one, a time when Bob's words were blasted full volume, blasted beyond the grave, my mother grieving her double loss.

These sounds, these scents, I will always associate with my first sight of Lukey, lying on a fluffy white towel, spread out on the rainbow-coloured quilt of my parents' bed. Seeing him there, evidencing no sign of blood or breath, I thought him a lifeless doll-baby. Thought, *This ugly-sweet creature cannot be* my *brother. He looks like the toy baby my grandmother gave me for Christmas*. I imagined Lukey's body to be floppy-soft, and his pale, smooth head – showing none of the white-blond hair to come – to be as hard and as fragile as porcelain. Suspected that beneath the white nappy drawn up between his colourless legs my alleged sibling's sexless-doll status lay hidden.

'Take him, Arlene!' my mother would urge me. '*Hold* your brother! He's as light as air. *Come on!* Take him in your arms!'

Hands clasped behind my back, fingers nervously entwined, shaking my head, I would offer some lame excuse and back from the room, refusing to hold Lukey for fear of breaking his 'doll's' head.

I was five years old that winter, and had been at Whitehouse Primary for four months. And yet no rose-tinted memories of a favourite teacher or a much-loved playmate have travelled with me through life. All childhood memories I own, all I can recall, have Lukey at their centre. From the start, my brother was the centre of my world.

'Stop, Daddy! Stop!'

I was fearful, too, should I catch Lukey being swung in my father's long, strong arms. His tilting carousel swings having a frightening energy, a degree of danger that caused my heart to race, my voice to yell, '*Please* stop. Think of Lukey's baby brain!'

Lennie.

He always called me Lennie because, as my mother later admitted, he had hoped for, had wanted me to be, a boy.

'He's a flesh-and-blood baby. He not made of glass. He won't break.'

Unconvinced by my father's assertions I would remain, watching fearfully, hoping my agitated presence would calm the trajectory of those rock-a-bye swings. Wait until, safely back in his cot, I could pull the honeycomb blanket over Lukey's fragile body.

And throughout that first year I believed my brother to be no ordinary flesh-and-blood baby. Believed him born of a more mysterious alchemy than the everyday love that had made me. Imagined he came from some faraway, fairy-tale land: a land of snow palaces, white knights and whey-faced princesses who slept on goose down and bathed in milk. To me, Lukey was too pale a creature to possess such a life-giving, life-taking liquid as blood. My whiter-than-white brother. The child I see now, swinging in his father's dark brown arms.

Our father came from Grenada.

'Do they have snow there, Daddy?'

It was Lukey's first summer.

'Do they have rivers of milk?'

'No, crazy chile. Grenada, she have sunshine, she have blue sky, she have nutmeg an cinnamon, an ginger...' Looking out at the grey July day, then turning to beam down at me, and, with an enthusiasm that made me want to taste it, 'And she have *rum!*'

Had it been just me, my father and my mother, had Lukey not been lying in his white cot, I might have said, *Can we go there, Daddy? Can we go live in* Grin-nay-dah, *with its blue sky, its sinner-man and rum?* But somehow I knew, before I knew why, that my mother would not sanction Lukey going there.

Dad must have known it too, because, sitting on the nursing chair beside Lukey's cot, he said, 'Come 'ere, Coffee

Bean.' (I was either Coffee Bean or Lennie. Never Arlene.) 'These locks is comin undone. What's your mother doin these days? Not plaitin' that boy's hair, for sure.' And I stood between my father's legs, my hands on his knobbly knees, as his bony fingers deftly plaited my unruly hair, feeling safe in the pincer grip of his long-limbed presence. 'Y'know, Lennie,' he said, 'blue sky can get a bit borin' day after day. An' a man can have too much rum.'

'Even a *sinner*-man?'

'*Specially* a sinner-man. Those sinner-men would ave done well not to ave touched it in de first place. But men is weak, Lennie-girl. Men is weak.'

'But Lukey won't be weak!'

His big hands gripping my small shoulders, my father turned me round to face him. '*Lennie*. Your brother is special, like any chile is special, an he'll need to be strong, for sure, but that boy won't be no saint, an I hope he won't be no sinner-man either.'

'He won't be,' I said, with all the certainty of the innocent. 'He *can't* be. Lukey's *extra* special.'

Back then, I think my father might have loved Lukey more than my mother did. Loved Lukey in the way he needed to be loved. Perhaps, foreseeing the dangers of a boy like Lukey having we two worrying women always about him, my mother knew that too. Maybe that was why, despite loving my father with a forgiving passion while he was with us, she hated him with an unforgiving passion after he left us.

My brother became my mother's precious possession, her prized piece of porcelain. One to be kept in a box, in the dark, lest it break. This boy whose skin more closely matched her own winter flesh was an embarrassment. He was not brown, not coffee-coloured, not black, but *white*. Whiter than the winter breasts to which she pressed his new-to-the-world head, Lukey's bleached mouth reluctantly accepting the watery milk leeched from her dark nipples. This pigmentless boy had let the side down. The beautiful woman from Grimsby, who had fallen for the beautiful man from Grenada, had wanted, had expected another coffee-coloured baby, just like me.

'My!' she would say, rubbing cocoa butter into my legs, 'what a *fine* colour! I'd love skin like yours, Arlene. No more sunbathing. *Ever.* You are *such* a lucky girl.'

I considered myself neither lucky nor unlucky. While, in spite of the stories I would tell him of snow queens in cloud-covered ice castles in the sky, knowing Lukey to be the unlucky one – especially after Dad left. For who would treat him like a real live boy now?

My mother had a job by then – on and off. Which meant I would sometimes have to skip school to look after Lukey, our curtained flat a stuffy mausoleum in which I conjured frozen wonderlands to escape to.

'The Ice-Cream Giant, Arlene! Tell me the story of the Ice-Cream Giant *again!*'

He was five years old and about to start school.

Three years later, I by then in my first term at Windsfield Comprehensive, Lukey ran away from Whitehouse Primary.

'I wanted to go to Iceland,' he told the policeman who found him sitting on a wall opposite the supermarket of that name. 'Wanted to meet the Ice-Cream Giant and the

Frosty-White Knight...' Managing to say, before bursting into tears, 'But they weren't there!'

I wasn't overly concerned then. For didn't all small children have such fantasies? And surely Lukey needed a make-believe world where milk-washed boys were superheroes to be worshipped, not weirdos to be scorned.

'Think I'll go there some day,' Lukey said, apropos of nothing.

We had just got home from school. I was in the kitchen, filling the kettle.

Despite everything, I had made it to the sixth form. Lukey had recently joined me at Windsfield Comp. Although, according to his form teacher, most of the time, my brother was 'in a world of his own'.

'Think I'll stay there,' he said, shuffling into the living room.

'Where?' I asked, following him.

'North Pole,' he answered, wandering out onto the balcony.

'*Luke Williams!*' Our mother, jumping up to expose her exposed breasts to half the street. 'Get your sunglasses *and* your hat before coming out here!'

'Yeah,' Lukey said, 'I'll *definitely* stay there.'

Hey there, Coffee Bean, my father wrote. I could hear his voice: deep and dark, and bittersweet. *Yer see, Lennie-girl. A man can be a sinner-man without even takin a drop a' rum.*

He had sent a photograph: his dreadlocks had grown longer and his skin looked darker against the dark blue sky.

He missed us, he said, but had *t'get a bittah sunshine for a while*. He would come back in a few weeks.

He came back in a few years.

He wore neither scarf nor gloves, and his coat was way too thin. I could hear his teeth chattering as he shivered at the graveside, my mother, an angry distance away, managing to be both grief-stricken and indignant.

As Lukey's coffin was lowered into the ground, snowflakes floated from the weighty winter sky to settle on the gleaming walnut.

I reached out for my father's hand. 'Don't you have any gloves?' I whispered, touching his frozen fingers.

'Don't need no gloves, Lennie-girl. Need to feel the pain of it. Need to hurt *more*.' And he squeezed my hand so tightly I thought my fingers would break. But I didn't wince, did not withdraw my hand from his, thinking, *Break them, Dad. Break them all. Let me hurt forever.*

I wrote a story on Lukey's back once. I can see my brown finger now, moving across the sweaty whiteness of his parchment skin. A scorching summer's day. He was seven years old.

Our storytelling game had begun three years before.

'Give me your hand, Lukey. No, don't look! You're to *feel* the letters.'

O-N-C-E… U-P-O-N… I shaped the words on his palm. Dad had left that March.

'Wuh-un-sah… *Once upon a time!*' Lukey cried out. 'I can do it, can't I, Arlene? My skin can read!'

'Sure you can do it, Lukey. *You* are the cleverest boy in the universe.'

—∿—

I was away at university. A year of retakes and I'd finally got a place. Though not the place I wanted: not a place close to home, close to Lukey.

It was snowing again. The previous weekend I'd not managed to get home, and, that week, hadn't spoken to Lukey for five days. He'd been in hospital for three of them. His eyes again.

'How'd it go?'

It was a Wednesday evening. Mum was out. She had been out a lot lately, he said. I hated to think of him alone in that claustrophobic little flat.

'Oh, y'know, Lennie,' Lukey said. He'd not called me Lennie for years. Not since our mother had insisted on reinstating Arlene, soon after Dad left. 'Same old shit.'

He sounded cheerful enough, in that world-weary way of his: Lukey not having a great deal to smile about, not one to smile a great deal.

'I'll be with you Friday,' I said. 'The weather forecast's pretty good.'

'You're always with me, Lennie-girl.' He was barely fourteen, but his voice had a deep resonance that reminded me of Dad. '*Always,*' he repeated.

He was found spreadeagled in the snow, his eyes (unprotected by the sunglasses Mum insisted he carry with him at all times) gazing up into the crystal-clear blue that followed the sub-zero temperatures of the previous night, his mouth frozen in a smile.

'I hope that's of some comfort to you?' the doctor who had attended the scene said.

It wasn't. But has since become so.

'Maybe you've gone home?' I whispered, as I touched Lukey's hand, turning to the doctor. 'May I?'

'Of course,' the doctor said. 'I'll be outside.'

L-O-V-E... Y-O-U... A-L-W-A-Y-S, my finger wrote on my brother's bloodless palm. *Maybe*, I thought, *somewhere where the sun shines down on everyone, Lukey's skin might 'read' these words, might never forget them.*

'Let's go for Christmas!' my husband says. 'Your father still writes, *Come visit* on his cards. And think of Nat, Lennie. His grandmother can carry her bitterness to the grave, but the boy should get to see his grandfather before he gets too grown-up for grandfathers.'

Our eight-year-old son has his father's fair hair and his maternal grandmother's sun-loving skin. He is bright and sporty, and has several friends, several of whom treat our house as their own. He even has a 'girlfriend'.

'Let's get ourselves some winter sunshine!'

'Well,' I say, 'I suppose I could at least write to him.'

'Uh-uh. You could at least *call* him. Break the ice, Lennie. Call. Call and say we'll go see him.'

'Go see who?' our very own superhero asks, dumping his schoolbag and slumping down beside me on the sofa. My fingers ripple through the sun-bleached waves of his hair. *Pretty soon*, I think, *you'll find this too close for comfort.*

Dick's Life

My wife slips quietly from our bed, silencing the programmed alarm clock before time, so as not to disturb her sleeping husband. But her husband is awake; I have woken before her, and feign sleep as she moves about the darkened room.

She takes underwear from the chair (removed from the drawer with the jingling brass handles the night before) and pulls on the obligatory panty girdle: of the kind she took to wearing after our daughter was born, almost thirty-six years ago, believing the firm support offered by the two-way stretch tummy panel was needed to restore her post-partum body to its pre-partum shape. Not needed at the time, over time it has become necessary. My wife, seeing no need to change this habit of a lifetime, possesses several of these corrective garments, washed from their original virginal whiteness to an aged slush-grey.

She bought one in black once: the two-way stretch satin tummy panel having converging lines of scarlet stitching running down it, a small red bow attached to its V-shaped centre resting just below her navel. 'I rather like those,' I told her the first time she put it on. 'More attractive. And more practical than white.'

'I'm not sure...' she said, 'I'd need to change my bras as well.' And this daredevil piece of decadence, this moment of middle-aged madness, was consigned to a dark corner of the jangly-handled drawer, never to be seen again.

She sits, oh so gently, on the end of our bed. I can see the fuzzy outline of her back, the curved shoulders a little too rounded now, as if she has spent a lifetime wrapping her arms about herself. 'It's the menopause, I expect,' she says.

'There's HRT,' I say.

'Not safe,' she says. 'And does nothing. It's all right for men,' she goes on, 'they don't have to worry about such things.' But does *she* worry about such things?

She fumbles with the hooks of her regulation no-frills-no-fripperies white bra. How would she respond, I wonder, if I were to put my hand... just there? There in the small of that not-so-small back. If I drew her back into the cooling marital bed; if I pulled off the warming white dawn-chorus vest that hides her head from me now; if I tore her ghastly green sweatshirt from her hands; if I threw those old lavender tracksuit bottoms – that should've been thrown away years ago – across the room and forced her to lie beside me, just for the love of lying there.

She pulls on the tracksuit bottoms, bends down to pick up her trainers, and I watch my shadow-play wife tiptoe from the room and, oh so gently, in case she disturbs me, close the bedroom door. Heaven forbid that she should disturb me. At times like this I find it hard to believe she ever did.

I roll over, pull her pillow on top of mine, and watch the dawn light seep in behind the heavy lined curtains. The pillow still holds her warmth. And a dying part of me wants to leap up, scramble into my clothes and follow Gwyneth to the source of her new-found serenity. 'Come *with* me!' she has said. 'It's something we could share.' Pausing. 'Something positive.' Already knowing what I am thinking, already knowing what I would never say. 'Come?' she repeats meekly. But I resist. Have resisted. And she no longer urges me to share her joy, going alone to meet her fellow twitchers. No longer declaring, 'The spring dawn chorus! To be amongst it; it is *such* a privilege. It's life-affirming.'

The last time she urged, 'Come! I promise you'll never regret it', I almost said, *Gwyneth. What if I already do? What if I regret the promise I made to you? What then? Will listening to your feathered friends tweeting across those blue remembered hills make me feel any better?* But it's not the sort of thing a man says, is it? Not after almost four decades. Not chivalrous. Not done.

I stretch out my body across no man's land. The sheet feels cold. The bed has lost its comforting warmth. I am wide awake, yet have no wish to move, no wish to stay. I am indifferent. Powerless. Have I always been thus? Was I thus thirty-seven years ago? Is neutrality my natural state? Was I waiting to be conquered? If not by Gwyneth, then by some other overwhelming woman: one who, tiring of my passivity, might have soon spewed me out. As my wife must frequently tire of her lukewarm Laodicean.

I look over to the clock. More than three hours have gone by, but still I lie in neutered stupor, my body weighted to the bed.

'Don't worry,' Gwyneth says, 'it *will* pass. It always does.'

She's right. It does. But is she making light of it, not wanting to expose the 'it' that is passing to closer scrutiny? And so she chivvies, she cossets, she chirrups. Twitching breathing new life into the month of April, for Gwyneth, at least.

I see her coming toward me through the half-light, a slim, flowing form: long hair, long skirt, Apache scarf tied around her forehead, its ragged edge trailing over one shoulder. She's toying with a string of beads dangling around her neck, slipping them into a knot before slipping them over her shoulder, so that they hang down her straight, straight back – so she might more easily toy with me. I can just make out a pretty, if unremarkable face.

My deflowering took place at the advanced age of twenty-two. It was the autumn of 1968: that year of protest and revolt. Though I made no timely protest of my own as, in a hazy daze, my first experience of sexual abandon sent my virginal petals fluttering to the floor of Bren's bedroom.

One's first sexual experience, it is often said, is never forgotten. But, after its overwhelming vehemence had died down, I wonder if mine might have faded into the misty memories of my marijuana-fuelled social life, had things turned out differently.

It was another of Bren and Callum's frequent parties. Frequent largely because, in Bren and Callum's eyes, a party required minimal effort on their part. Food was most certainly not a prerequisite for two guys whose idea of a square meal was four pints of Guinness and a box of Ritz crackers. For Bren and Callum, their large and eclectic record collection lined up in apple-pie order at the start of the party (the only order in their run-down, messy flat), a dozen cans of lager, a wine box in the fridge, a stash of weed and skins in the sitting room, and, if they were *really* pushing the boat out, half a dozen packets of crisps and a couple of salted peanuts shaken into a few chipped bowls dotted about the place, was all that was needed.

Whilst still in my virginal state, I have a vague recollection of a pleasant time spent in the kitchen, where an incongruous chunk of Parmesan cheese had been found lurking behind an empty wine box in the fridge. And after the green crust had been pared from it, cheese, knife, and current joint were passed around the group, each one of us coming up with increasingly bizarre theories as to why such an exotic comestible could have found its way to Bren and Callum's food-free refrigerator. I cannot recall a single face from that group, just hands passing cheese, knife or joint one to the other – my future wife's hands might well have been amongst them. Perhaps she had already set her cap at me? Though that contraceptive turn-off came later.

Back then, in Bren and Callum's kitchen, I was a carefree, sexless zone, at one with my solitary self, with no desire to spread my seed hither and thither.

As a boy I had used the conventional method of relief to good effect and, aided by a selection of top-shelf stimulation, had continued in this way to my complete satisfaction. But I had yet to be blessed by the white-breasted whirlpool of sexual energy that was Gwyneth Bronwen Jones, yet to be consumed by her Charybdian charms, to be drowning inside her.

And so it happened that, while my college chums were high and happy, laying any swinging, pill-taking chick they could lay their carefree hands on, I was venturing where no twenty-three-year-old should ever go: I was moving not *out of*, but *into* suburbia! My feet had been reluctantly placed on this 'ladder of life' by courtesy of Gwyneth's affluent parents; my new wife and I ensconced in a pleasant, tree-lined avenue which – and I cannot recall if this is fact or fiction – in my memory, had a burial ground at its end. It was, appropriately, a cul-de-sac!

I see my pregnant wife shuffling about our pride and joy: a snazzy fitted kitchen. See her hands massaging the enlarging bump. '*Our* bump!' she would say. *Why* our *bump?* I would think. *The bump is patently in* your *body. The bump is being cooed over in your Welsh wood-pigeon coo. The bump is caressed more often by your hands than by my own. You have been the force of its creation.* Your *bump. Your damn bump!*

Gwyneth had decided our snazzy kitchen drawers must be lined with wipe-clean contact paper. I see her cutting along the red-lined grid, see her peeling back the backing paper, see her hands smoothing the green-and-white check, scattered with yellow lemon slices, on the bottom of the cutlery drawer. For some reason this banal memory cannot be wiped away. And there I am, perched on one of the two most uncomfortable stools ever made, watching Gwyneth while thinking, *This cannot be happening to me. This cannot be* my *life! This cannot be the woman who, a mere eight months ago, overwhelmed me at Bren and Callum's, who, to all intents and purposes, raped me! This Stepford wife must be an impostor. I have plans. Dreams. I have to escape! If only that guy in the kitchen hadn't run out of cigarette papers.*

I had gone to Bren's bedroom to get another packet of Rizlas from my coat pocket. Not bothering to turn on the light, I'm searching through the mound of coats when I hear the door being gently closed behind me. I turn to see the murky form coming toward me, and feel pleasantly disturbed by it. And, suddenly, I'm on top of the mound, and the murky form's on top of me. On top of me like she couldn't wait, like she'd been working up to this moment for quite a while. I can hardly breathe, half suffocated by sheepskin, the brass buttons of someone's Sgt Pepper jacket grinding into my back with every groan this unknown whirlwind emits.

Was it really *my* Gwyneth who uttered those words all men long to hear – 'Wow! You're *still* hard!' – before slipping from me, dropping her long, fringed skirt to her ankles, and floating silently from the room? Leaving me in a post-coital daze, my duck broken, my dick smarting with a more satisfying kind of satisfaction.

I have sometimes thought, if Gwyneth had stayed, if she had lain beside me, doe-eyed and adoring, giving me one of those where-do-we-go-from-here looks, my whole life might've been different. She might have remained forever the unknown woman of my first lay. But this woman appeared not to give a damn. Appeared to be of the 'she saw, she came, she conquered and she left' variety: a wicked, quick-shag, queen-of-the-night kind of woman. Every twenty-something's wet dream. Except, I suspect, even whilst shagging me amongst the sheepskin, there might've been a hint of the puppy-dog-and-slippers stratagem nestling in Gwyneth's subconscious, because, as it turned out, this particular conquest wasn't just for Christmas. It was for life!

Staggering to my feet, buttoning up my flies, I find her pants hooked around a button, attached by their label: St Michael; turquoise-blue cotton knit, a hint of minimal lace around the legs; nothing to get excited about, nothing to get off on. I should've seen those knickers as a bad sign. On the surface, the sexy siren. Beneath the skirt, bog-standard knickers. Knickers not used to regular exposures at orgies; unaccustomed to being hooked around a slain fella's fly button.

I believe it is said that a woman doesn't reach her sexual peak until her mid thirties, while my poor sex, sad unfortunates that we are, begin slithering down the flaccid slopes to impotence from the innocent age of eighteen. Gwyneth's Ben Nevis moment came that October evening in the nineteenth year of her life.

Gwyneth is cotton knit through and through. I have never been able to wean her off its utilitarian comfort. Though I have tried.

One birthday, some fifteen years ago, I presented her with an expensive pair of French knickers in red silk – a hint we might spice up our flagging sex life. She wore them once. 'But didn't they feel nice against your skin?' I asked her.

'They cut into my crotch,' she said. 'How could that feel nice?' And soon they joined the black panty girdle somewhere in the nether regions of her underwear drawer.

My wife, you see, has never been quite the same 'down there', down in that furry foreign country, since Claire's birth. A hatchet job made of the episiotomy. Done in haste because 'baby' was in foetal distress. Or so Gwyneth told me. I was dashing through the city to Waterloo station as my wife's waters broke. 'Baby' arrived too early. Husband arrived too late. Too late to see my only child breeching her way into the world. Too late to witness Gwyneth's perineum being mutilated by a pair of pinking shears. 'Obviously, sex is best avoided for a little while,' the midwife informed us. 'But, after a few weeks, everything should be fine down there.' Well, she got that one wrong, didn't she? Sex was off the agenda for months. Or was it years? It certainly felt like it. Though, episiotomy or not, I doubt that either of us was up for it anyway.

As the bump had grown, as our proto-baby began to make her disruptive presence felt, so Gwyneth grew overprotective – a mother's intuition, you might say. She said sex felt uncomfortable. Didn't feel 'quite right'. Said it might 'harm the baby'.

'That's bollocks!' I said. 'The baby'll be fine!'

'What do *you* know?' she said.

Nothing at all, it seems.

I used to wonder what might have become of us if Gwyneth hadn't become pregnant. We had a pretty good time at the beginning. Even *after* we were married, before the bump became too big. Our honeymoon was quite a bed-in. Could have knocked John and Yoko's into a cocked hat. Not Amsterdam in our case, but Nice: a nice family-run hotel, familiar to, and generously paid for by, Gwyneth's well-heeled parents, keen as they were to welcome me to the bosom of their family. It was hot stuff down there, my whirlpool wife, as warm and inviting as a Jacuzzi, bubbling over my accepting body – if a *little* less ferociously.

Naively, the fact that the nameless maelstrom's knickers couldn't have twisted themselves around my fly button never occurred to me. I stuffed them into my pocket, giving my skinny profile added pizzazz, and joined the partying throng.

About half an hour later, through the smoky haze of the hall, I see her standing by the bathroom door. 'Hi there,' she says, shuffling from one foot to the other. 'Wish whoever's in there would get a bloody move on. I am *desperate!*'

'I've got something you might need,' I tell her, pulling her pants from my pocket.

'You certainly have,' she says, and pulls me in there with her.

I watch her pee. Watch her wipe her unmutilated fanny with the turquoise knickers – Bren and Callum's hospitality not stretching to the additional bog roll required by female partygoers.

'Don't need these, do I?' she says, looking up at me, doe-eyed, and she drops them in the loo.

I feel her mouth envelop mine… And we do it again, there in the bathroom. I turn on the tap to muffle her expressive moans: the hot one, by mistake, and pretty soon we can't see each other for steam. And Callum's banging on the door screaming, 'If whoever's in there is so *fucking* desperate for a soddin bath, they can go down the soddin road to the Porchester Hall! Not drain our soddin gas meter dry!'

I reach out to illuminate the clock: 7.45; Gwyneth will soon be home. With effort I drag my torpid body to the window and pull back the curtains. Blinding spring sunshine fills the room. My squinting eyes look down at the garden. Black-stemmed bamboo sways in a gentle breeze; tulips, the colour of ripe plums, poke their heads through a sea of custard-yellow euphorbias. And I marvel at my wife's artistry, at her ability to weave this changing tapestry of texture and colour from plug and pot, and seed and sapling; envy her ability to find this conduit for her prodigious love.

We moved here twenty-six years ago. For Claire's sake. A place had come up at a good school nearby; we still had hopes for our daughter, back then. 'You're very fortunate,' we were told. 'Such places are like gold dust.'

How lucky we were.

Gwyneth soon put the little energy she had left into bringing the neglected garden back to life. As Gwyneth nurtured the garden, the garden nurtured Gwyneth, and I watched my wife, if not blossom, then at least regain some of her vigour, a faint bloom returning to her cheeks. 'It's meditative,' she informed me. 'I forget everything when I'm out there. If it works for me…?'

But I was still a young man! I was only thirty-five! I felt my biological clock had been tampered with. Felt my life hurtling toward middle age, old age. Death. 'How *can* we forget?' I yelled. 'How in *heaven's name* can we?!'

She brushed a tear from her cheek, put on her gardening gloves and walked out to the terrace. It was April, of course. A month that Gwyneth has learned to love. But April can still bring the black dog howling at my door.

I go into the bathroom, turn on the shower, and see her through the steam; remember those bright blue eyes, their dilated pupils a nose-tip from mine, see her slip the bandana from her head, see the moistened blonde waves rippling over her face.

'Hi there, hard man. I'm Gwyneth!' And Callum's still banging on the bathroom door as this woman is skilfully adjusting my equipment, and buttoning up my flies, in a way that suggests she has done this many times before.

'You couldn't be more right,' I say. 'I'm Richard, Richard Hardmann.'

'Well, hello, Dick!' she says, slithering down on her haunches to kiss my crotch. Looking up, 'Can I call you Dick?', stretching her arms around my neck, swinging her legs around my waist, and kissing me long and hard.

'I'd rather you didn't,' I say when I get my breath back.

And we cling together in the clearing steam in silent, reckless oneness, our bodies hot and damp, her naked fanny pressed against my half-buttoned crotch, my hands supporting her smooth-skinned buttocks, until she says, 'So! How do we get out of here? Is there a window we could escape through?'

'Nope!' I say. 'We'll just have to open that door and face the music. There is *no* escape.'

How right I was.

'She's a gift from God, all the same. *All* children are,' my mother informs me, when I telephone with the news that her beautiful new grandchild is destined to remain a child for the rest of my mother's grandparental life. 'But of course,' she adds, 'you'll try again soon, won't you?'

Not *quite* such a gift, then.

It was around the time of my puberty, at the start of my long passage to adulthood, that my own stealthy fumblings under the candlewick caused me to consider my fate as an only child; an only child whose mother confessed to being a 'strict' Catholic.

An early memory of my mother is of her at the lunch table: her long neck stretched up, her eyes gazing beyond the cracked ceiling rose, the dusty glass chandelier, to Our Father's spotless home on high. Then, chin lowered, closed eyes cast down to hands clasped in benediction, an incantation was uttered over the food before us. This only serving to make me suspicious as to the contents of my lunch. My mother, I concluded, rightly unsure of her culinary powers, had seen fit to plead for assistance from the Lord should her family be struck down after consuming the pea and ham soup she had prepared, and, as a consequence, the contents of my bowl remained untouched.

Though, that evening, when both of my parents appeared in robust health at the supper table, I deemed it safe to consume the tiniest piece of tinned salmon. This regime of limited sustenance continued for several days, until I became satisfied I would not be poisoned by my mother's kitchen sorcery – nor by God's. And thus I grew to skinny, suspicious pubescence, while believing my mother to be poisoned, nonetheless.

She would attend daily Mass; she would light her candle; she would go to confession. And I would wonder what it was she had to confess – save for the two almighty sins of overcooked cabbage and lumpy custard – while coming to realise that my mother was right in one respect. For she was laden with guilt: the guilt of embracing the Lord and of not embracing life. Life was borne out with a sufferance by my mother. Life was what she had been forced to go through in order to return to her Father again – since we were all 'gifts' from him in the first place. A gift of the worst kind: a gift with conditions attached. No gift at all, in fact.

I would also wonder – good Catholic that she was – why my mother had not managed to deliver a few more gifts for me, her only son: a ribbon-tied sister, one or two tag-playing brothers. Denial, I concluded, had played a large part in my mother's life. A *self*-denial, should she still desire my father, or a privation of sexual pleasure denied my father, should *he* still desire her. Or else an unspoken disavowal of her supposed 'beliefs'. A further option later occurred to me – one deemed too depressing to consider in those drab years of my childhood: the possibility that my parents no longer loved each other enough for the whole risky business of sex to ever take place.

For, amongst her 'God-given gifts', the gift of love was not heavily bestowed upon my mother. Claire, our precious little gift, was only a gift in my mother's eyes so long as

Claire remained *little*. My mother could not adjust to the awkward, lumpen teenager, to the overweight, dribbling adult her grandchild became. But who am I to cast stones? I would not visit our daughter for weeks on end. Months, at one point. To the extent that Gwyneth gave up urging me to do so, while she herself would drive there almost every day to wipe the drool from Claire's mouth, to spoon the baby-mush lunch into her mouth that would have to be wiped all over again. On one occasion Gwyneth insisted our fifteen-year-old child had uttered the word 'Mummy'. *Straws in the wind*, I thought. *Imagined sparks to lighten the gloom.*

I should have gone with Gwyneth more often. The guilt remains. But then, I had never declared, as my mother had done, never faintly considered the ghastly trick of fate that was our daughter 'a gift'.

I think my parents were attracted to the idea of living out their last years in Spain largely because it was a long way away from their grandchild. A gift-wrapped present twice a year was all the God-given love they could handle after Claire hit twenty-one. And it didn't look quite so ludicrous, did it, didn't feel *quite* so embarrassing to fold pretty paper around that Farmer John animal puzzle, or that bumper colouring book, knowing the postman would deliver it, not you yourself.

I dress slowly and go downstairs.

In the kitchen Gwyneth has put coffee in the pot, ready on the stove, and croissants in their tin, waiting to be heated: our Sunday-breakfast treat. 'The Burgundy brochures are on the table, Richard,' she has said. 'We *must* decide this weekend!'

Love, Gwyneth once said, when I suggested she ease up on her visits to Claire, is a hard taskmaster. Was I jealous of my wife's ability to give love? Or resentful of her, because of my own *in*ability?

I used to imagine a different life for myself. One completely under my control. A life in which I meet a woman, in full curvaceous bloom, whom *I* overwhelm, who succumbs instantly to my charms, and who I leave panting for more. To do the same the next day with a different woman, and the next with another, and the next, and the next. With no responsibility, no consequences… with no love.

'Ten days in Burgundian wine country,' Gwyneth pronounces, handing me the brochures. 'It'll be a nice birthday present for you!'

'But, Gwyneth,' I say. 'There's Claire…?'

Since those carefree days before my twenty-second birthday, this annual day of celebration has become a source of sadness to me. For an extra birthday gift arrived, seemingly in good order, just two days after the anniversary of my own birth. Though that second bottle of champagne, purchased for our special delivery (expected in early June), was left unchilled.

Gwyneth, unconvinced by the midwife's stamp of perfection, was, she confessed, more prepared for the news than was I. A mother's instinct, she said.

For better or worse, I go with Gwyneth now, as often as I can, and *always* on Claire's birthday. For some time our daughter came home for the day. But even Gwyneth had to admit Claire had become too big a baby for her to deal with. Now we spend the day there – well, midday until 7.30, when they usually put Claire to bed. Gwyneth reads her a bedtime story, then we slip away, feeling we've done our duty.

'We'll go see Claire the weekend before,' Gwyneth says. 'She's hardly going to notice the difference, is she? *We* need a break, Richard. We've each other to think of.'

I hear my wife's car on the gravel, light the coffee and turn on the oven. I reach the corner of the terrace as she comes through the side gate. She's smiling as she walks toward me, her body swaying in the same girlish way that, in spite of everything, she has never lost, her face beneath the extra pounds still pretty in that unremarkable way and, I think, more interesting now that suffering has etched depth into it. She wraps a green sweatshirted arm around my waist and we walk in silence into the kitchen.

'Did you sleep better last night?' she asks me, putting butter and milk on the table. 'I hope I didn't disturb you.'

'No,' I lie, 'you didn't. And yes, I slept better. I'm surfacing.'

Her hand strokes my shoulder. 'It always passes, doesn't it?' she says softly, stooping to check on the croissants. While I watch an orange-tip butterfly, its wings spread out on the brick wall outside the kitchen door, glinting in the sunshine.

'We must book this *now*!' she says, fluttering the fan of brochures under my nose. 'You may be able to say no to the birds and the bees, but not, I *know*, to a decent drop of Burgundy.' She flashes me a cheeky smile, and we are back in Bren's bedroom, we are there with Callum banging on the bathroom door, and I smile too, smile for the first time in weeks.

She puts the tray of crisped croissants on the table, reaches for a pot of jam from the cupboard, raises a warm hand to my cheek, and says, 'That's it, Dick. Keep that pecker up!' And her touch is not sexy, but soft; her look not lust, but love. And I feel hope returning. It always does.

Gwyneth pours coffee into our Sunday coffee bowls (bought on a trip to Brittany two years ago) and I feel the black dog skulking away. It gives a pathetic growl before slinking to the door. Perhaps, if I learn to growl back, it might stay away forever? If I don't roll over and allow myself to be conquered by it.

'Did you say you wanted to go to the garden centre today?' I ask my wife.

'Yes. But I can pop there myself, in my car.'

'Mine's got a bigger boot!'

She looks so pleased, so grateful. I kick the drooping dog still lurking on the terrace. It yelps, and I feel a tremendous sense of power.

'It's beautiful out there,' I say. 'I'd like us to share the day.'

The black dog whimpers and limps away into the bright April morning.

That Day

That Day

The partying on TV had brought it back to him; that and the way she'd turned her head, a glass in one hand, a bottle in the other, saying, 'Let's celebrate!'

She had worn a red dress that day. It had a halter neck and buttoned down the front: large white buttons that began beneath the line of her exposed cleavage and ended, a little too soon, he'd thought at the time, halfway down her thighs, so that when she sat down, when she crossed one smooth leg over the other, way too much flesh was revealed. 'That is *not* a dress to sit down in!' he'd told her, the day she bought it.

Her hair was still long back then. It tumbled over her tanned shoulders; it brushed her smooth back. 'OK?' she'd said, eyeing her reflection in the mirror before looking over one shoulder to where he stood in the doorway.

'OK,' he'd answered. 'Fine.'

Irritated by his under-reaction, sighing, she had lifted the weight of hair from her neck, briefly exposing her pale, vulnerable nape. And from where he stood, the backless dress had given the impression that, like some Etruscan maiden, her breasts were also exposed. *How beautiful she looks from behind*, he'd thought, watching her loop a wayward strand of hair behind her ear, feeling the pull of her body reining his in.

'Right, then!' she'd snapped, her piercing green eyes flashed briefly in his direction, 'Let's get this show on the road!' Striding past him, a blaze of red. He left to inhale her perfume trail, his gaze drawn to the narrow bands of leather rising from the soles of her sandals to criss-cross like two blood-red kisses before buckling around her ankles, as the high stacked heels took their first tentative steps down the stairs.

'She'll have a temper on her with that hair,' his mother had pronounced on first meeting her son's new girlfriend. As if Raye's wild mane might curl inside her scalp as well as out: coiling around her neurons, twisting her dendrons, screwing up her axons until they screamed for release – as he sometimes silently screamed. Raye would not give up the fight until he joined in. His mother had been right – not that he had told her so. For, like Raye in the years to come, his mother, in the years before he had come to know Raye, had grown used to getting her own way. This red-headed girlfriend was clear evidence things were going to change on that score.

He and Raye had quarrelled that day. Or, rather, had quarrelled the day before that day, their disagreement spilling over into the early hours of the day marking his wife's fortieth birthday.

He had imagined Raye entering the world in much the same way as she'd entered the bathroom that last evening of her thirty-ninth year, red-faced and raging, suspecting

Raye's parents might have intended naming their daughter Rage, but the clerk had mistaken the G for a Y.

Rarely could he recall what misunderstood word, what hapless slip of the tongue, what misconstrued phrase or action had fired Raye into Rage. Moments before he might have been looking out onto a peaceful enough panorama – a little murky maybe, not exactly a cloudless sky, but set fair enough, *he'd* thought – and then, funnelling out of nowhere, blowing him sideways, there it was. And try as he might, he could not bring its swirling violence to an end. Their course was set. He must be blown along it until all energy was spent.

Afterwards, Raye appeared oblivious of the wreckage all around her: the shocked silence of the house, the way everything felt 'flattened'. *How many times can a relationship stand up to this?* he would ask himself. But, like reversed film footage of a dynamited tower block, within days it had righted itself, he trying not to see the cracks, the fissuring fractures, the fallout brushed under the carpet.

Frequently energised by these harrowing experiences, Raye did not want release from them; had, she said, found in him the one man who could make her happy. Had told him so, yet again, at four in the morning that day, as he lay sweaty and exhausted, wishing they had not sent out all those invitations – wishing he had not agreed to Raye's idea of *A Garden Party!* A party that began at three in the afternoon and ended... 'When it ends,' she'd answered. *When it ends.*

When it ends, he'd thought.

After the storm would come the lull.

If the storm had hit him during daylight hours then this would be when Raye might be heard humming a wordless tune as she moved about the house in a state of energetic serenity, often deciding to clean the cooker, wax the floor, or to take up some other postponed domestic chore her recharged Rage batteries had given her the energy to complete. While he, deflated, run-down, head spinning with words said or not said, with love turned sour by idiocy, could barely move with the oppressive weight of, as he saw it, their failure to relate.

But, even so, come the night there would come that familiar sigh – *Never go to sleep on an argument*, was Raye's motto – her arm stretching out, her body rolling across the cool-sheeted demarcation zone, her hair curtaining his face. Sometimes she would twist a thick lock of it between thumb and forefinger, would use it like a brush. On his chin, his forehead, his nose. Anywhere! Would tickle his fancy, so to speak. It usually worked. Like Samson, Raye knew where her strength lay. Only afterwards would she speak.

Why did he give in to her so easily? Give in to the pointless war. Accept the phoney peace. This was why *she* was happy with him. She had found herself a poor schmuck who could roll over and play dumb.

'You're the *only* man for me,' she'd say.

It was 1970. He was twenty-six. His father had been dead for five years. He wasn't certain how long he himself had been dead, he only knew it felt a helluva lot longer.

Six months before he had found himself a flat. Not much more than a bedsit: a kitchenette divided off by plasterboard, which did not reach the ceiling, so that, if you were tall, as he was, you could stand on your toes and peer over into the next 'room'.

'Whatever do you want to move for?' his mother said, aghast at the very thought. 'I'll have *two* spare rooms now.'

'Two lodgers, then,' he'd replied. 'Double the income!'

In a huff, she'd gone to top up the teapot, returning to sit at the table in frosty silence.

But soon 'a nice young man' was found to fill his room: a tall, quiet, brown-haired young man, who her neighbours still believed to be her son. So he was as interchangeable as that.

He continued to help out at weekends. His mother moving south to be with him made it his duty.

'No, Mum,' he'd told her that Friday, 'can't make it tomorrow.'

It was as if he'd announced his intention to emigrate to Australia.

'But the shopping? Tea later on?'

Heavens! She was fifty-nine, not *seventy*-nine. She did not need a helping hand. Although he did enjoy the routine of it: the walk up The Broadway, the slow meander down the crowded, colourful market, her arm linked in his, his importance in her life since his father's death.

'Sunday lunch, surely?' Her voice strained with the worry of it. 'I've already bought the lamb.'

Stepping out at Sloane Square he felt he had entered an entirely different world. Felt reborn by this one act alone. To be Mike Redpath strutting his stuff along the King's Road.

To *not* be the Mike Redpath who helped his mother with the weekly shop: the young man who often felt himself too old for his time, and yet, at the same time, not quite old enough.

He was perched on a stool, sucking milkshake through a stripy straw – feeling both grown-up and free and foolishly childlike – when he saw the helmeted, purple-clad figure swinging one purple leg from the shiny black-and-chrome motorcycle, the leg, the swing of that leg, the entirety of that body-tingling shape shooting through him like an electric charge, causing him to grip the edge of the stainless-steel counter. He watched the purple arms reach up to remove the helmet. *Jesus!* The colour of it! The sun dancing on it as it tumbled to her waist. His eyes could not move from its dazzling brightness. Never wanted to turn from her again.

Depositing the helmet in the chrome pannier she turned to mount the steps to the entrance and, seeing him looking down at her, held his gaze. He had never felt further from death than at this moment.

As a child, the black ash on his father's clothes, his father's face, his father's body, the black bathwater, the black ring when the filthy black water was drained away, seemed to herald his father's death. Were forerunners for the filthy black lung hiding inside the white, scrubbed-clean, dying body. This flame-haired, purple-clad woman outside the Chelsea Drugstore at 2.28 on the afternoon of August 15th was the antithesis of blackness, was the antidote to death.

And there she was beside him. 'Hi! I'm Raye!' Her head bent forward as she'd perched on the stool, her hair brushing his cheek, gripping his heart.

'Mike. I'm Mike.'

He was waiting for her to acknowledge her mistake. Surely she'd thought him someone else? She was looking down to the overlarge watch on her wrist – finding an excuse to leave, no doubt. The man behind the counter was signalling to her.

'*Shit!* I've gotta make another delivery. Whaddaya doing *next* Saturday, Mike?'

He should lie. He should feign popularity.

'Nothing special,' he said, as nonchalantly as he could.

'Well, you are now!' And, pulling a red flyer from the breast pocket of her purple jumpsuit, she laid it before him. 'My birthday party! Be there or be square. And *don't* be late,' her lips brushed his cheek, 'or *I'll* be spoken for.' And, skipping over to the counter, she took the boxed pizza held out to her, turning back to say, 'See ya there!' before hurrying down to the street.

He watched as she put the pizza in one pannier, took the crash helmet from the other, twisted the wondrous hair on top of her head, covered it with the chrome helmet, mounted the bike and, in seconds, without a second look, was gone.

And suddenly life was glorious, was *the* most wonderful thing.

He paraded the entire length of the King's Road in a magical-mystery-tour dream. He bought two new shirts, of a kind he'd not worn before, tried on several outlandish jackets – wondering if his sideburns could be grown a little longer in six days – and, on impulse, invested in some colourful underpants: purple printed with red roses, and blue bedecked with yellow submarines, a single appropriately placed speech bubble reading, *Up periscope!* Would he ever dare wear them? Anyway, it was most likely a wind-up. There would be no party. Or else she would pretend they had never met – which they barely had.

'Dun'be crazy, Mikey.'

She might call him Mikey when she was drunk. He had liked it at first.

'You *know* I'd-never-do-id-with-anyone-bt-chew.'

She had removed the high-heeled sandals by now, but was still swaying a little as she said this.

They were gathering up the glasses that day – although, in truth, by then it was already more than three hours into the next day.

'Leave'm!' she instructed with a lackadaisical wave of her hand that so disturbed her axis, it caused her body to tilt back precariously. Fearing she might topple to the stone terrace, his body felt inclined to rise to prevent it doing so. But his mind had other ideas. What did he care?

'Lezzdo-it t'morrer,' she said.

He remained on his haunches, picking up the broken pieces of glass, dropping them, one by one, into the plastic bucket, and in spite of getting through several glasses of wine himself that long, long day, feeling disgustingly sober, and somewhat depressed that the idea of drunken escapism should appeal to him now.

Despite her inebriated state, Raye had managed to half-fill the large round tray she was carrying with glasses. Holding it close to her body, beneath her breasts, the breasts, half-exposed by the plunging halter neckline, appeared to be resting on it, like an offering. And, despite what he was feeling (or was not feeling), looking up at her, he wanted to 'do it', there and then, amongst the broken glass on the terrace, wanted to roll over it, wanted to feel the shards stabbing, painfully, into his flesh. Moreover, he wanted Raye to feel the pain of it. And yet, at the same time, wanted never to touch her, *never* to want her again.

'But *you* wanted to, didn't you?!' he insisted. 'You wanted to do it with him. You've wanted to do it with other people many times before now. You just daren't take the risk.'

'Mikey,' putting on her fake little-girl pout, 'y'*know*, if-I-wannid-enuff, ife-no inni… inni… bizions-on-thad-score. Whoevver-iddiz.'

And, lowering the wobbling tray to the terrace, she proceeded to unhook the halter neck, undo the large white buttons and let the dress fall on top of the glasses on the tray. Why, he wondered, looking up at the smooth curves of her thighs, her buttocks, those breasts, beautiful to him in the glow of the kitchen light, had she chosen to spend the entire day without pants?

'C'mon, Mikey.' A hand held out.

The lawn was wet with dew. Her mouth tasted of sour wine. Her hair smelt of cigarette smoke and hash. It was the best of times and the worst of times. He remembers shivering inside as her naked body shivered against his. 'Lez-getta-bed,' she said, getting up and swaying to the kitchen door.

Lying there, he heard the croaking of a toad and thought he would much prefer to sleep alone in the garden.

'*Mikey!*' Her breasts and hair hanging from the bedroom window. 'Dun-forgedda-lockup!'

Breasts and hair. Surely he loved more of her than that?

'*Mmm, mmm, mmm-mmm, mmm, mmm-mmm, dah de-dah dah...*'

She was tunelessly humming along to it. Perhaps with that tune one could do little else?

'Is that your third glass or your fourth?'

'I dunno. Anyway, it's your fault for not going halves with me on the bottle. If this isn't cause for celebration, I don't know what is. *To the future!*'

She chinked her glass against his teacup, and he sees her that day, remembers the moment he decided it was all over between them.

She had been talking to a man. He has long since forgotten who that man was. Maybe he never knew. The man and Raye had been sitting on the low wall near the barbecue, his wife showing way too much thigh. Had she got off on the frisson of knowing how exposed she was under that exposing dress? Turning from the man, tossing her silky hair over one shoulder, Raye had seen him there: leaning against the warm brick wall of the house, a glass in his hand, looking back at her.

Until that moment he had been feeling reasonably at ease with the world, untroubled by his wife's need to toy with another man's affections. It was a harmless game. She had played it before. And this was *her* day. She was beautiful. Was desired by others. But was his. It had been the way of things for thirteen years. Raye's ballsy brazenness was a small price to pay. Until that brief glance he had taken pride in his wife's ability to pull a man so far, but no further, and to still want to 'do it' with her husband.

She had been laughing, her milky-smooth neck arching back, hair rippling down, when, turning from the man in question, across the expanse of garden, their eyes met. Hers saying, *Heavens! It's my husband. I'd almost forgotten he existed.* His: *Until this moment I was convinced you loved me. Now I see it's all a game to you.*

D:Ream were still singing that damn song, the champagne bottle beside Raye was almost drained, and Raye was still beside him. A dream come true, or a nightmare? Sometimes, he supposed, it was a bit of both.

He said, 'Do you honestly think "things" are going to get better?'

'Sure they are. He's a good guy. Genuine. You can tell, can't you?'

'Can't say *I* can.'

Not sure I ever could, he thought, taking another mouthful of tea.

'Life is but a D:Ream,' he said.

'What?'

'Never mind.'

It was a similar time of year as this: late April; the Easter holidays, he supposes. Unusual, his parents holidaying at Easter time. Though by then, he realises now, they must have known their time together was limited and had resolved, as his father used to say, *to make the most of it.*

To escape their claustrophobic company – his mother forever fussing over him, his father, as if still at home in his green armchair, his head in a newspaper, the sad irony of the never-had-it-so-good headlines apparent only to his parents – he had ambled over to Filey Brigg. His mother's warnings of the danger of starfish and of climbing too high ringing in his ears, he had clambered higher than she would have wished, relieved to be away from them, yet feeling himself a lonely, only boy who, like the limpets clinging to the rock pool's edge, might never be free.

Coming to rest on a rock, looking back up the beach, he saw them, set apart from the smattering of families strewn about the sand: two isolated figures on their fold-up stripy chairs, heads close together, the blue-and-yellow windbreak protecting them from the buffeting breeze. And seeing them there, so small, so far away, so distant, he wanted both to escape their love forever, to shake its smothering weight from his skinny shoulders, and at the same time to scramble down the rocks and race back across the sand to bind himself to them forever.

Was there something in him that sought to silently rail against those he held dear? A stubborn perversity. A kind of cowardice. At least, he considered, watching her raise the last glass of the champagne to her lips, Raye's anger, irritating as it may have been, was out in the open. Was honest. As was her overt fondness for wine – should she be in party mood, for alcohol of any description.

Had his own obsessive tea-drinking, itself bordering on an addiction, been purposely developed as a counterweight to his wife's excesses? Proof of his own purity?

It was the same back then. His father being a coal miner had produced in him a congenital aversion to all things manual, all jobs in which a man might blacken his hands. Jobs George Orwell might glorify. But there was no *pier* at Wigan. There was no *glory* in coal dust. No superiority could be found in slogging your guts out to fuel other people's kettles when, in the end, you yourself would lose the power to lift your own teacup.

Heavens! She was singing those godawful words now. Christ! They were *all* at it: Prescott, Mandelson, Kinnock, standing like a load of groupies waiting for their newly crowned 'king', smiling from ear to ear just like him.

'A new start!' Raye was saying. 'With a dynamic, young Prime Minister. Isn't that something to smile about? Things *will* get better.'

'You reckon?'

'Yeah. Sure they will.'

All childlike enthusiasm, she pulled her legs up onto the sofa and, tucking them beneath her, turned away from him to give the celebrations on the South Bank her full attention.

She said, 'We should've gone down there!'

And suddenly he felt inordinately fond of the increasing flesh of her chin, the drooping profile of her breasts beneath the red-and-white top, her belief in a future that that would never come to pass – or, if it did, would pass all too quickly.

'I suspect things will remain much the same,' he said. 'That is, they'll swing back and forth in the same old ding-dong, swingometer way, but, ultimately, nothing much'll change.'

Though Raye's swings had changed: they were less violent now. And now she could blame her hormones, she would often apologise for her moods; sometimes, but less frequently now, 'apologising' in bed, sometimes, her lips brushing his cheek, saying, 'Sorry, Mike. Fucking hormones', before turning over and turning off the light.

It was cringe-making, watching them all crowded up to the barrier, swaying back and forth: the political equivalent of watching your parents dance the twist at your sixteenth birthday party. 'England Swings (Like a Pendulum Do)'. Crappy songs then, crappy songs now.

'...now that I've found *you!*' she joined in, looking back at him, her glass raised.

'For better or worse!' he said, raising his teacup to the screen.

'Boring old cynic,' she said, downing the last of the champagne.

Another Time

Another Time

'**M**y God!' you say. 'Is it?'

Wondering if a negative response might please you just as much as a positive one, if, face to face, you've had no choice but to react in this way, might have walked on by had you caught sight of me from a distance, reverting to the insecure young woman you once knew, I hear myself say, 'I'm afraid it is.'

'Well, well,' you say, still blocking the entrance to the café. 'My oh my!' As three people push past us and I fear I might lose the vacant corner table I'd spied through the window. Wonder this while wondering how you *could* know me now, could recognise me in this bustling crowd? Since, as far as *I* know, as far as I've been told (by those who know me better than you ever could), I look quite unlike the brown blob of a girl who once worshipped at your feet. And yet, at a glance, you have seen through the sheen of red on my hair, seen beneath the carefully applied lipstick, the blusher brushed just so, so as to bring out the cheekbones risen through that comfort-eating girl's fleshy face. Your recognition of these facts, recognition of that girl, annoying me.

And, even more annoyingly, you do not say, *My, how you've changed. You look* great! No. Your face turning from mine, opening the door, as casual as you please, you say, 'Let's grab ourselves a catch-up coffee!'

As if you and I had *caught up* like this months ago, not eighteen years ago. The city that offered you up then, offering you to me now, out of the blue. Typical you, popping up on this bright blue day. No mizzled greyness for you. Oh no. You must shine. *Do* shine. Sparkle as you stride to the corner table I would have taken had I been allowed to stride before you.

Nor do you ask if I have time for this *catch-up coffee.* Assuming, as far as *you* are concerned, I am always available.

'You look well.' Said as if I had just emerged from a weekend at a health farm. How could I not look well compared to the way I looked the last time you saw me? Yet there is no embarrassment on your part, no desire to make amends, to apologise in any way. 'Cappuccino?'

As if a hit of caffeine and a few teaspoons of chocolatey froth is all it will take.

'Actually,' I say, 'I was coming in here myself. Coming in for lunch.'

'*Lunch?* Ooh...' Looking down at your watch, wondering if you've bitten off more than you can chew. Wondering if, despite the red hair, the green jacket, the veneer of sophistication, I might become that wailing witch of a woman you ran from, talons clasping at your wrists, begging you not to go. Would you have stayed if *I* had promised you heaven? Not bloody likely. Not you. 'Well... I suppose... um... Yes. *Yes!* Why *not* lunch?'

'What I meant was, I am *meeting* someone here for lunch.'

And, taken off guard, unused to anything resembling a rebuttal – especially from me – you reach for the scarf you'd slung on top of the briefcase on the empty chair beside you. 'In that case—' you say.

'No need to rush,' I say, softening as always, 'I'm early. Promised to nab a good table, you see.'

'Your husband?' Relaxing now the pressure's off. 'Partner? Whatever the correct term is these days.' Elbows resting on the good table you yourself had claimed, picking up the menu, flicking it over. 'How about I order us a bottle of wine? A glass of vino and a few olives will do me. You and your… *companion* can have the rest on me. White or red?'

'Red.'

You smile approvingly, remembering the spritzer-drinking mouse you loved to shag. You yourself more than capable, quite masterful, in fact, after a whole bottle of Cab Sav.

You hail the waitress. She comes in an instant. You like that. *Loved* that. 'Oh,' you'd say, 'over already?', delighting in the power you had to turn me on.

You order the wine without checking what they have. The waitress nods. Of course they have it. Why would they not?

'And some mixed olives and breadsticks. Pronto! If you don't mind.' Turning back to me, 'Yes,' you say, 'you were often early. And *I* was frequently late.' Said with some pride.

Wishing I'd not been so eager, had had the courage to appear not to care, I say, 'I was late once.'

'Oh?' you say, pretending to recall meetings long since wiped from your memory bank. 'I don't remember.'

We take turns spiking the olives, you the black, me the green, and move on to safer ground. Politics. Your subject then and now. Except now you are no longer a lecturer in it.

Now you are 'a political advisor to the Labour Party'.

'Does it still exist?' I say ironically.

You raise an eyebrow above one of your darkly beautiful eyes. 'OK,' you say, '*New* Labour', and go on to tell me you have co-authored their manifesto, *New Labour, New Life for Britain*. 'I'm rather proud of my input,' you tell me.

I'm not surprised. You always took great pride in your achievements – in everything you did. 'Hence the red scarf!' I say.

You smile and take a large gulp of wine.

'Though, come to think of it, shouldn't it be pink?'

Still smiling, perhaps surprised to find you remember something else about me, you say, 'You always were a radical in sheep's clothing.'

'Would that be a woolly liberal, now, do you think?'

'*Very* good!' Adding another olive stone to the pile on your side of the dish. *He loves me, he loves me not, he loves me…* 'Still sharp beneath all that woolliness.'

Your attention diverted, your gaze, drawn to someone who has just come in, moves from my face. It's quite like old times. You appear captivated by this person, who must be weaving through the tables toward us. Coming to our table? I don't turn around, don't wave a welcoming hand, but continue looking at you, trying to gauge that look. Admiration? Taking pleasure in beauty? Or lust? The lech in you unable to lie down. I was not the only one. Perhaps after me they got even younger?

'Hi!' She leans to kiss my cheek, sits down, takes a breadstick from its tall glass, snaps it in two, sinks her Hollywood-white teeth into one of them.

'My daughter: Rhiannon.'

'Rhiannon? Unusual, yet familiar.'

'My grandmother's middle name,' Rhiannon tells you. 'Mum's half Welsh. But maybe you already knew that?'

'Maybe I did.'

A kind of honesty, I suppose.

You ask Rhiannon what subject she's taking at university.

'Not there yet!' she tells you. 'A Levels next year.'

You tell her she looks older than seventeen. She likes that. Is charmed by you already.

'Then Cambridge, I expect.'

'There's confidence for you!' Looking at me as if to say, *Obviously not inherited from her mother.*

'Where did you go?' Rhiannon asks you.

'Oxford,' you tell her.

Rhiannon says she *might* go there 'if forced to'. And smiling at her audacity, you swig the last sip of wine from your glass and prepare to leave us.

We look up at you, risen from your chair, Rhiannon turning to look at me, looking at you. Gazing into the shallow darkness of your eyes, I wonder what I ever saw in them. Know I never got beyond them. Yet something in me still wants to move towards you. If I did, would you draw me close to that soft black roll-neck, to the speckled wool of your jacketed shoulder? Would I feel anything if you did? And yet, to have that rush, to want someone like that again…

I watch you loop the red scarf around your neck, tuck the black briefcase under your arm, and think how beautiful you look, even now. Your student, your slave, your subject, still objectifying your film-star looks, still caught up in the Tinseltown glitter that travels with you. What a fall guy

I was. What a fool. In admiring you I was attempting to admire myself, was hoping to turn myself into someone I *could* admire: that insignificant, mouse-coloured girl who had trapped a cat as cool as you – for a little while.

Trying to read Rhiannon's inscrutable expression, it comes to me: that one time she saw your face. A dull autumn day. Trapped in that tiny, gardenless flat. Going to the photograph album to bring you back to life, back to *my* life. Do you remember? Of course you don't. Why would you need to?

I had bagged a passer-by. Felt bold in doing so. Although at first, not looking best pleased, you complied, a long-fingered hand on my hair pulling me close, tucking my head into your neck. You didn't ask for copies. I didn't force them on you. But we did look happy in those photographs taken on Brighton beach. Our holiday snaps. Our weekend away – or rather, our one night. Rhiannon must have been seven when she saw them, I almost twenty-seven, but feeling much older, and no doubt still dreaming of getting you back. Ridiculous. I had never possessed you in the first place.

Did my daughter question the way I looked at your photograph then? Or was she drawn, as her mother was drawn, to the tanned face, the brown-tinged blackness of your hair, that smile? Did she ask who you were? I don't recall mentioning your name. But may have done. I expect it was one of those talking-to-myself, sobbing-to-myself sort of days. There were quite a few. The drizzling bleakness of the sky, my whingeing daughter spraying her tears every which way. Why should I not leak your precious name; repeat it to someone other than myself?

'Right!' you say. 'Better leave you to eat.'

'Why not stay?' Rhiannon's eyes fixed on yours. 'Eat with us!' Then, in a strangely coquettish tone, 'I know so little about you.'

'Another time,' you say, producing neither card, address book nor mobile phone on which to record contact numbers, adjusting your scarf, thinking, *How do I get out of this in my usual charming, disarming way without appearing a bit of a heel to this beautiful young woman?*

I feel the warmth of your hand on my shoulder.

'Enjoy your lunch,' you say, stepping aside to let the waitress pass. Then turning, flashing that smile in our direction, you move through the tables with the swagger of a born optimist, a New Labour man full of New Life for the New Britain he believes is coming his way. The old Britain written off. Redundant.

Do I want you to turn around? I used to want it so much. Want you *never* to walk away from me. Used to look down from my bedsit window willing your eyes to look up. Used to stand on the platform willing your head to turn, your hand to wave as the tube train disappeared, watching you go again. Hoping. Dream-catching. But dreams *do* unwind. And love has a way of screwing up your mind. It was a favourite song of yours: 'Rhiannon'. I would sing it then, but not believe it. I believed in you, you see. Believed I was living a dream having you, believing you loved me.

'*Wait!*' Rhiannon's voice loud in my ear. 'Wait a minute!'

The couple at the next table turn to stare at us, to stare at you.

'*Dad!*'

And this time you do turn around. This time, stopped in your tracks by that one syllable, your head spins in my direction. And, for a moment, the face that turns to us is drained of charm, looks middle-aged. There is an emptiness in that look. A sudden, recognisable loss. For what you might have had then? Or what you might lose now?

You are moving back through the tables towards us. Loosening the red noose round your neck, you sit down, look first at Rhiannon, then at me. 'My eyes,' you say.

Yes. *Your* eyes, wondering if you had wondered that several minutes ago, had known who you were walking away from, as I look at you both across the table: father and daughter, side by side, two peas in a pod.

'Christ!' The man who co-wrote New Labour's manifesto shakes his head, unable to string more than two words together.

'Here!' Rhiannon hands you the menu, as cool as you please. 'I've already decided.'

Should I chastise my daughter for this? Or be grateful to her? I admire her for it. Marvel at her ballsiness. *Now that could only have come from her father*, I think, as in stunned silence you pretend to scan the menu.

'Jesus!' Your fingers anxiously combing through your dark, silky hair.

Only then do I notice the narrow gold band on what some might call their ring finger. You never wore a wedding ring back then. What a new man you've become, coming out in this way.

A Woman Walks Into a Bar...

A woman walks into a bar... No. Let's get this joke right from the start.

An *Irish* woman walks into a bar, sees a man perched on a stool by the bar in this bar, walks up to this perched man and says, 'I think,' – get this – 'I *think* you might be my husband.' And then, here comes the corker, the line that'll make you laugh fit to piss yourselves, 'Could you tell me... *are* you my husband?'

Well, I don't know whether to laugh or cry.

You see, she's not exactly my type, this woman. Looks to me to be a tad older than my own forty-three years. Not that, in normal circumstances, I'd mind an older woman coming on to me right now. It's just, this one's let herself go a bit. Would have been a looker a few years back. Could be still, I suspect. Thing is, she has the weather-beaten, dishevelled look of – how can I put this politely? – an *outdoors* woman. Though I'm pleased to say the resultant bodily odours incumbent of that lifestyle – and I'm not talking magnetic, fuck-me pheromones here – have been mercifully suffocated, but not *entirely* smothered, by the distinct whiff of alcohol exuding from her. Cheap beer? Cider? Meths? Though something in her face tells me she's not quite reached the rock-bottom meths stage yet.

This is how it starts, fella, I tell myself; *it starts with you perching on this bar stool at three in the afternoon.* Tell myself this as her questioning green eyes search my face.

She's got a fading bruiser of a black eye (puke yellow with a tinge of yuck green between the crow's feet) covering half her cheek. And although I've had a couple of beers and a chaser – or was it a couple of shots and one beer? – and although I know for certain I am *not* this woman's husband (though, if I were, would I admit it to her, the state she's in?), I hear myself saying, 'No, I don't think I am.' Thinking, *What the hell do you mean by that, you idiot?! This is not the sort of woman you want to encourage, now, is it? Life can't be that bad, surely. I mean, you're hardly going to take her back to your flat.*

Well, hardly a flat. Barely more than a room. A *studio apartment*! What joy! I'm back where I started twenty-two years ago. But bijou as my studio apartment is, it still manages to eat up a large part of the small pizza-the-action left to me after the bulk of my dosh is consumed by my ex-wife (who I know is not this wino) and my two kids (fast becoming my ex-kids), who I might consider disowning should they walk into this bar and say, *Excuse me, are you the man who was once our dad?* Except they wouldn't say, 'Excuse me', since under their lazy mother's laissez-faire management, there appears to be a downward slide when it comes to the manners side of things. No. If my teenage offspring *had* walked in here right now, they'd most likely have said, *Oi, mate, you look sorta like the arsehole who used to live with our mum. Are you that particular waste-of-space wanker?* Familiar, familial forms of abuse picked up from their mother over the past few years.

She's still looking at me, this woman: scrutinising my face as if checking me out to see if I've made a mistake.

Meanwhile, I'm looking down at her hands. See that, apart from the dirt under her nails and the nicotine stains between her fingers, the skin on their bony backs is quite pale, quite unlike that of her worn-out face. A few seconds of silence leaves a door open for her to say, 'You're sure?'

Come on, *lady,* I'm thinking, *you are really not in a condition to do the hard sell on this one. What more can I say?* Thinking, come to think of it, it was *three* shots and *two* beers. Well, it's been a bummer of a week. A week that's not getting any better, if I'm the sort of man that looks like husband material to this lost and battered soul.

'Yes,' I tell her, 'I am sure.'

Was there a slight Sean Connery slur to that S? Maybe it was *three* beers and three shots?

Still she stares at me. And, for some reason, the look on the face looking into mine makes me say, 'Sorry about that. But why don't I buy you a drink anyway?'

And she smiles, as any alky would at the offer of a free drink; as I might if anyone were to offer one to me. As I would.

Out of the corner of my eye I catch sight of the barman, at the other end of the bar. See him shake his head, while taking money from the only other sad fucker with nothing better to do than prop himself up on alcohol this fine autumn afternoon. See the barman moving down the bar towards me with an *Eh, mate, you are* distinctly *lowering the tone* look on his face.

'Just a quick one!' I add, not wanting this woman, or the barman, to get the wrong idea. 'I've to be somewhere in twenty minutes.'

If only that were true.

She asks for a whisky. I buy her a double. The barman slams the glass on the bar with a *Nice to have your dosh, mate, but this better be your last order* look on his face.

'And another beer for me!' I say.

He scowls some more.

'Make that an alcohol-free one, if you please,' I add, imagining a nightmare scenario where I actually *do* take this woman back to my place.

Christ almighty! What *am* I doing?

The barman slams down the beer in the same weary way, a worried look cast in the woman's direction, who, hand on the seat, is contemplating taking up the perch next to mine.

'And I'd be grateful,' the barman says, giving me my change, 'if you'd be so kind as to escort your *girlfriend* over there to the table by the door. Or, better still, take her outside, where the air is fresher.'

I see the woman's hand slip from the leather seat and feel… well, *feel* for her, feel for the state she's in.

'These stools have only just been re-covered, you know,' the barman says. Adding, 'We were *attempting* to go a bit upmarket!'

'*I say!*' I say. 'Though aren't you bucking the trend? Thought things were levelling out at last in our them-and-us society. Come the revolution, we will be one people.'

'Pull the other one!' the barman says, turning to empty the dishwasher.

And the woman who is not my wife and I take our drinks outside to one of the half-dozen empty tables littering the pavement.

'Sorry,' is the first thing she says.

'No problem,' I say.

She tells me her husband's name was Patrick, that she thinks I might resemble him in some way.

'Was he a good husband?' I ask her.

She hesitates. 'I'm not sure,' she says. 'It seems so long ago. I remember a few good times. The good times were OK, I think. My memory…' She looks down into her whisky. 'I've forgotten so much…' her voice trailing off into barely a whisper, 'lost so much… So little left to hang on to.'

'Well, here's to the here and now, then!' I say, for want of something better, while realising it's a pretty crass thing to say, and we clink glasses.

'Thanks for this,' she says, taking a large gulp of whisky. 'This helps!' Pausing to gaze into the depleted glass, before adding, 'Or hinders.'

And I give her a five-minute résumé of my trouble-and-strife divorce.

'Now my kids despise me,' I finally say.

'I don't have kids,' she says, 'thank God. Or they sure as hell would despise *me*.' And she smiles a sad, ironic smile. A pretty smile, had she been cleaned up a bit.

A dirty, bulging canvas backpack sits on the chair beside her, all its pockets stuffed full to busting, one with a hole in it. She catches me eyeing it.

'My life!' she says, patting it in the way you might your pet dog. 'It has come down to this.'

And I'm thinking what a sweet voice she has, that faint Dublin twang. *Has she been down and out there as well as in London?* I wonder, as we sit inhaling traffic fumes beneath the darkening sky. Wonder how such a sweet-voiced, gentle-sounding woman *could* come down to this. And, suddenly, I snap myself out of such wonderings. Christ almighty, I don't *want* to wonder about some strange woman I don't know. I have my own problems to pull me down without bothering about yours, lady who walked into a bar. And, jumping up, I say, '*My God!* Just noticed the time! I'll be late! You take care now!' And I hurry away without so much as a backward glance.

Though, back 'home' in my dishevelled studio, I rather wish I *had* looked back, had turned to smile in her direction. Had wished her luck, at least. Even wish I'd stayed a bit longer, seen if I could've helped her out somehow. Not that I've got any money to spare. There was a gentleness to her I liked. A gentleness that made me fear for her survival on the streets.

'I'm Katherine!' she'd called after me. 'What was *your* name?'

'*Matt!*' I called back, not looking back. '*Matthew!*'

I'm with someone else now. Polly and me may just stay the course. It's not a bed of roses, she and I. But neither is it the prickly scratch-game gamble it was with the ex and me.

Just when I'm getting it together with Polly, getting my life back together, the ex comes over all sweetness and light.

The kids still haven't managed it, though. The ex says she's working on them on my behalf. Knows it must be painful for me. *That's rich*, I think, *coming from you. Since it was you who turned them against me in the first place.*

I think of her sometimes: the woman who walked into the bar. Katherine. Twelve months on and she still comes back to me every now and then.

Sometimes I'll picture how she might look after a few weeks of decent life, all scrubbed up, a spot of make-up on, a splash of scent behind her ears. Think of her and wonder, *Has she managed to pull herself up from the gutter? Or did she fall deeper still? Is she six feet under?* I've even imagined her and me as an item – her all spruced up, of course.

And once, would you believe it, I had a wet dream about her. Felt a bit sick when it came back to me next morning.

Went looking for her a couple of weeks after that. Something in me said, *Perhaps she was on to something, that woman.* This was before I met Polly, of course. Though I confess to having an occasional flash since Pol and me shacked up. A recurring madcap thought that won't quite go away. Perhaps that woman intuitively knew, in less straitened circumstances, we'd have made a go of it, she and I?

I roamed the streets in that part of town for several days. Walked from one street hang-out to another, from cardboard-city squares to occupied underpasses that have become no-go areas.

'I wouldn't go down there if I was you!' a woman at a nearby bus stop warned, my foot on the top step. 'You either take your life in your hands with the bloody traffic, crossing over the top, or risk being robbed, or worse, venturing down through that health-hazard hellhole! I leave fifteen minutes earlier these days. Wait here for the bus to get me over to the other side.'

'Think I'll risk it,' I tell her.

'Council should clear 'em out!' she says.

'Or house them?' I suggest.

'You reckon that lot'd pay the rent?'

'More would than wouldn't, I suspect,' I say. '*If* they were given a job – and a chance. Better crack on!'

And I descend to the Underworld, leaving her still moaning.

There were a lot of them down there. But no sign of the woman who walked into the bar. I asked quite a few – those that were together enough to listen and answer: the silent, voiceless majority.

'There was this red-headed woman I once met,' I'd say. 'Her name was Katherine. Don't suppose you've seen her around lately?'

But no. No luck.

It's two years later, a couple of months after my father's sudden death, that I come across it.

I'm back home with my mother, looking through a big box of photographs – as you do at these times – when my hand settles on a group shot; a family party: an anniversary, birthday, something like that. Must be nearly fifty people trying to squeeze into the frame.

Why are you studying this photograph? I ask myself. *What is it to you? You who doesn't own a camera. You who no longer takes holiday photos. You who doesn't even have a couple of treasured shots of his kids framed on his desk at work: those sweet little kiddy-kins who were going to be your entire world. You who has even deleted the two school shots you kept in your wallet for a decade – I mean, come on, there's only so much bad-mouthing one man can take from his own flesh and blood before he cracks.*

I take the photo to the French doors, open to the garden, stopping at the bureau en route to get my dad's old magnifying glass from the drawer in order to examine these small faces as systematically as Sherlock Holmes. I note the old brick wall behind the smiling throng is the one I look out to now – now half-hidden by ivy – and see it was taken in the garden of my childhood home. Panning down the pile of partying people, I see a young girl in a green dress, long red hair trailing over her shoulders, pale face smiling at the camera. See her again, this time not through the magnifying lens but in my mind's eye, her face gazing up into mine. See the two of us standing beneath the mistletoe in the front hall of the house I'm standing in now. The girl would have been thirteen or so, I a couple of years older.

Returning to the sitting room with a tray of tea, my mother says, 'You know, Matthew, now your dad's no longer with us, Bekkah and Jude have started coming over for Sunday lunch again. I do the usual roast. Which is good for me, and goes down well with the two of them. Claire was never much of a cook, was she?'

'Not up to your standard, Mum, no. But she was hot stuff with the oven chips and fish fingers when the kids were small!'

'Anyways,' Mum goes on, 'I was thinking, why don't you come and join us next Sunday? It'd be a way of keeping up with them, of healing the wounds.'

'I dunno, Mum. It might just open up those wounds some more. I might end up driving them away from *you*. And we don't want that, do we?'

'Course not,' she says, 'but I honestly don't think that'd be the case, Matthew.' Walking over to where I'm standing. 'I'll just let that tea brew for another minute.'

'Seems my kids don't have too high an opinion of the men in this family,' I say.

'They're teenagers,' she says, 'they'll get over it.'

Ever the optimist, my mum. She had to be, marrying my dad.

'You reckon?' I say.

She peers at the photograph. 'Have you found yourself in there yet?' she asks. 'It was our silver wedding anniversary. We pulled out all the stops. Remember? There's you! Look! There! Just behind… Now, what was her name? *Katey!* That was it! Sweet little girl, she was. She had quite a crush on you, didn't she?'

'Did she?'

'I think *you* rather liked her.'

'Did I?'

'But she was just a young, quiet country girl, moved over from Ireland. And you were keen on that Petra at the time, weren't you – or thought you were.'

'Was I? Petra…?' But nothing comes to mind.

'Tall, skinny, bleach-blonde punk hair,' my mother reminds me. 'Left for art school. Remember?'

'Vaguely,' I say.

'She broke your heart for at least a month afterwards.'

'Did she now?' Still nothing. 'And Katey?' I ask.

'I'm sure her young heart was broken when they had to move suddenly like that. Her father got the sack, didn't he? And there was some family trauma I can't recall. In any event, they had to up sticks. They'd only moved in the year before, poor things.'

'I kissed her under the mistletoe once,' I confess.

'You flirt, you!' my mum teases. 'And you mooning around over that haughty Petra. But no doubt Katey's heart mended almost as quickly as yours. The young don't hurt for long, do they? Wish that were true of the old,' she adds mournfully.

'And of my kids,' I say, putting an arm round her shoulder.

'Here's hoping!' she says.

She's been there since that afternoon, has Katherine: lodged somewhere at the back of my mind. Sometimes walking into the foreground, sometimes coming to me in a dream, all cleaned up. And sometimes she'll return as that pale, freckle-face girl, those green, watery Irish eyes looking up at me, looking for all the world like she loves me.

Now here's a funny story. Here's a real good one.

A woman walks into a bar, goes up to a man perched on a bar stool by the bar and says, 'Could you tell me, are *you* my husband?'

And the man looks into the woman's green eyes and says, 'No, I'm not your husband. But if you clean up your act I might be willing. Let's give it a try, shall we?!'

And the woman looks up, all smiles, looks as if she doesn't give a fuck that I'm *not* her husband, she just wants to be with *me*.

Now that's the kind of joke that makes me wanna cry my eyes out.

A man walks into a bar, a bar he has not frequented for a couple of years or more, perches on one of the battered leather bar stools and says to the barman, 'Looks like you've been letting the wrong clientele in here since the last time I passed by.'

The barman looks at the man quizzically.

'I mean,' the man goes on, 'these leather stools were newly covered back then. I should've thought they would've *improved* with age, not worn out. Did you decide to lower your standards after all? Let anyone in off these mean streets of town?'

'Eh?' goes the barman.

'Look at the state of them!' the man goes. 'The leather's all cracked!'

'That, my friend,' the barman informs the man, 'is more to do with the bog-standard *so-called* leather I was flogged, than *our* clientele.'

'You mean,' the man says, 'you were sold a pup?'

'It might've been better if we'd been sold several pup *skins*. No, turns out we were sold liquid cow!'

'*What?* Hope it doesn't come in a bottle. Hope you're not selling it!'

'Did you know,' the barman explains, 'they grind up the crap bits and spray on the flippin' stuff? It was cheapskate,' his index fingers make speech marks in the air, 'leather!'

'Well, tan their hides!' the man says.

The barman looks at the man for a minute, looks at me a bit like she looked at me that day, and says, 'Hey! You look familiar. Yeah… It's coming back to me now. You're the guy who came in quite a bit a year or so ago.'

'A bit more than a year ago,' I say. 'And I came in a bit too much. But yeah, that could have been me.'

'Yep! *You* are the weirdo who brought a filthy wino into my bar and bought her a drink!'

'*Excuse me!*' I say to the barman. '*I* am the guy who was sitting on this very stool, innocently sipping his drink on an autumn afternoon (and, I might add, steadily increasing your profit margins), when a down-and-out woman, seeing me from the open door, walked into your bar in the mistaken belief I was her husband.'

'*Christ!* Is that a fact?' He continues polishing the glass he's holding, then says, 'And were you?'

'What?'

'Were you – *are* you – her husband?'

'No! I *was* not. *Am* not. But, in retrospect, I think I probably should've been.'

The barman gives me another quizzical this-guy-is-bonkers look and says, 'Reckon you might have saved her from a life of grime, do you?'

'Pretty damn certain I would have. Yeah.'

'What can I get you, Saint Saviour?' the barman says.

Fifteen minutes later, about to go on my way, I'm slipping off my perch when the barman says, 'Thought you'd be staying for another one or three.'

'Nope. Not this man. I've decided I want to live. With or without ex-wife, ex-kids and ex-lovers.'

'It must be that charm of yours that drives them away.'

'Must be. Au revoir!' I say, turning to walk to the door.

'Ciao!' the barman says. And then, 'Hold on, mate!'

I do a U-turn. 'Oh...' I say, slipping my hand into my breast pocket.

'No,' he says, 'put that wallet away! You're all paid up! All those exes of yours brought it back to me. Another one of your many lovers was in here a few weeks back, asking after you. At least, your description fits the bill. I seem to remember... weren't you... John? Mark? No. Hang on, you were that other saint... Matthew, wasn't it?'

'I was and am that mortal man,' I say. 'Well done, you!' Thinking, *Could it be...?* 'Did she have red hair and green eyes?' I ask him.

'She had red hair. Don't recall the eye colour.'

'Did she look in a bad way?'

'Well, let's put it this way: if *that* was bad, then bring on the good. Lovely-looking woman, she was. Quite a cracker. Wondered if I had an address or phone number for you. Said she wanted to thank you for something.'

'Has she been back?'

'Not to my knowledge. But I'm not here day and night – though it sometimes feels like it. Gavin, my other half, might have had the pleasure and not told me. Though if he has, he's toast! I wrote her name down... He opens the till. It's in here somewhere...'

He pulls out a scrap of paper. 'Here it is! Katherine was her name.'

'The woman who nearly soiled your fake-leather stool!' I inform him.

'The wino? *No way!* This woman was well-groomed, well-dressed, and smelled of something a tad more seductive than cheap cider and street piss.'

'I assure you it was the very same. *Must* have been. I know no other Katherine.'

'Who knows, after a few shots, you might have had a quick fumble and forgotten. It happens.'

The silly thing was, my heart was racing like the clappers. I'd not felt so happy, so patently alive, for years.

'Don't suppose *she* left an address, a number?'

He shakes his head. 'You suppose right. Just said to say thanks, if I see you, and that she might pop in next time she's in the area.'

A man walks into a bar. 'The usual?' the barman says.

'Make that a *double* orange juice,' the man says, 'and throw in a packet of pistachios, if you will.' And he perches on one of the newly covered leather stools.

'Don't suppose I could encourage you to partake of a double Scotch every once in a while?' the barman says. 'My maths isn't super hot, but the slowness at which you sip those juices vis-à-vis the amount of shuffling your arse does every other day on that expensive leather I've had to fork out on, means your residency on that stool is currently running at a loss.'

An hour later the man orders a tonic water and a packet of crisps. 'Just one for the road, Joe,' he says to the barman, 'then home, James.'

'The name, as you well know, my good man, is *Harry*,' says the barman.

The man swings around on his stool just as a woman walks in: she is tall and skinny and bleached blonde.

'Now *that's* the sort that would do for me,' says the barman.

'No she *wouldn't*, Harry!' the man says. 'You're *fucking gay!*'

'I know,' Harry says, 'but a gay girl can dream every once in a while, can't she?'

'You're a joke, Harry,' says the man, putting down his empty glass. 'Catch you in a coupla days. Trust you've still got my contact info safely in the till, just in case?'

'*Yessir!*' Harry says, standing to attention, hand to his brow in mock salute. 'And *I* know who the joker is in this bar, Matt, my man, and it ain't me, babe.'

'See you later!'

And the man walks out into the cool autumn evening.

Appetites

The strange thing about those first empty weeks without her was his ability to carry on as before: to sleep, to eat, most afternoons, to even spend time in his studio, though producing nothing of worth, the clay resistant to his touch, unable to be shaped to his will. And yet he could still go in there, could still structure his day with breakfast, lunch and supper, the scaffolding without which he might fall apart.

But how could he eat breakfast, lunch and supper as if nothing had changed? How could he prepare food, desire food, without the only woman he had truly desired sitting opposite him? Was this ability of his a healthy or *un*healthy one?

He would ask himself this question, standing at the chopping board, listening to the radio, no longer listening out for his wife's key in the front door, occasionally looking up to gaze out into the garden. From time to time, even taking pleasure in being able to hear every word of the programme, which, until that moment of realisation, he must have been genuinely absorbed in, no longer distracted – frequently irritated – by Vita's evening chatter overriding the presenter's words.

'It's known as conversation, Adam,' she would say; '*con-ver-sa-tion*. It's what most people take part in at some point in the day.'

Perhaps he had fallen in love with the proper noun that was her name before he had properly fallen in love with Vita? Liked the sharp, decisive sound it made cutting through silence. '*Vita!*' she'd said, quick as a flash. 'My name's Vita.'

Unusual, he'd thought.

Her mother's choice. There had been a distinct waft of Bloomsbury about his mother-in-law. '*Marry?*' she had questioned, when, a little too politely, he had formally declared his intentions. 'Do you want to love my daughter,' pausing to remove her sunglasses in order to fully scrutinise his face, 'or to own her?'

'Love her,' he'd answered. 'Love her more than life itself.' Not certain even that would be quite enough for someone as demanding as Virginia Somerville.

'Ah well,' she'd said, taking off her straw hat to flap a wasp away from the jam jar, 'marry if you must.'

'I must,' he'd said.

'Hmm,' she'd murmured, picking up a drained lemonade glass and upturning it over the wasp, now distracted by the sugary crumbs littering the tea table.

Had he, he wondered, slowly grating himself a pile of Parmesan, tried to own Vita? Might his wife be with him now, he considered, draining the last of the wine from a bottle opened eight days before? Before... He sighed to himself. Might he be pouring a glass for Vita at this very moment, had he not needed her quite so much? And if he had needed her so much, then why, instead of sipping this small glass of red – for all the world as if Vita was about to walk into the kitchen at any second – was he not drowning his sorrows downing crates of the stuff? As any decent, loving man should at such a time.

He slid the grated cheese into a bowl: one he'd made some twenty years ago. The green glaze was a little cracked – he had noted a small chip on the rim – but the bowl itself was intact. Things survive, he thought, flicking the switch of the kettle to boil water for pasta, *if* you take care of them.

It was two days later that the offerings began. Word must have got around.

An anonymous cottage pie came first; a note, should he think it any old supermarket ready meal or a rejected Meal on Wheels, peeking out from beneath the foil container, declared it *Made this morning!*

A shiny red tin followed, a Bruegel painting, *The Hunters in the Snow*, on its lid, a large snow-white envelope propped against it, his name, *ADAM*, scratched out in spiky, backward-leaning capitals as if 'written' by a hopping-mad blackbird. The delicate water-washed violet of the irises on the card – having none of the vivacity of the real thing – had, he read on the back of the card, been painted by a member of the Mouth and Foot Painters' Society. Except, at first, he had read it as the Hand-to-Mouth Painters' Society, bringing to mind the two-ringed Baby Belling, the north-facing windowsill co-opted as a fridge, and Vita's twenty-something voice bemoaning their 'hand-to-mouth existence'. *Thinking of you at this time*, someone had written inside the card, adding only a large *M* and a small, scratchy *x*. But what to do with so many fruit scones? He had never been much of a carbohydrate man. And where and to whom to return the tin?

He knew of three Ms. Knew the handwriting of two of them and imagined the third, a psychologist friend of Vita's from way back, a woman of considerable sophistication, would possess the elegant forward-sloping hand befitting its elegant, intelligent owner. Had Myra, he wondered, in a moment of madness, considered scone-baking a way back to his heart? Not that Myra had ever *had* access to his heart – or to any organ or any part of any organ, for that matter. There had been a certain frisson, that was all. An atmosphere that had been far from unpleasant. One that had induced him, on one or two occasions, to imagine Myra naked. She was rather shapely back then (*Perhaps still is?* he thought), less bony than Vita, and he had wondered what it might feel like: that softness.

But Myra had moved away years ago. A university somewhere. Salford? Bradford? Somewhere with a '–ford' in it. What's more, a woman with an MSc *and* a PhD would certainly not own such retrograde handwriting. And, anyway, Myra would have rung the doorbell. Myra might have offered her soft, rounded shoulder as solace.

There followed an avalanche of offerings: beef and beer casserole in a Tupperware box (*Just three minutes in a saucepan!*); a fish pie, the mashed potato lid piped on in decorative rosettes; a colourful, carefully arranged salade niçoise 'gift-wrapped' in cling film, the black and green olives, the artfully placed hard-boiled eggs, the criss-crossed

French beans all in disarray as he peeled back the film. A roast chicken wrapped in foil arrived on Saturday morning, a home-baked Dundee cake arrayed with almonds on Sunday afternoon. Several kind notes were slipped silently through the letter box, several kind arms thrust quietly across the threshold. Empathetic, sometimes tearful eyes had gazed into his, some unable to disguise a questioning, *Why, Adam, are your eyes not tearful too?* look, before looking down to the bowl, the plate, the tin in their hands, as if to say, *If we could heat up Vita and bring her to you, we would, but since we can't we've brought you this.* 'Well...' they would say, standing there, he not inviting them in, they not wishing to intrude, 'Well... better not keep you...'

Well, he would think, *well...*

And, in one sense, he had been well. Had, as they say, kept body and soul together. Well, had until now. Until all this cooked-up love, this manna from heaven had invaded these early empty days. How could he, faced by all this ready-cooked food, now spend his evenings cooking supper?

Now he snacked. Something he had never done – not even in his years at university. Now he scooped a mouthful of kedgeree straight from the bowl, gazing out to the studio he had not set foot in for days, leaving the bowl on the worktop; later, throwing the rest away. Now he cut himself a slim slice of a mushroom tart, not bothering to make salad. Not even using a plate. Pieces of mushroom slipping to the floor, and remaining there; he could see a piece now, covered with dust, festering beneath the breakfast bar.

Now he gnawed at a spicy chicken leg, felt revolted by the taste of flesh, and tossed it in the bin, despising his own wastefulness, his rejection of these ephemeral acts of love he was leaving to desiccate, decompose, be composted. *Eaten at last!* he would think, thinking of the utter wastefulness of life. Thinking of Vita.

He had expected to suffer. Had wanted to suffer. Was not suffering part of the package? What life throws at you when death comes calling.

'I'll go first, for sure,' he'd once told her. 'I'm three years older than you, and I'm a man. With luck, you'll be rid of me when you're in your prime. You'll still look young. You'll *always* look young. Someone'll snap you up soon enough.'

He had been twenty-eight when he'd said that. Why, with so much life ahead of them, had he brought up the subject of death? Vita standing at the window, eyes welling. '*Don't*, Adam! *Don't!* Please stop!' He crossing the empty room to wrap his arms around her.

The scene had returned to him as he'd returned from the hospital that last day: Vita's tearful young voice filling the empty house. And although there had been two – no, three – houses in between, it was as if he were back in their first two-up two-down terrace. He barely noticed the Victorian tiles of the hall floor, the rust-coloured carpet, the spacious yet cosy sitting room, the leather chair by the window. All he could see was the young couple they'd once been, standing in their small, empty living room, waiting to fill it with the meagre contents of a few boxes. Waiting to unpack their lives.

Slumping in the leather chair, watching a blackbird pulling a worm from the lawn, he thought of Vita, boxed up by now. *I can't bear to think of life without you*, he heard her young voice say, remembering the pale hand going up to wipe tears from her smooth, young cheek, yet glad he himself was still alive.

Their friends (or rather Vita's friends, for without her social skills they would have been virtually friendless), the Maids of Honour, as he'd dubbed them, had brought on this creeping anorectic regret. *Too much food!* he would think each time another life-giving dish was presented to him. *Too much food, Adam!* he heard Vita's voice complaining, recalling the look of horror on her face the first time he had presented his new girlfriend with what he considered a medium-sized supper. *You know I don't have your appetite.*

'You know, there's really no need,' he'd told Rachel that afternoon. 'I *am* coping.'

Did none of them remember that he, Adam, had been the main provider in this house? Surely they knew that without his '*provisional* love' Vita would have been living on coffee and air – supplemented in earlier times by a few meaty Marxist theories, watered down later on with a sprinkling of vegetarian liberalism, and, more recently, balanced out with great dollops of Green rhetoric? Had they forgotten what a new man this old man was? Had they not complimented him on his pastry, practically levitated with delight at the lightness of his cheese soufflé, swooned over the authenticity of his vegetable curry? Did they think, no longer having Vita to sustain, he had reverted to some protean specimen of mankind: one unable to lift a finger unless it was to bash a mammoth's brains out?

'It's no trouble,' Rachel said, 'no trouble at all.'

Rachel, who had bathed his wife's feet with a hot flannel, the orange cloth lain over Vita's milky skin, Rachel's tanned hands massaging in the sweet-smelling cream, Rachel's voice saying, 'Well, it can't do any harm, can it?' He, looking up, thinking, *Nor can it do any good, Rachel.*

Though Vita's best friend insisted she had heard a moan of pleasure from the other end of the bed. 'Did you hear that, Adam?' she'd asked.

Adam had been reading about recent improvements in the treatment of breast cancer when Rachel said this. Looking up from his newspaper, seeing Vita lying there with closed eyes, closed mouth, close to death, he had wished she could be lying there awake, but riddled with carcinogens, so he might speak to her, one last time, of love.

'Maybe, Rachel,' he'd answered her. Since, who knows? Amongst the shuffling of his newspaper, the hum of the monitor, the blip of the drip, not to mention the comings and goings in the corridor, there might have been something. 'Maybe,' he repeated, eyeing Rachel's soft hands and thinking of the number of times over the past four weeks they had stroked the backs of his own hands, Rachel's palms cupping his cheeks, Rachel's voice quietly saying, 'There's still hope, Adam.' He responding with, 'There's always hope, Rachel.' Each one lying to the other.

'Vegetable lasagne!' Rachel announced, putting the terracotta dish on the worktop. 'I remember Vita saying it was a favourite of yours. And don't forget! Whenever you feel up to eating with us, just say the word. Recognise it?' She tapped the side of the ovenproof dish with an index finger. 'Adam Harris, circa 1998! I'll pick it up on Friday.'

In fact he had cooked himself vegetable lasagne shortly before the onslaught of food had begun. He had driven to Happensfield, a town where he knew no one to speak of or speak to, and where, since his wife's death – or rather, since his wife's accident, which amounted to the same thing – he had done all his shopping. He had no wish to discuss Vita with anyone. The only conversation he could comprehend having was the one he could no longer have. And to be caught in flagrante delicto, buying aubergines, olives and good red wine at Hampton's deli in the High Street (where he'd previously shopped several times a week), well... What would they think of him? What would he say to them? *Ah, well! One has to live. Life goes on.* They might be able to say that to him. But was *he* allowed to say it to them? Say it so soon, at this early stage in the game of death? To be so brazenly alive, so patently determined to *stay* alive? Well, it wasn't done, was it? And for every caring neighbour or friend wishing to breathe new life into the bereaved spouse, for each one suggesting he keep his chin or pecker up, there must surely be an equal number, *more* than an equal number, who drew some form of moral sustenance from a grieving partner ready and willing to toss him- or herself onto the mental funeral pyre.

His wife was dead! He should feel hollowed out. Empty. Perhaps he did? Perhaps that was why, at the beginning of all this, he could still eat as he did? He had been *attempting* to fill the void: that vast, empty space where Vita's life had been. But had he, he asked himself, been enough to fill Vita's life?

'You'd manage fine without me!' she'd once said. 'Your emotions are all out there. They're as transparent as gossamer. They flail about with the wind. But, deep down, Adam Harris, you're as tough as old boots. You've a resistant inner core that's as hard as the Rock of Gibraltar. Hellfire won't crack it!'

'Is that where I'm heading?' he'd asked her.

'We're going nowhere, you and I.' Her cool, clear eyes looking from the asbestos-covered door, to the polystyrene ceiling tiles, to the threadbare carpet beneath her bare feet. 'We're here! Let's concentrate on the here and now, shall we?'

Their early bedsit days. Vita was nineteen. He had known her for six weeks.

Three days after hearing his wife's voice for the last time he had gone to the box room to search for his old diaries. Nineteen sixty-seven! He'd found it. July 23rd: the day he had faithfully transcribed Vita's damning summation of him. *Does this woman know me better than I know myself?* he'd scrawled beneath it. *Or not at all?* He pictured Vita standing before him in her blazing red Che Guevara T-shirt, her dark brown hair flowing down, covering half of Che's face.

He had wanted her life-giving presence from their very first meeting. Whatever she'd said about his emotions, when it came to Vita, he had been rock-solid from the start.

'*Adam!*' Prising herself away from him. It was nine months into their relationship. They had been apart for six whole days. 'For Chrissake, let me breathe!'

'Stay with me, always,' he'd pleaded. 'Live with me forever.'

She had forced him down onto a chair, hands on his shoulders, holding him there. 'Get real, Adam! We've got to study. We've got to work. We can't *always* be together.'

Had their appetites always been a little at odds? Food. Work. Socialising. Sex, to a certain extent. Where he wanted more, Vita wanted less.

'You're such a vampire!' she'd told him. 'You want to drain me of life.'

And then, more than two decades later, without a word to him, at forty-five, after a decade of working from home, Vita had got herself an in-house job, writing for some artsy-fartsy magazine.

'Don't look so upset! Anyway, it'll be healthier,' she'd insisted.

How, when they would no longer meet up for healthy salad lunches, home-made soups in winter, no longer on fine days, if their work schedules allowed, take long, health-giving walks before supper, could it be *healthier*?

'We'll have more to talk about,' she told him. 'We will actually *miss* one another.'

'I miss you now,' he told her. 'I miss you if we're apart for four hours.'

'You don't. You *can't.*'

'I do and I *can.*'

'In that case,' she'd said, 'this'll *definitely* be healthier for us.'

'All that driving!' Adam complained. 'Why not take the train?'

She would need the car for interviews, she told him, for research.

And soon she was rushing off in it each morning, frequently without breakfast, eating the only thing Vita did slowly.

Resigned, Adam would pour himself a second cup of tea, before drifting down the garden to his studio, less driven himself now that Vita was no longer working in her study at the front of the house, and feeling more like his wife's father than her husband. Had he, he wondered, always felt a little like her father? A dull sort of father to Vita's high-spirited, high-minded child, to the wayward teenager she became in middle age. Were they unsuited to the 'incestuous' life they'd shared?

'*Vita!* Eat up, for fuck's sake!'

The fork, carrying three spiked beans, hovered halfway between Vita's plate and her mouth. Observing the hardening egg yolk, the barely diminished pile of beans, he realised that in this all-important part of life his brand-new girlfriend was singularly ill-named.

'I thought,' she had said, spearing two more beans, 'we were having a rather interesting discussion. Don't you think, if we're like this now…?'

Adam, watching the candle wax dripping from wine bottle to enlarging petrified pile on the wooden table, had run a thumbnail beneath its warmth, saying nothing. He had no wish to think. He wished only that Vita finish the simple supper he had prepared for her before it was stone cold.

'I mean,' Vita went on, 'we sometimes have such different desires.'

'We do?' he'd questioned, getting up to make coffee, turning to see the fork finally make contact with Vita's lips.

'And what about me?' he'd asked her when she told him what she had done. 'Don't I have a say in this?'

Had all Vita's life-changing decisions been made without consulting him? What else had she done without need of his approval?

'No!' she said emphatically. 'You don't.'

'What about, *With my body I thee endow*?'

'Come on, Adam. You know damn well we went through all that palaver to please your folks. Neither one of us gives a fig about marriage, about religion. Anyway, it's all done and dusted. It's what *I* feel is the right thing to do.'

'Dust to dust, then,' he said.

Then, remembering his young wife crying at the thought of her husband's death, tears welling in his own eyes, opening his arms to her, he'd said, 'Come here!'

She had come to him a little stiffly, her newly blonded head resting, somewhat reluctantly, on his shoulder, and he'd wondered, *Would she? Could she? Has she?* But weren't they too old for such dalliances? He himself had always been too old for them. Or, maybe, not quite old enough? But Vita? Vita was still out there in the greedy, consuming world of work, of divorced men, of married men, of men who got more excited by sex than did her boring father figure of a husband. Men who were far *better* at sex than was her boring father figure of a husband. All those office frissons. Those flighty flirtations. Who knows what went on in the wicked world of work?

'After all,' Vita said, pulling hers away from his, 'it *is* my body.'

'Mine too!' he declared, wondering how many men got to sixty-four with only two notches on the bedpost, a hand reaching out to stroke her hair.

'Do you like the new look?' she'd asked him.

'Sure, I like it! But then, I liked the old, greying look just as much.'

Reminding him of her fervent atheism, telling him it was the right thing to do, she'd said, 'Join me, why don't you?'

'I'll join you in a suicide pact at ninety-five! Pills and booze? Or walking into the sea? What's your poison?'

'Pills and booze!' she'd answered. 'But make that one hundred! Me. Not you.'

And suddenly the sun came out.

We'll be fine, he thought. *We'll be fine until the pills and booze.*

It was four in the afternoon, five months later, when the doorbell rang.

Turning off the wheel, his dripping hands reaching out to grab a cloth, he ran through the garden, alarm bells ringing in his head.

Vita – part-time now at the artsy-fartsy magazine – had dashed off somewhere that morning: 'Interviewing someone!' she'd called out, when he'd asked where she was going.

Would she never slow down? Would she never stop?

If I were to lose you to someone... he'd thought, the flailing, gossamer-winged fears aflutter once more. Why had he not the confident belief in his wife's love that Vita so obviously had in his? Was it because he was the weaker personality? Or because his was the stronger love?

Rising sixty-two, Vita had, over the past decade, developed a subtle sheen, a patina of glamour. It was as if her busy inner life had seamlessly merged with her attractive outer self, and was saying to the world, *This is me, folks! The complete Vita Somerville. Take me or leave me.*

Had she been taken, he wondered? Had another man injected glamour into his wife's seventh decade?

He opened the front door.

'Mr Harris?'

He froze.

Two police officers stood on the doorstep: a man and a woman.

She was not dead. At least she was not dead. There was relief in that. The car was a write-off, but Vita was not dead. Vita was still alive.

'Where was my wife's car?' Adam asked.

'Hamdown Road,' the policeman said. ''T'other side of crossing.'

The policewoman moved toward his swaying body, her right hand going out to support Adam's left arm.

'Ah!' he said, dropping the clay-stained cloth to the hall floor, suddenly aware of the watery red slip running down his arms, dripping off his elbows like muddy blood. Aware of two clay-smeared hands – were they his? – hovering in the air, one either side of his face, as though, instinctively drawn together, fearing their supplication might become permanent, they had stopped short of prayer.

'Was there anyone else in the car?' he'd asked them.

'No, sir. No one else. Though skid marks on the road suggest another car might've been involved.'

The ambulance had taken Vita to Saint Joseph's Hospital.

He remembers nothing of the drive there. Remembers little of what he was told that evening. Remembers only Vita's sleeping face. Vita's alive but lifeless hand in his. And then the waiting. Waiting for the woman who would never slow down, to be switched off.

'Of course,' some jovial relative of a patient in the main ward tactlessly commented at the coffee machine, 'it could be locked-in syndrome?'

'They say not.'

'But they don't always know, do they? Don't let them rush you. It's *your* decision.'

No, it's not, Adam thought, wanting to be rushed, wanting it to be their decision. *How could Vita live with locked-in syndrome?*

'A party to celebrate Vita's life!' a few friends smilingly suggested, appearing to see her cursory cremation and, when he shook his head at the notion of a party, the lack of a party as a personal slight on them.

'Maybe later?' he said to keep them quiet.

How could he 'celebrate' Vita's life when he was furious with her for dying like this?

'But your body? What will be left of you?' he'd asked her, when she told him what she'd done.

'Weren't you supposed to be going first?' she'd responded cheekily, wrinkles rippling her smiling fine-boned face. 'Anyway, you and I have a suicide pact. What'll we need with a burial plot in consecrated ground? Back by dusk!'

'*À bientôt, ma cherie*,' he'd responded, his flailing emotions stabilised, fearless at that moment. 'Think I'll rustle up a veggie pasta for supper. Four cheeses. Finish it off in the oven.'

'Great! Y'know, I'm a pretty lucky woman.' Hurrying away, as happy as Larry.

'You're a pretty woman, for sure,' he'd called after her, thinking, *God, how I love you.*

'*Adam!* Really!' Rachel, horrified at the very thought. '*Vita?* With someone else? Are you mad?! Anyway, in that unlikely event, you know Vita, she would've come right out and told you.'

Of course she would have. What had he been thinking of? Voicing his flailing fears had wiped them all away.

'Though,' Rachel said, reaching over to take Adam's empty plate, 'Vita might have kept one little secret from you…'

He felt his body stiffen. Felt his heart thumping in his chest.

'Did she tell you she hooked up with Myra a couple of times?'

'No! But why ever wouldn't she?'

'Why d'you reckon, old son?' Rachel's husband Stan said.

Adam shrugged.

'Checking Myra out, old mate. Seeing if it was worth the risk.'

'*Risk?*'

'*Jesus*, Adam!' Rachel sighed. 'Surely you're not that naive? Myra's moved back this way, apparently. Other side of Grazeborough somewhere.'

'More importantly,' Stan went on, 'Myra's got herself divorced! I mean, that woman was dangerous enough married. Can you imagine her footloose and fancy-free? She tried to pull me, too, y'know – hard as that is to believe.'

'And Jacob!' Rachel added. 'Merial said Esther almost left Jacob over it. I imagine Vita thought it safer to keep Myra out of the picture for good.'

'Safer?' What a fool he had been. What an insecure, egoistic fool.

'Come on now,' Stan said. 'There were overtures, weren't there?'

'Just an innocent, flirtatious game, that's all. Played out in the public arena.'

'Ah! Trouble is, Adam, old mate, Myra took her game-playing *pretty* seriously. It took someone as loving and trusting as Vita – and you – to invite her as close as you did. Vita always saw the good in people, didn't she? Well, you both did.'

'We did?'

'Sure you did!' Rachel said. 'You two were an example to us all.'

A warm glow enveloped Adam's entire body. He felt better than he had done for months and months. Was it really two years?

'You never did have that party, did you?' Rachel said.

'No. Been thinking I might manage something at our place sometime soon, though.' He could never say, 'my place'. Vita would always be there. 'Might cook up a curry, like I used to. Or a tagine? I've just finished a new range. Selling quite well, apparently. Invite Jim and Fazia. And you two, of course.'

'I'm there!' Stan said.

'Great!' Rachel said.

He'd been putting it off, could not bear the thought of her trickling through his fingers, but, two months ago, as requested in her will, he had sprinkled Vita's stardust remains into a pile of red clay and rolled it out into long, snaking coils, rolling them slowly, not wanting to stop rolling them, before hand-building the earth-coloured bowl – he could not bear the thought of throwing her onto the wheel.

Turn me into something curvy, she had written in an addendum to her will. *Make use of what's left of me, Adam. Use me up!*

He had scratched a V on the base, a heart shape encasing it.

Sometimes he finds himself talking to the bowl as if it were Vita; sometimes cursing her for being on that road, for not being at home with him; sometimes thanking her for being true to her name in death as in life, pleased, now, that his wife's corneas, kidneys, heart and lungs are still alive in the world, still journeying on in other people's bodies. And, sometimes, while filling the bowl with a large pile of grated Parmesan, he thinks he hears Vita's chastising voice coming from it. *Too much cheese,* she says; way *too much cheese, Adam.*

'Oh!' he said, I forgot to tell you. I've donated my organs, too. Did it online last week.'

'Good on you!' Rachel said.

'Mmm,' Stan equivocated, reaching for the wine bottle.

'The ultimate in recycling,' Rachel added, putting the cheeseboard on the table. 'Help yourselves, you two.'

'Uh-uh,' Stan declined, a hand on his expanding waistline, conscious of his cholesterol.

'Love some!' Adam said, reaching for the knife.

Acknowledgements

Thanks to my partner, cartoonist Peter Schrank, for his support throughout the decade in which these stories were written – as well as before and, I hope, in the years to come. Thanks also to my two new wordaholic friends in this fine literary city: to singer-songwriter Holly Lerski for her enthusiastic encouragement, and for engineering, quite literally, the *On the Shelf* podcasts, and to novelist and translator Deborah Arnander for joining me 'up there' to talk about the pleasure of writing prose fiction and the pain of not being read.